ON

...was too long to play nanny to a bigmouthed mynah bird with a penchant for major mischief making.

...was too short to tire of the sound of the sea, the feel of sandy dunes beneath bare feet.

...was all Zoe had to uncover the meaning of the plaintive melody, the scent of lilac that haunted her waking hours.

For the month of June, Joe Piper was to be mistress of Gull Cottage.

It would be a month she would never forget.

ABOUT THE AUTHOR

Robin Francis is a lover of romance novels and baseball. After reading hundreds of romances, Robin decided to write one herself. Although she has a passion for baseball, Robin began work on her first novel during a World Series and found writing to be so addictive that *Charmed Circle* is her fourteenth book.

Books by Robin Francis
HARLEQUIN AMERICAN ROMANCE

Don't miss any of our special offers. Write to us at the following address for information on our newest releases.

Harlequin Reader Service
901 Fuhrmann Blvd., P.O. Box 1397, Buffalo, NY 14240
Canadian address: P.O. Box 603,
Fort Erie, Ont. L2A 5X3

CHARMED CIRCLE

**ROBIN
FRANCIS**

Harlequin Books

TORONTO • NEW YORK • LONDON
AMSTERDAM • PARIS • SYDNEY • HAMBURG
STOCKHOLM • ATHENS • TOKYO • MILAN

Published July 1989

First printing May 1989

ISBN 0-373-16301-0

Prologue

The shoes were custom-made, Italian. The suit was Savile Row. And the smile was classic McClellan.

There was charm in that smile and wit; a hint of mischief and a mouthful of gleaming white teeth. Yet for some reason, on this balmy spring day the smile equaled less than the sum of its parts.

Cora Piper slid back on the bench; her feet dangled clear of the floor. She craned her neck, trying to improve her view of the couple at the corner table, and spoke in a stage whisper to Cosmo DiSantis.

"Don't look now. Larry's about to make his move."

She scooted toward the aisle, and Cosmo grinned.

"Poor Laurence. Maybe I shouldn't have tipped you he was doing lunch here."

"Nonsense," said Cora. "I only want to talk to him."

"Yes, but there's talking, and then there's *talking*—"

"Shh! He'll be along any second. The waiter's bringing the check."

"That's my cue to pretend I'm an innocent bystander."

Cosmo picked up his glass of club soda and left the booth, and with gleeful determination, Cora followed him.

At four foot ten—five one in her spike-heeled boots— she presented a minor obstacle. But despite her diminutive stature, the sight of her was enough to slow Mc-Clellan down.

"Larry! *Darling!* Fancy meeting you here!"

The greeting carried to the farthest recesses of the tavern. Heads turned as Laurence McClellan submitted to Cora's embrace. She clasped him to her bosom, kissed the air in the direction of his cheek, then held him at arm's length.

"This is the most delicious coincidence! I've been trying to reach you for weeks. If I didn't know better, I'd think you were trying to avoid me."

"Things have been hectic, Cora. My time is not my own. We'll get together soon, though. That's a promise."

"Why not now? As long as you're here, let me buy you a drink."

"Can't, love. Gotta run. I'm on my way to another engagement."

He tried to squeeze past her, but Cora stood her ground.

"Surely you can spare a few minutes for your oldest, dearest friend."

McClellan's eyes darted this way and that, searching for an escape route. Finding none, he ushered Cora into the booth. He affected an air of false heartiness until their drinks had been served, but once he was sure of their privacy he regarded her with less fondness than he would show a grease spot on his lapel.

"Congratulations, Cora. You're more resourceful than I realized. In the past week you've accosted me at my apartment, my office, the theater, and now here. I expect tomorrow I'll find you lurking in the steam room at the gym."

Cora laughed, unrepentant. "You just might, if you run out on me again."

His mouth thinned to a reproachful line. "Did it ever occur to you that I have no desire to speak to you?"

"Naturally it did."

"Then why are you making a nuisance of yourself and a public spectacle of me?"

She gave his forearm a playful swat. "Larry, sweetheart, I didn't get to be executive producer of *Passion's Children* by taking no for an answer, and I don't intend to start with you."

"Looks as if you'll have to, love, because I have no intention of doing a guest shot on your trashy little soap."

"My show may be trashy, but it's not what I'd call little. Millions of viewers never miss an episode—including a certain well-known drama critic."

Laurence scowled. "How did you find out about that? Which one of your spies told you I watch the show?"

"Frankly, I don't remember. All I recall is someone mentioning you're a fan of *Passion's Children*. But tell me, darling, what difference does it make how I found out?"

"Dammit, Cora! Have you any idea what would happen to my reputation if that sort of information got out?"

Her features softened; her smile grew pensive. "I imagine it wouldn't do you any good. After all, what would people think? You're the dean of critics, the arbiter of good taste. If you pan a play, it flops. If you praise it, ticket sales soar."

"Is that why you want me to join the cast? To prop up your sagging ratings?"

"My ratings aren't sagging, thank you very much. They're actually quite stable. But I have wondered if the McClellan seal of approval might help them survive the writers' strike."

"Ah, yes. Rumor has it the strike caught you with a woeful shortage of scripts."

"A slight miscalculation, nothing more," Cora replied dismissively with a breezy wave of her hand. But inside, she was quaking.

Passion's Children was her baby. With the possible exception of her niece Zoe, it was the thing she loved most in the world. She had rescued the series from near oblivion. She had nurtured it, revamped it, worried over it, and guided it to the top of daytime drama. She had invested the best years of her life in the show. She was not about to lose it. And if keeping her job meant trading punches, knocking heads, even twisting Laurence McClellan's influential arm, so be it.

Cora took a fortifying sip of wine and braced herself. The preliminaries were over. The main event was about to begin, and she planned to come out swinging.

"You know, Larry, I've heard a few rumors myself. About you."

Laurence smoothed his palm over his thick, silver hair. "I'm accustomed to being the subject of gossip, my dear. That's the price one pays for fame."

She saluted him with her wineglass, undeceived by his preening. "These rumors had nothing to do with your love life, darling. Your May-December romances are old news."

"I'm deeply wounded by your choice of adjectives, Cora. December's stretching it a bit. I'm barely into October."

"Have it your way," she conceded dryly. "But don't forget, I knew you when you wore knickers. That's why I'm concerned about you."

After a brief hesitation, Laurence shrugged. "Very well, I'll bite. What have you heard?"

"That you've put the East Hampton house on the market."

"There's some truth in that. I've listed it with a rental agent, but only for the season."

Cora removed a dog-eared memo pad from her shoulder bag, and foraged through the side flap for a pen. "What do oceanfront properties rent for these days? About fifteen thou a month?"

"Yes, about that."

She made a note of this figure. "If you find a tenant, will you spend the summer in the city?"

"Heavens, no! By the end of May I shall be frolicking through the South of France, vacationing with friends and penning my memoirs."

She looked at him, wide-eyed, admiring. "Your bio should make fascinating reading."

"I think so, too," said Laurence, "and I trust my publisher will agree."

His smugness was astonishing. Cora leaned forward, lowering her voice. "I don't want to shatter your confidence, but I've also heard that you've been gambling again."

"Life's a gamble, my dear."

He ran an idle forefinger around the rim of his glass, and she snatched the glass away from him.

"This is not a philosophical discussion, Larry. For God's sake, drop the act. It's common knowledge you're in financial trouble. You've always lived beyond your means—"

"Is it my fault Amaryllis took me to the cleaners? The divorce settlement alone was staggering. I had to mortgage everything but the children. Between the interest on the loans and the alimony payments, it's all I can do to keep my head above water."

"I understand, darling. Believe me, I do. I've made you personal loans, haven't I? And not once have I pressed you to pay me back."

Laurence threw up his hands. "If you want your money, say so. I still have a few knickknacks I can sell."

Cora sighed and shook her head. "You can keep your knickknacks. Money's not the issue."

"Would you mind telling me what is?"

"Well, according to the grapevine, you've welched on some gambling debts—"

"And as my oldest, dearest friend, the minute you got wind of it, you rushed over here to gloat."

"On the contrary. I'd like to propose a solution to your problem."

He gave her a measuring look. "If your proposition has anything to do with *Passion's Children*, I'm not available."

"I'd make it worth your while."

"Forget it, Cora. I may be one step ahead of the loan sharks, but I have my standards. My integrity is not for sale."

"I know it isn't. That's part of your value, so I wouldn't dream of asking for a rave review. But Gene Siskel and Roger Ebert have done guest shots. I saw them a year or two ago on *Saturday Night Live*, critiquing the skits, and that sort of exposure doesn't seem to have hurt their credibility. When you think about it, it's simply good PR."

Cora paused, giving Laurence a chance to consider her perspective. Then, with a meaningful glance at the row of figures she had jotted on the notepad, she went on.

"If you agree to do the cameo, I'm prepared to cut a deal that could be advantageous to both of us."

His expression soured. "The advantages to you are obvious. I fail to see how I might profit."

"Take a look at this, my darling, and you will." She angled the memo pad toward him. "In addition to your salary—which I think you'll admit is generous—there'll be publicity. We'd want you to make the talk show circuit, for which we'd pay you a bonus, and once you mention your guest role, you'd have the perfect opportunity to pitch your book."

"Would I have to plug the soap in my column?"

"That's entirely up to you. And the cherry on the cake is, I'd like to use your house for some location shots."

"You're planning a shoot in East Hampton? May I ask why?"

"You can ask, but I can't answer. Not without giving away details that should remain secret till the segments are on the air. All I can tell you is, we've been scouting location sites on Long Island. We're scheduled to begin taping out there in June, and if you agree to let us use your place, I can guarantee you two months' rent for one month's occupancy."

"A tidy sum," said Laurence.

Cora nodded. "Enough for you to feed the loan sharks and buy some souvenirs."

She underlined the column of figures, and handed the pen to Laurence so that he could work out the total for himself. She knew she had captured his interest when a mercenary gleam outshone the skepticism in his eyes.

He cleared his throat. "The house is yours if you'll take care of Boris."

Her jaw sagged. "You must be joking."

Laurence shook his head. "I never joke about Boris."

"But he hates me, and I must say the feeling is mutual. He's always hopping about and screeching at me, staring at me with those beady little eyes."

"Come now, Cora. You're exaggerating. I'll admit Boris is discriminating. There aren't many people he likes, but you shouldn't take it personally."

"I can't help it, Larry. Just the thought of being his nursemaid is enough to give me the hives. Can't you leave him with the vet?"

"Unfortunately, Boris gets homesick. I boarded him at the clinic last January while I was in Martinique, and by the time I got home he'd plucked out most of his breast feathers, and his wings were practically naked. Obviously, if his condition was that appalling after two weeks, I can't uproot him for the summer. The poor baby's terribly sensitive."

"Sensitive, my foot! He's an egomaniac. There's nothing wrong with that mynah bird that couldn't be cured by a swift kick in the tail."

Laurence stroked his mustache. "If you feel that strongly about it, I suppose I could make some adjustment to the rent."

"How big an adjustment?"

"Shall we say a thousand?"

"Come again?"

"Two thousand."

She cupped her hand to her ear. "Sorry, darling. Money talks, but you'll have to speak a little louder."

He gritted his teeth. "Four thousand—but you'll have to supply me with tapes of *Passion's Children* while I'm in France."

"Make it five, and not only will I tape the show for you, I'll also finagle Zoe in to bird-sitting Boris."

His frown vanished at the mention of Zoe's name. "It's a deal," he said. "Zoe's worth the extra thousand. I'll inform the agent I've found a tenant for June."

Cora gathered up her notebook and pen, beaming at him. "I give you my word, you won't regret this, Larry. I'll messenger the contracts to your office—"

"Not so fast, Cora. I've agreed to let you use the house. That doesn't mean I'll do your show."

She sobered. "I thought you understood. This is a package deal. It's all or nothing, and the terms are non-negotiable. No cameo, no rent—and the next issue of *Soap Opera Digest* will spread the word that the most celebrated man-about-town since Oscar Wilde spends an hour every weekday afternoon parked in front of his wide-screen TV, watching *Passion's Children*."

Laurence blanched. "You're bluffing. You're tough and pushy, but you're not deliberately cruel. You couldn't resort to blackmail. Especially with me. Why, the very idea is ludicrous!"

Cora had never thought of her maneuvering as blackmail. The idea took some getting used to. She tipped her head to one side, weighing Laurence McClellan's fair-weather friendship against her devotion to her career.

"You may be right," she said at last. "There's only one way to find out."

"And how, may I ask, is that?"

"Try me."

Chapter One

Zoe Piper woke up that Sunday morning, expecting her life to change.

Uranus was transiting Sagittarius. Venus was trine Pluto. By noon tomorrow retrograde Mercury would be afflicted by an opposition from Mars.

The signs were there in abundance, too powerful to ignore. She had foreseen a time of upheaval, but in her wildest dreams she could not have anticipated what form the upheaval would take.

She certainly never expected to find a lanky six-footer with sandy-brown hair asleep on her living-room sofa.

Zoe stared at the stranger, paralyzed by indecision.

Should she barricade herself in the bedroom? Should she tiptoe past him to the hall? Should she scream or make a run for it, or should she confront the intruder, demand to know what he was doing in her flat and how he'd gotten in?

She didn't know whether to feel threatened or outraged or simply curious, but she was sure of one thing. Somebody had some tall explaining to do.

Zoe shook off her inertia and retreated as far as the phone. She was about to dial 911 when she spotted Cosmo DiSantis's note.

"His name is Ethan Quinn. He assures me he doesn't snore, and I can attest he's housebroken. Merlin likes him, so don't worry."

Merlin did like him, Zoe realized, glancing toward the sofa. The marmalade tabby, generally disdainful of men, was curled up on the visitor's chest, purring for all he was worth.

Perhaps it was foolhardy, relying on the judgment of a cat, but experience had taught Zoe that virtually nothing escaped Merlin; he often detected character flaws she missed. Coupled with Cosmo's message, his feline stamp of approval tipped the balance in Ethan's favor.

If Merlin's willing to share the sofa with him, he must be trustworthy, she reasoned.

Suspicions lulled, deciding to play the gracious hostess, she went into the kitchenette and started a pot of coffee. By the time it finished perking, Merlin was on the prowl.

She heard a rush of wings as he leaped from the windowsill to the fire escape, startling a pigeon into flight, but the moment she opened the refrigerator the cat appeared on cue, alternately rubbing against her legs and nipping at her heels, demanding his weekly ration of half-and-half.

Zoe paid Merlin his tribute, then added a dollop of half-and-half to her coffee and cleared a space for herself at the drop leaf table, where she could keep tabs on Ethan Quinn.

Although they had never met, she remembered hearing his name. Since he was acquainted with Cosmo, she assumed Cosmo must have mentioned him, and it troubled her that she couldn't recall in what context. But the memory lapse was a minor disturbance, compared to the shock of recognition that shot through her when she got a closer look at his face.

The well-marked brows and high cheekbones, the wide, mobile mouth and stubborn chin—all were familiar and dear.

Without ever having heard him speak, she knew the resonance of his voice. Without having felt his caress, she knew his touch would warm her. And without having seen his eyes, she knew they would be blue—not gray-blue like Aunt Cora's or the color of forget-me-nots like her own, but a clear, pure indigo, reminiscent of distant horizons and twilight skies.

She knew his eyes would reflect his moods; knew it so precisely, she could see them bright with longing and dimmed by despair. She saw the way they would crinkle at the corners when he smiled, and even as this image formed, she asked herself where it came from. But she never doubted its accuracy, for in that instant another memory surfaced.

She was standing on a hillside, surrounded by darkness and by the fragrance of lilacs. And somewhere, someone was playing a piano. The notes of the nocturne filtered through the shadows, twinkling like fireflies before the breeze snatched them away—

The memory was a fragile thing, as ephemeral as the melody, and as poignant. It filled her with nostalgia, and faded before she could identify it.

Mystified and more than a little intrigued, Zoe sat at the table, studying Ethan's face.

When he looked at her, would he feel a twinge of déjà vu, or had he forgotten—

Forgotten what? she wondered.

This was the most intriguing question of all, but before she could pursue it, Ethan rolled onto his side. His eyes slitted open and his gaze traveled about the room, puzzling over the row of crystals on the lamp stand, the star charts on the wall, the brick-and-board shelves that sagged beneath the weight of the books they housed.

He blinked once or twice, as if he were astonished to find himself in her fourth-floor walk-up, then focused on her with surprising intensity.

Her first reaction was disappointment because his eyes were brown. Her second was discomfiture because he'd caught her staring. But despite her uneasiness, she didn't look away.

"If you'd like to wash up, the bathroom's the first door off the hall."

Ethan hauled himself erect. "If it's not too big an imposition, do you suppose I could have some of that coffee when I'm done?"

"How do you take it? Cream and sugar?"

"Please."

His voice was deeper than she'd imagined it would be. Huskier. And the cadence of his speech was wrong. It should be slower, less clipped, more like a waltz than a march.

Zoe listened to him splashing about in the bathroom, and when he emerged, her feeling of recognition vanished like a puff of smoke in a gale.

Buttoned down, spruced up, and decidedly less rumpled, Ethan Quinn bore little resemblance to the mythical man her subconscious had dredged up.

He's a stranger after all, she thought. And in the wake of this thought came consolation.

She had been mistaken on most counts, but she was right about one. He had a dreamer's eyes, and when he smiled, tawny flecks of gold leaped into the midnight languor of the irises.

"Scorpio," she murmured.

"Pardon me?"

"Scorpio," she repeated. "Maybe Pisces."

Her scrutiny shifted from his eyes to his feet, drawing Ethan's attention to the hole in his sock.

One of his loafers was where he'd left it, next to the coffee table; the other was nowhere in sight. He dropped to his knees and began fishing for it under the sofa.

Zoe swung her feet off the floor and wriggled her toes. "Do you have trouble finding shoes that fit?"

"No. Do you?"

"Constantly. That's why I prefer to go barefoot."

Beneath the sofa, his fingers encountered something soft and furry and combative. He jerked his hand away, and one marmalade paw whipped after it, claws unsheathed.

"Merlin! Behave yourself."

Zoe's reprimand didn't stop the cat from taking another swipe at Ethan's hand, and when he abandoned the search for his shoe and joined Zoe at the table, Merlin streaked after him, and established a new beachhead under his chair.

"You seem to have made a friend," she observed.

"I'd have said enemy."

"No. That's Merlin's way of showing affection."

"In that case, I hope he doesn't get to be too fond of me." Ethan glanced warily at the cat. The look he gave Zoe was equally wary. "What was all that about Pisces and Scorpio?"

"I was just trying to figure out your sun sign."

"And?"

She offered him a mug of coffee and an engaging gamine grin. "It's obvious one of the water signs is prominent in your chart."

"What's obvious about it?"

"Your eyes. They're very distinctive, you know. There's something compelling about them."

He couldn't suppress a smile. "I'm afraid right now the most distinctive thing about my eyes is that they could use a little more sleep. But thanks anyway, for the compliment.

And thank you for that lovely clue, thought Zoe. She slid the sugar bowl toward Ethan and followed it with the carton of half-and-half, studying him all the while.

"Scorpio. Definitely Scorpio."

Ethan stared at her, bemused. "Should I be impressed, or was that a lucky guess?"

"There's not much luck involved. Your skepticism gave you away. It's typical of Scorpios, but you really should try to rise above it. You won't realize your full potential until you acknowledge your interest in the occult."

He helped himself to the sugar, the picture of indifference. "What makes you think I'm interested in the occult?"

"You're a Scorpio, aren't you? And you're a friend of Cosmo DiSantis."

Ethan shrugged. "Mr. DiSantis and I are business acquaintances, nothing more. We met for the first time last night."

"Then what are you doing here?"

"DiSantis said the painters hadn't finished work in his guest room."

Zoe's gaze was as wide and unblinking as Merlin's. "I suppose you couldn't go home."

"As it happens, I couldn't. Not to East Hampton. DiSantis is quite a spellbinder. We got to talking, and I lost track of the time. I didn't notice how late it was till I'd missed the last train out."

East Hampton? But that meant— "You're the man who's in charge of the Seymour Collection!"

"Among other things," said Ethan. "I'm the executor of my great-uncle's will—"

"I'm sorry," said Zoe. "I didn't realize you were related to Mr. Seymour."

"He was my grandmother's brother, but condolences aren't necessary. They'd had a falling-out. To the best of my knowledge, they'd had no contact with each other for fifty or sixty years. If my mother hadn't written the old guy to inform him of Grandma's death, he wouldn't have known I existed, so I can't honestly say that I knew him very well."

"He must have regretted the estrangement," said Zoe.

"I doubt it. From what I saw of Uncle Hiram, he was too busy nursing old grudges to be capable of sentiment."

"Yet he named you his executor."

"Yes, and I'd be honored if I didn't have the feeling that wherever Uncle Hiram is, he's laughing his head off at the spot he's put me in."

"Is his estate that complicated?"

"No, it's fairly straightforward. Most of his assets go to charity, but my uncle left his house and his library to me, and it's the library that's the problem. You wouldn't believe the number of inquiries I've had about the portion of the collection that deals with the mystic arts."

"Oh, but I would," said Zoe. "The Seymour Collection is practically a legend. If the works are authentic, going public with them would be like unveiling the Golden Fleece and the Rosetta Stone, rolled into one."

"I can't vouch for the authenticity of any of the works, but I can tell you one thing: they've attracted every kook in the state. And while I can appreciate the value of the library to the bona fide student of psychic phenomena, my employer frowns upon an officer of the trust department associating with clairvoyants and swamis and other assorted nuts."

"Your employer being?"

"The Long Island branch of Merchants Bank."

"You have my sympathy," said Zoe.

The hint of frost in her reply was not lost on Ethan. He looked at her sharply. "Sounds as if you have a low opinion of banks."

"To tell you the truth, I don't know much about them, except that they put profits ahead of people, and they won't approve a loan unless you can prove you don't need one. Based on that limited knowledge, I might conclude banks are overcautious. I might assume their only concern is presenting an image that convinces depositors their money is secure. I might think bankers are too conservative, or that they have weird priorities, but until I was better informed, I'd hesitate to call them nuts."

Moments ago Zoe had been smiling. She'd been open, friendly, even flirtatious. Then in the blink of an eye Miss Congeniality had disappeared, and in her place was an aloof, unapproachable Snow Queen whose icy demeanor made Ethan feel as clumsy as a schoolboy.

"I—uh, it seems I've offended you," he said.

"I'm usually offended by bigotry, especially when it's directed at my friends."

Oh, God! His crack about the psychics was coming back to haunt him. When would he learn to censor his remarks? How could he have forgotten that his uncle's bequest had plunged him into a lunatic fringe, where the eccentric was considered the norm and he was considered the oddball?

But Cosmo DiSantis seemed normal enough.

For that matter, so did Zoe. A bit bohemian, perhaps, in her tie-dyed skirt and peasant blouse. A scarf tied gypsy-style about her head subdued her unruly mane of hair without subduing the color. The flyaway curls that spilled across her shoulders were a vibrant red-gold, a molten hue that seemed to radiate heat.

Those wild red curls hinted at a fiery disposition, but the cool blue eyes tempered the fire and promised emotional depths.

Ethan thought, if her passions were aroused, this lady might be too hot to handle. Then again, she might be at war with herself. But basically she seemed sensible. Down-to-earth. Even when she'd talked about sun signs, he'd felt comfortable with her. Drawn to her. Almost as if he had known her for years—

I can't afford to antagonize her, Ethan realized. She's my ticket back to the well-ordered world where people can go for months without worrying about karma.

He exhaled on a sigh, resigned to eating the requisite bite of crow. "I've been tactless, and I apologize. From now on, I'll try to keep an open mind."

Zoe spared him a pitying glance. "Are you sure that's possible?"

"Of course. Why wouldn't it be?"

"You're a banker, aren't you?"

Ethan pushed his chair away from the table with a suddenness that sent Merlin scrambling for the no-man's-land beneath the sofa.

"This is getting us nowhere," he muttered.

"Then why are you still here?"

"Because— Dammit, I need your help!"

The admission seemed to stick in his throat, but he breathed a bit easier when astonishment chased annoyance from Zoe's face.

"*My* help? With what?"

"My uncle's library."

She lifted her chin a notch higher. "Since it's such a nuisance, I'd advise you to sell it."

"I plan to, as soon as it's feasible. The catch is, I have no idea what it's worth."

The angle of Zoe's chin became less severe. Her mouth turned up at the corners. "So *that*'s why you met with Cosmo."

"That's why." Now that the danger of fireworks had subsided, Ethan reclaimed his chair. "I needed an honest appraisal, and people tell me DiSantis is as reputable as they come."

"He is," said Zoe, "and he's an authority on astrology."

"He says the same about you."

"There's no comparison. Cosmo's a gifted teacher, but I've barely scratched the surface."

"He says you've surpassed him. He also said you might be persuaded to catalog the collection."

"Cosmo said that about me?"

"You are Zoe Piper, aren't you?"

Ethan chuckled and Zoe laughed with him, but her eyes remained solemn, her expression thoughtful.

She was flattered by Cosmo's confidence in her, and excited by the prospect of working with the Seymour library. Not just for the quality of its fabled first editions, but for its letters and personal diaries, as well.

Reading the correspondence from the world's leading astrologers, numerologists, psychokineticists and spiritualists would be a revelation. Authenticating the manuscripts would be a privilege, the chance of a lifetime. This was the kind of opportunity veteran astrologers would give their eyeteeth for, but it was not an opportunity to take lightly. And while Cosmo apparently had faith in her, Zoe was less certain of her own abilities.

She had been studying astrology for only three and a half years. Before then, like Ethan, she hadn't taken it seriously. Sometimes she'd read her daily horoscope, and now and again she'd been struck by the aptness of a forecast, but they were so general, she figured an occasional prediction *had* to be right. Although she tended to be fatalistic, she had dismissed any connection between fate and the stars—until she met Cosmo.

Her aunt had introduced them the evening Zoe arrived in New York City.

"This is my niece," Cora had said. "The one who's my inspiration for Sheila Gentry."

"So this is Zoe." Cosmo bent over her hand, and she caught a glimpse of his bald spot, sparsely covered by thinning dark hair. She had stared at his shining pink scalp, thoroughly charmed by the courtliness that seemed at odds with his coarse, battered features and pugilist's build.

At a loss, she'd blurted out, "No one's ever kissed my hand before."

Cosmo exchanged an amused glance with Cora. "You were right about this one," he said. "She's that rarity of rarities, an honest woman."

"But I'm nothing like Sheila," Zoe protested.

"No one's like Sheila." Cosmo pressed Zoe's hand, then released it to sketch an hourglass figure in the air. "Sheila's larger than life. Everything about her is exaggerated. Depending on your point of view, she's either high tragedy or low comedy. She's overblown, oversexed, overglamorized—"

"But sympathetic," Cora broke in, rushing to defend the lead character in her soap. "Sheila gets more fan mail than any of the actors on the show. Women idolize her and men adore her. They seem to find her fascinating."

Cosmo's eyes twinkled behind his horn-rimmed glasses. "I'll grant you, she's never boring."

"Which makes her the perfect soap-opera heroine." Having won a concession from Cosmo, Cora turned her attention to Zoe. "Story ideas aren't thick on the ground, my darling, but if you object to my adapting some of your experiences for Sheila, just say the word and I won't do it anymore."

Zoe did object, not only because Sheila's escapades threatened to invade her privacy, but also because Sheila's fictional life was so much more romantic than her own. If Zoe bumped her head, Sheila developed amnesia. If Zoe dated a man more than once, Sheila had an affair. And when Zoe had received a refund on her income tax, Sheila had inherited a fortune from her long-lost Uncle Sam.

But *Passion's Children* meant the world to Cora, and after her aunt's many kindnesses, it seemed to Zoe the least she could do was to provide a little grist for the mill.

"It's not that I mind," she replied, "but I wish you wouldn't tell people—"

"Say no more, sweetie. I quite understand, and I wouldn't embarrass you for anything. The only person I've told is Cosmo, and he's the soul of discretion."

DiSantis nodded agreement. "In my business, I have to be."

The quiet dignity with which he made this claim piqued Zoe's interest. "What sort of business are you in, Mr. DiSantis?"

In reply, Cosmo had given her his business card, and an invitation she could not afford to refuse.

"If you're looking for a job, stop by and see me. I might have something for you."

Zoe made her way to the address on the card the following morning. While the rush-hour swarm of taxis and buses flooded the streets, she strolled by Chinese laundries and Korean groceries, seedy bars and posh cafés. She passed a newsstand, a tobacconist, a flower shop, a boutique, a number of elegant brownstones she identified as yuppie enclaves.

By nine o'clock she was standing outside a building just off Columbus, wondering if the job offer was a put-on.

According to his business card, Cosmo DiSantis was the proprietor of The Second Story, a shop dealing in "Rare Books, Out-of-Print Books, First Editions, New and Used Books." But the physical evidence belied the advertising on the card.

The ground-floor windows of the brownstone were shuttered. A neon sign in the window closest to the door offered Rolling Rock on tap. A lunch menu had been taped to the glass beneath the sign, and the limited choices on the bill of fare seemed to indicate that the tavern was a neighborhood hangout. But the wine-colored awning above the stoop bore the name that supposedly belonged to DiSantis's bookstore.

Zoe compared the street number on the building with the address engraved on the card. She checked the sign on the corner of Columbus to make sure she was on the right cross street, and finally marched into the tavern and took a seat at the bar.

The bartender glanced up from the glass he was polishing. "What'll it be, miss?"

"I'm looking for Cosmo DiSantis."

"He expecting you?"

"He asked me to stop by."

"You can use the back stairs, then." With a flip of his towel, the bartender directed her toward the rear of the tavern. "Straight ahead, through the kitchen, and hang a right."

Zoe followed his instructions, and one flight later she followed her nose from the stairwell into some sort of storeroom, which led to an office, which led to a reception room, which led to the salesroom of a shop.

She paused in the alcove to get her bearings, but the distinctive odors of leather and paper and library paste, blended with a not unpleasant mustiness, confirmed that this truly was a bookstore.

Snatches of conversation drifted to her from the front of the shop, and using the voices as her guide, she wandered through a maze of tall oaken shelves, crammed floor to ceiling with an amazing array of books. Here and there a stack of volumes spilled onto the floor and blocked her path, requiring her to backtrack.

By the time she found the center aisle, she was awestruck by the dimensions of the display, and appalled by its randomness. Without discernible logic, fiction mingled with nonfiction and poetry with parody. Recent paperbacks were wedged into the gaps between hardcover classics.

She leaned down to pick up a hardbound collection of Shakespeare's sonnets that had fallen off the shelf, and put it next to a copy of *Twelfth Night*. At eye level, two shelves above, she spied *King Lear* and *Hamlet* and another volume of poetry, and she automatically reshelved those, as well. And once she had brought that miniscule bit of order to the chaos, she found she couldn't stop.

It was quarter to ten before Cosmo DiSantis and his customer appeared from a smaller room at the front of the shop, and by then she had finished a row of Shakespeare and was busy arranging Shaw—both George Bernard and Irwin.

DiSantis saw her and waved a greeting. "Be right with you," he called.

"There's no hurry," she answered. Time was one thing she had plenty of.

"Can I get you anything while you're waiting?"

"I could use a dust cloth."

He brought her a feather duster from a bin behind the cash register, then returned to the register to ring up the sale. He was seeing his customer to the door when the phone rang, and while he was on the phone, the jingling bell above the front entrance announced that another customer had come in.

"Hey!" said the newcomer. "This really is a book-store."

Zoe finished with the Shaws and started organizing Steinbeck.

Twelve o'clock came and went, and she still hadn't had her job interview, but she'd served tea to one of Cosmo's clients and learned to recognize first-time visitors to the shop. Without exception, they walked through the door saying, "This really is a bookstore!"—or words to that effect.

She had worked her way up to Thackeray before the shop was quiet. Cosmo complimented her on how much she had accomplished, and suggested she take a break. "It's after two," he said, "and I'll bet you haven't had lunch yet."

Zoe admitted she hadn't. Her groaning stomach reminded her she hadn't had *breakfast*.

"Come up to my apartment. We'll see what we can find in the fridge."

Cosmo put a Back at 3:00 sign on the door of the shop. He talked about the amenities of the brownstone as they climbed the stairs to his third-floor flat.

"The best thing about the building is, I own it," he said, "and the worst is, I own it. Since I bought the place, I've discovered I don't like being a landlord any more than I liked dealing with one."

"Is it hard to find tenants?"

"So far I haven't had to worry about that. I'm still renovating the units on four, and I inherited the tenant on the first floor. My original plan was to have the bookstore down there, but I couldn't overcome the tavern's longevity. When word got out The Second Story was losing its lease, the regulars mounted a protest. I got so many complaints it became obvious, if I shut down the tavern, I'd create nothing but ill will for the store."

"Is that why you used the name?"

"That's why. It's a condition of the new lease I worked out. I also became part owner of the tavern—"

"Which makes you your own landlord."

Cosmo laughed. "I never thought of it that way, but you're right."

Over pastrami on rye, Cosmo told her about the job. "The retail end of the business is a sideline. I do appraisals and consultations as well as a fair amount of speaking, so I'm away from the store a good deal of the time. I'd hoped to find an assistant who could eventually manage sales, but this position can be whatever you choose to make of it. You can confine yourself to the scut work, or let me train you in my specialty."

Zoe nodded eagerly. "What is your specialty?"

"Astrology."

Her eagerness vanished. She felt deflated. With her checkered employment history, she knew a little bit about a variety of things but, she admitted with some reluctance, "I don't know anything about astrology."

"I regard your lack of knowledge as a plus, my dear. It means you're not burdened by preconceived notions."

"No," she replied. "I'm not."

"Are you willing to learn?"

"If you're willing to teach me."

"Are you prepared to devote long hours to your lessons?"

"Yes, assuming you offer me the job and I decide to take it."

Cosmo's eyebrows shot to horrified peaks. "You must take the job, Zoe. That's all there is to it. After the way you've redistributed my stock, I won't be able to find anything."

She held his gaze, and thought, *Either he's joking, or this is the strangest job interview I've ever had.*

"Mr. DiSantis, before you hire me, shouldn't I tell you something about myself?"

"You can if you want to, my dear, but it might be more appropriate if I were to tell you about yourself."

Cosmo handed her an apple from the fruit bowl at the center of the table. She took it, mute with surprise. He polished his own apple against his shirt sleeve, and offered a disarming smile.

"You're searching," he said quietly. "You have been all your life. You've traveled around so much, done so much job-hopping that even the people you're fondest of accuse you of being fickle. They think you're frittering away your talents and urge you to settle down. Recently you've begun to worry that your loved ones may be right, but rest assured, they're not. The trouble is, you don't know what you're searching for—"

"Do you?" she asked.

"Only in the broadest sense, but I can tell you this much. Whatever it is you're looking for, you'll know intuitively when you find it. So even though the search may be painful, even though subconscious memories draw you into the past, it's imperative that you go on with it."

Over the next quarter hour, Zoe ate her apple in uneasy nibbles while Cosmo told her many things about herself, some of which she had known for years, some of which she was just beginning to recognize.

He talked about her fear of the water and advised her to overcome it. "The sea is your natural element," he said. "You're more likely to flourish if you live near the shore."

He told her he'd never had a moment's doubt that she would stop by the bookstore. "When someone makes a request of you, you find it impossible to say no, even if the request is unreasonable, even if it causes you inconvenience. There are some who take your helpfulness for granted, but still you feel obligated. You expect a lot of yourself, but you must learn to be selective and not spread yourself too thin. Otherwise, there may come a time when you promise more than you can deliver."

He gave voice to her deepest secret. "Your independence is protective camouflage. You long to be swept away by a grand passion."

"How do you know all this?" Zoe marveled. "Did my aunt tell you?"

Cosmo shook his head. "Cora told me the date, time and place of your birth. Your natal chart told me the rest."

"It's uncanny."

"Perhaps it is, but it's also astrology's greatest gift. Correctly interpreted, the stars can alert us to our shortcomings and help us rise above them. They can highlight our potentials and define our goals. They can even help us reach them. And in your case, I have the sense astrological guidance would be particularly beneficial." Cosmo peered at her over the rims of his bifocals. "Would you like to learn more about it?"

Would I! thought Zoe. But her answer was cautious. "Do you think I'd bc any good at it?"

Cosmo gave her a smile of singular sweetness. "My dear, I think you're a natural."

WITH THAT INDUCEMENT, Zoe had accepted the assistant manager's job, and in the time since then, she had worked hard and studied diligently, exploring the ancient wisdom of astrology.

Toward the end of her second year at the bookstore, Cosmo had tested her progress. He'd asked her to draw up a natal chart for a specific birth date, and with the chart as her only clue, figure out which of his clients it belonged to.

She'd passed the test with flying colors, and her analysis revealed a rare talent for investment counseling.

"The subject's a Jekyll and Hyde," she'd declared. "On one hand he's a conformist. He's fond of tradition, maybe even staid, and he has remarkable powers of discrimination. But where money's concerned, he's a gambler. The longer the odds, the better he likes them. He usually comes away with a profit, but that's more luck than skill. And just now, Neptune's conjunct Jupiter in his second house, which makes him prone to self-deception where finances are concerned."

"Interesting," said Cosmo. "And most enlightening. If he were your client, how would you advise him?"

"I'd tell him to retrench. Stick to safe investments, read the fine print on any contracts, and be careful to count his change. If he's in the stock market, I'd advise him to get out, at least temporarily. But I wouldn't expect him to listen. Not with his ego."

"Neither would I, but I'll relay your advice just the same." Cosmo drummed his fingers against the chart. "So tell me, Zoe. Who is this mystery man?"

"My guess is Mr. McClellan."

Cosmo beamed at her. "Absolutely right, my dear! Go to the head of the class."

With Cosmo's encouragement, her confidence blossomed. Over the next six months, she began applying her lessons to practical matters, and by last summer Cosmo had been sufficiently impressed with her insights that he sometimes referred financial questions to her.

And then in September, during her weekly consultation with Laurence McClellan, she had made a prediction that brought her an unwelcome spate of publicity and made her a laughingstock.

On the Tuesday after that fateful appointment, she arrived at the shop and found Cosmo at the sales counter, poring over a newspaper. She knew he was upset the moment she walked in. He scowled and shoved the paper toward her.

Her name leaped out at her, and Cosmo's, and above them, in bold type, "Stargazer Sees Wall Street Crash."

"The next time you have a yen to forecast stock market trends, I'd appreciate your leaving my name out of it."

Cosmo issued the rebuke mildly, and after a hurried scan of the article, Zoe marveled that he hadn't screamed at her. The tone of the column was scathing, almost blistering in its attack.

Economic indicators have rarely looked healthier. With the easing of inflation and the market over 2500, leading experts have projected continued growth. Even the least optimistic brokers expect only minor corrections as a result of profit taking. But where there are optimists, there are pessimists. Where there are monetary profits, there are prophets of doom. And where there are financial wizards, there are peripatetic wizards who will do anything for a buck. Onc

of these wizards, an itinerant astrologer who calls
herself Zoe Piper, has turned a jaundiced eye on the
heavens and concluded the sky is going to fall in October, and bring the market tumbling with it. According to Ms. Piper, "The Dow could lose as much
as 20% of its value."

The article went on to discount the forecast, and accuse
Zoe of biting the hand that offered the handout. It referred to her as "the sorcerer's apprentice," poked fun at
those who believed in astrology, and implied that its prac-
titioners were either charlatans or fools. By the time she
reached the end, Zoe was furious.

"How could Laurence do this?" she fumed.

Cosmo folded the newspaper and dropped it into the
wastebasket. "He's a journalist, my dear."

"But my comments about the stock market were private. I had no idea he'd share them with anyone else."

"I'm sure you didn't, and I doubt that Laurence intended to see them in print. Chances are he simply mentioned your prediction to the wrong person."

Cosmo's calm acceptance sharpened her pangs of guilt.
"How can I make it up to you?" she cried.

"You can't, Zoe. The damage has been done. But I've
weathered worse, and I imagine you have, too. What's
important is that you learn from this fiasco, and that you
exercise more restraint the next time you talk to the press."

"There won't be a next time, Cosmo. I promise you,
there won't."

Whatever his intentions, Laurence McClellan had violated the sanctity of the client-adviser relationship. He had
violated her trust. And because he hadn't kept a confidence, she had been held up to public ridicule.

What was worse was that Cosmo had been dragged into it, and despite his stoic exterior, despite his talk of weathering the incident, she knew how sensitive he was to adverse publicity.

That afternoon, when Laurence McClellan stopped by to apologize, she gave him a chilly reception. But in the end, at Cosmo's urging, she accepted the apology.

McClellan stayed for tea and to watch the day's installment of *Passion's Children*. When the show was over and the teapot empty, he left the store, all smiles.

In the late-afternoon lull between customers, Cosmo closeted himself in his office. Zoe did some paperwork and studied her current assignment.

On the surface nothing was changed. But the first article spawned others just as scathing, and over the next six weeks she sensed an increasing coolness in Cosmo's attitude toward her.

She was living in the fourth-floor flat by then, and they still spent most evenings studying. But as September blended into October, Cosmo became less enthusiastic about her lessons.

A distance was opening between them, and it seemed there was nothing she could do to reverse it. Zoe considered giving notice, moving out of the flat, returning to her Aunt Cora's. She thought about leaving New York. She had already stayed in the city longer than she had meant to. Perhaps it was time to move on.

She had actually bought her bus ticket the day the bottom dropped out of the market. Cosmo had left early that morning for a lecture tour upstate, so she heard about it from Laurence. He phoned at two o'clock and asked if she'd heard the news.

"What news?" she inquired.

"Turn on the TV," he replied. "God, I wish I'd taken your advice!"

Laurence hung up before she could question him, but the desperation in his voice told her what had happened, even before the CNN news team confirmed it.

For the next three hours she remained glued to the television set, stunned by the reports from Wall Street. When the phone rang, she ignored it. When it rang again, she took the receiver off the hook.

Although she had foreseen a drastic fall in prices, she had not envisioned the scope of the disaster. With each update, the size of the loss grew. One hundred...two hundred...three hundred points. And as the newsmen pointed out, the volume of trading had made the ticker tape lag behind. When the final tally was in, the loss could be devastating.

Zoe switched to a local station, as if the news might be better on another channel. It wasn't.

She tuned in an interview with the CEO of a major brokerage house, and listened to him compare the present debacle with the crash of '29. An economist joined the discussion and talked about the weak dollar and programmed selling, margin calls and institutional investors. He spoke of "recession" and "depression," and wondered how today's events on Wall Street would effect the Tokyo exchange.

"Of course," he concluded, "we must keep in mind that this is primarily a paper loss."

Zoe listened to the economist, and understood enough of his technical jargon to translate the plunging stock prices into terms of human suffering. A special bulletin graphic flashed on the screen, followed by a grave-faced announcement from the anchorman that the market's decline had exceeded five hundred points, and she thought about fortunes lost and hopes shattered, careers in ruins and futures destroyed.

She turned off the TV and reconnected the phone, preparing to close the shop. As soon as she replaced the receiver, another call rang through.

"Ms. Piper, this is Arnold Sorenson with the *Daily News*. I read a number of articles about you a few weeks back, and in view of what you said in them, I wondered about your reaction to what's happening on Wall Street. Do you feel vindicated at all?"

Zoe hung up without answering, appalled by the reporter's suggestion that she might be gloating over other people's misery.

Cosmo phoned from Albany that evening. "I've been trying to reach you for hours, Zoe. Is everything all right?"

"Everything's under control," she said. "I haven't spoken to the press."

"To hell with the press! It's you I'm worried about."

"You needn't be. I'm f-fine." She trailed into silence, aware that the quaver in her voice had given her away. She had never been a good liar. "It's just— Oh, Cosmo, I feel so *responsible*!"

"You're not, Zoe. Believe me, you're not. You merely predicted this panic. You didn't create it."

"But if I'd pursued it—if I'd insisted—"

"It wouldn't have made any difference, my dear. Unless your audience is willing to listen, all the talk in the world won't sway it. And human nature being what it is, given the choice between confronting disaster and hoping disaster will pass them by, the vast majority of people would rather play ostrich."

Cosmo had common sense on his side. He also had Zoe's respect. But his arguments raised more questions—

questions that kept her awake that night, browsing through her astrology texts, searching for answers.

The following morning most of her doubts remained, but she'd managed to resolve one issue.

As long as Cosmo was willing to teach her, she would go on with her studies; she would not let him down again.

As for Laurence McClellan, if she tried very hard, someday she might forgive him. But if he attempted to take advantage of her again, he'd be in for a nasty shock.

She might look like a pushover, but she had a long memory, and she *never* made the same mistake twice.

Chapter Two

"Never," said Zoe. "Never, never, never!"

Ethan rocked back in his chair, startled by her vehemence. "Never say never. Not till you've heard me out. If you agree to catalog my uncle's library, I'll make it worth your while. In addition to a generous salary, I'm prepared to grant you, as DiSantis's agent, first option on any sale—"

Zoe held up one hand. "Money's not a problem."

"Well, if it's the time that concerns you, I'm sure we can work something out. I'd hoped to schedule the auction for later this summer, but if you can't get out to East Hampton for a while, we can make whatever arrangements are convenient to you."

She shook her head. "Timing's not a problem, either."

Ethan tipped forward, allowing the front legs of his chair to settle on the floor. "Would you mind telling me what is?"

"Two things, actually. The first has to do with a personal weakness I've been trying to overcome. You see, I used to have a hard time denying people favors. Rather than disappoint a friend, I let myself get roped into doing all sorts of things I'd rather not do. So I promised myself, when someone asks for my help, instead of an automatic yes, I'd force myself to say no."

"Sounds like a wise move," Ethan replied with some impatience, "but I don't understand what it has to do with me. Mr. DiSantis gave me the impression you'd want to catalog the library. He said it'd be a feather in your cap."

"It would be," she allowed. "And under ordinary circumstances I'd be delighted to work with the Seymour Collection."

"What's wrong with the circumstances?"

"Coincidence, Mr. Quinn." *And the feeling she was being manipulated.* "Until a month ago, I didn't know where East Hampton is. Now, all at once, I have two invitations to visit the town. Yours and my Aunt Cora's."

Not that she considered Cora's nagging an invitation. It was more like a command. For the last three weeks, not a day had gone by without Zoe's receiving a call from her aunt, imploring her to bird-sit Boris.

Cora had tried cajolery, flattery, bribery, threats. She had even resorted to tears. But no matter what approach she took, Zoe had remained adamant. She'd had the misfortune to meet Boris, and a few minutes in his company had convinced her that the mynah was as treacherous as his owner.

And while half a year had passed since Laurence McClellan had leaked her Wall Street prediction to the press, she hadn't forgotten his betrayal.

Flimsy as the evidence was, Zoe had a right to be suspicious. Cora's pestering and Laurence's penchant for exploitation gave her that right. For all she knew, her aunt had prevailed upon Cosmo to send Ethan Quinn her way. Ethan's proposition could be another gimmick to lure her out to Long Island.

But what if the offer was genuine? What if Ethan's only guilt was by association, his only crime living in East Hampton?

She glanced at him and he spread his arms in an expansive gesture, withholding no compromise, no accommodation that might win her cooperation.

"Say no more," he told her. "I'm flexible. If you want to spend time with your aunt, you can set your own hours, work at your own pace."

Zoe studied him, unimpressed. "Do you know my aunt?" she inquired.

"No, I don't believe we've met."

"What about Laurence McClellan?"

"I know him by reputation."

"So Cosmo didn't tell you that my aunt's rented Gull Cottage for the month of June?"

"Not that I recall. But I'm familiar with the place."

"Do you think I'd enjoy staying there?"

"I don't know why you wouldn't. If you took a poll, I think you'd find that most New Yorkers would jump at the chance to spend a month in the Hamptons. And McClellan's cottage is ideally located. It's on Frigate Alley, right on the dunes, and it has a fantastic view of the ocean."

Ethan fell silent, aware that he was beginning to sound like a one-man chamber of commerce. Zoe was watching him as if she were weighing his honesty, and he suddenly felt as if every lie he'd ever told was branded on his face.

His ears were hot, his collar too tight— Damned if he wasn't blushing.

He shuffled his feet beneath the chair, and Merlin attacked his pants cuff. He reached down and scooped the cat onto his lap, welcoming the distraction.

He cleared his throat, trying to figure out where Zoe's questions were leading, and added, "It's up to you, of course. If you'd prefer to stay at my uncle's house, there's plenty of room there, or I could get you a room at The Maidstone Arms or one of the bed-and-breakfast places."

"That won't be necessary." Zoe braced herself, preparing to announce she must decline his offer, but Ethan sensed what was coming, and flashed his most persuasive smile.

"I really need your help," he said. "If you take the job, I swear you won't regret it, but you don't have to give me an answer today. Take your time. Think it over. Check me out with DiSantis. When you've made your decision, let me know."

"How do I contact you?"

"You can reach me at the bank during business hours, or at my home phone after five."

Ethan handed her his business card, then consulted his watch and deposited Merlin on the floor. Zoe felt her resolve weakening as she helped him retrieve his loafer from beneath the sofa and followed him to the door.

Still smiling, he said, "Are there any other questions?"

"Only one," she replied. But considering how feebly she resisted temptation, this final question might be the most vital of all.

He turned to look at her, his features taut with expectation.

"What's your birth date?"

He relaxed visibly. Laugh lines fanned out from the corners of his eyes. "November 2."

The Pluto decan of Scorpio, she thought. Unless other planets in his natal chart offset the impact of Pluto, a man born on that date would be competitive, driven, enigmatic; fully conscious of his power and not afraid to use it—

Just as Ethan was now. Turning on the charm. Smiling into her eyes as if she were the only woman in the world.

And although she knew it was deliberate, she was not immune to his charm. She sounded slightly breathless as she inquired, "What year?"

"I'm surprised you have to ask. If astrology is as revealing as you claim, you already know everything worth knowing about me."

She lifted a winging, red-gold brow. "I know a Scorpio evasion when I hear one."

"But you obviously don't recognize when you're being teased."

"I take my work seriously, Mr. Quinn, and it seems I must remind you, I'm an astrologer, not a fortune-teller."

The laugh lines deepened. Ethan's voice dropped an octave. "Very well, then. I'm thirty-three. You can figure out the year for yourself. And, Vangie, in case you're wondering, I'm not married, not involved, my sexual orientation is hetero, and given the proper incentive, I advocate mixing business with pleasure."

A bewildered look clouded the amusement on Zoe's face. "Who's Vangie?"

Ethan regarded her narrowly. After a brief hesitation, he shrugged. "I give up. Who is she?"

"You tell me. You just called me by her name."

"Why would I call you Vangie when I've no idea who she is?"

Zoe mimicked his shrug and his hesitation. "I give up. Why would you?"

Ethan frowned. The gold flecks left his eyes. "That's an interesting question, Zoe. And I'd like to get to the bottom of it as much as you would, but just now I've got a train to catch."

"Then I guess Vangie's identity will have to remain a mystery till the next time we meet."

Zoe's laughter was soft and musical—and oddly familiar. Ethan stared at her, wondering if they had met before. But then he thought, *If we'd met, I'd have remembered it. She's not the sort of woman I'd forget.*

"Can I expect to hear from you next week?" he asked.

"Oh, yes," she said. "One way or the other, I'll be in touch."

Even as she stalled, Zoe sensed that in the end she would accept Ethan's offer. And over the next few days this feeling was borne out. As Cosmo succinctly put it, "The chance to work with the Seymour library is too good to pass up."

"But you're passing it up," she argued.

"Only because I have a prior commitment. I promised your aunt I'd act as technical adviser on her show."

"Don't tell me Sheila's getting into astrology."

"No," said Cosmo. "I think she's about to become possessed by the spirit of her great-great-grandmother."

"Didn't that happen once before?"

"Not to Sheila, and not on *Passion's Children*. But it is a standard concept for daytime drama."

"So Cora's really scraping the bottom of the barrel."

"It's the writers' strike," said Cosmo. "She's hoping the special effects will hide the hackneyed story line."

Zoe glanced at him quizzically. "Do you believe in possession?"

"Not the way they'll do it on the soap, with two identities fighting over one body, but I know for a fact that unresolved issues from our past lives can carry over into the present."

"How do you mean?"

"Well, I myself, for instance, led one former life in eighteenth-century Spain, during the reign of Carlos III—who, by the way, was quite a progressive ruler and the homeliest man I've ever known. In that existence, you see, I was preoccupied with physical beauty. I was a ringer for Ricardo Montalban, and I made the most of my appearance. Not always wisely and, I'm afraid, not always honorably. I was vain, narcissistic, and let me tell you, I cut quite a swath with the ladies. And now, for my sins, I look like Fred Flintstone."

Zoe wasn't sure whether she should laugh or sympathize. She couldn't always tell when Cosmo was joking. His mention of former lives sent a chill of foreboding down her spine, but the realization that he would be at Gull Cottage was reassuring.

"Sam Kellogg and Brynne Loringer are staying there, too," Cosmo said, "and your aunt's been in a tizzy, trying to choose which of the second leads should have the extra bedroom. But if you join the party, we'll have a full house. Cora can book everyone but the stars of the cast into the local inns, and there won't be any bruised egos."

Which provided a neat resolution to Cora's predicament, but raised a problem for The Second Story.

"If we're both in East Hampton, who'll mind the store?"

"I'll get into town once or twice a week for consultations with my usual clients," Cosmo replied. "And for the days I can't be here, I'll hire a temp to answer the phone and deal with walk-ins."

"Will you be available if I run into any difficulties with the library?"

"My dear," said Cosmo, "I wouldn't have it any other way."

On Wednesday of that week Zoe had lunch with Cora, and agreed to bird-sit Boris.

"You're a lifesaver, my darling!" Cora gushed. "With you in East Hampton, who knows? I might find fresh inspiration for my turkey of a plot. Which, if you'll excuse the pun, is rather like killing two birds with one stone!"

Zoe was touched by her aunt's display of gratitude, and although she didn't much like being compared to a rock, on Thursday she telephoned Ethan and informed him she had decided to take the job.

"We'll be driving out to East Hampton the first of June," she told him. "Perhaps we could get together that evening to work out the details."

"If you'd like, I could pick you up about eight and give you a preview of the library."

"I'll look forward to it," she replied.

Now that she had made up her mind, she was eager to see the Seymour library. And, oddly enough, she was also looking forward to seeing more of Ethan Quinn.

Chapter Three

From what she knew about Laurence McClellan, Zoe expected Gull Cottage to be luxurious and elegant, with a certain amount of glitz.

In most respects she was not disappointed. In some she got more than she'd bargained for.

East Hampton was smaller than she had thought it would be, the houses statelier, the streets shadier, and the village green more bucolic. Hook windmill, which revealed the influence of Dutch colonial days, came as a picturesque surprise, and the shops that lined Main Street might have served as models for Disneyland's Main Street U.S.A. But a glance at the price tags on the offerings in the store windows dispelled the theme park illusion.

After strolling through several boutiques, Zoe arrived at a rule of thumb: the more understated a garment, the higher the cost.

Minimalist art commanded outrageous prices. A white-on-white canvas ran to five figures, and the "simple is best" code applied even to groceries. Some foods, she discovered, were fashionable; others were not. Madame Makarova's deli supplied such staples as thirteen-dollar eggplants and five-dollar cabbages, fresh chopped basil worth its weight in gold, and tins of beluga caviar, ounce for ounce more expensive than the costliest perfume.

"Half the battle is marketing," Cora explained. "Madame Makarova happens to be the former food editor for *Izvestia*, and Larry tells me anything authentically Russian is much in demand this year."

At least in East Hampton, thought Zoe.

They lunched on pelmenie Siberia—which was not unlike wonton soup—served with sour cream and hot Russian mustard, then climbed back into the network limousine and drove on to Frigate Alley.

As Ethan had told her, Gull Cottage was situated on the dunes. Its steep roofs and tall chimneys made an imposing silhouette against the windswept sky. She could smell the salt tang of the sea even before she got out of the car, but she didn't get her first glimpse of the Atlantic until she stepped into the foyer.

French doors dominated the southern wall of the living room, and offered breathtaking ocean views. Zoe stood at the windows, dazzled by the display. She watched the surf roll onto the beach and fancied she could feel the tug of the waves as they retreated.

With Merlin tagging close behind, she wandered out to the deck and from there to the solarium, where the ceiling soared a full two stories past a copper-hooded fireplace, exposed oak tie beams, and round dormer windows that admitted streams of light.

A glass-fronted cabinet held a gallery of photographs, and Zoe stopped to look at them.

A few of the pictures featured the McClellan family, but most were of Laurence with celebrities whose performances he had touted or whose careers he had "made."

More photographs of Laurence lined the walls, along with a collection of playbills and silver-framed copies of his best-known reviews. One began with a gibe: "A tragedy occurred at the Music Box last night. Unfortunately, the farce that made its debut on stage was supposed to be a comedy." A second paraphrased George S. Kaufman: "Am watching your act from the last row of the balcony. Wish you were here." A third referred to Cora as "the doyenne of daytime drama," then borrowed a quote from Fred Allen to lampoon *Passion's Children*: "Television is called a 'medium,'" Laurence had written, "because it's rare when it's well done."

A raucous two-note whistle reminded Zoe that the Seymour library wasn't the sole reason for her presence at Gull Cottage. The solarium was Boris's bailiwick.

She turned and saw that Merlin had climbed onto a chair back to get an unobstructed look at the mynah, whose cage occupied the one shady corner of the room. Boris was teetering on his perch and leering at her.

"Cat got your tongue," he taunted, and with another shrill whistle hopped down from his perch.

Zoe approached the bird cautiously and gathered up the half dozen Post-it notes Laurence had taped to the base of the cage.

"Read the instructions. Read the instructions."

"Thank you, Boris. I will."

"Out loud," the bird prompted.

Zoe read the first note, keeping a watchful eye on Merlin. "This one says, 'Never tease a mynah. It will quickly learn to retaliate—'"

"That's a lie!" Boris shrieked. "You can reach me through my lawyer!"

"That may take a while," Zoe answered absently. She finished glancing through the notes and tucked them into her carryall for safekeeping. "Is there anything I can get you in the meantime?" she asked.

Boris ruffled his breast feathers and cocked his head to one side so that he looked almost sheepish. In a remarkable imitation of a Southern drawl he confided, "I have always depended on the kindness of strangers."

"So have I," Zoe murmured.

She couldn't help laughing, and as she rounded up Merlin and went off to find her bedroom, it occurred to her that she might have more in common with Boris than with any of the humans who would be staying in the house.

LATE THAT AFTERNOON the tenants of Gull Cottage gathered around the pool for predinner drinks. "This house is a treasure," Cora Piper declared, and no one disagreed with her.

Cosmo said, "The solarium should lend itself quite nicely to your hypnotism scene."

"I should think so," said Cora. "It's a fabulously visual room."

Sam Kellog praised the shingle-style architecture and its intrinsically pleasing proportions. "I'll bet every room in the house is photogenic," he said.

"I simply *adore* my boudoir," Brynne Loringer remarked in her overemotive italicized way. "Pink is *such* a flattering color. I just *know*, when I'm lying in my sweet little canopy bed, I shall feel as if I'm sleeping in a seashell."

Zoe sipped her tonic water and wondered if Brynne might be persuaded to trade accommodations with her.

Perhaps from a misguided sense of guilt, Cora had assigned her the master suite, and the bed in Zoe's room was a set designer's reproduction of Cleopatra's barge, swagged and tapestried, covered in hieroglyphs, with gold-leaf serpents slithering up its legs.

The bed was bigger than her flat, yet the thought of climbing the ladder to the sleeping platform made her feel claustrophobic. Even if the altitude didn't bring on a nosebleed, she doubted she would be able to sleep with the curtains closed around her, surrounded by stylized animal totems.

Zoe wondered if the fact the bed was a stage prop would carry any weight with Brynne. She wondered whether any of the others had slot machines in their bathrooms, but before she could ask, Cora inquired how she was getting along with Boris.

"It's too soon to tell," she replied. "So far he's been on his best behavior."

"Larry said he'd left you some notes."

"I found them," said Zoe. And she had read the directions for the daily care and feeding of the mynah, tips about meals and baths and cleaning the cage and for the daily vocabulary lessons Laurence had requested. "We'll have to be careful what we say in front of Boris," she warned her aunt. "Mynahs are very imitative, and Boris seems to be an especially quick study. He's already learned to imitate Merlin."

"I'll be careful," Cora promised. "And I trust you will be, too. I shudder to think how Larry might react if that cat did anything to harm Boris."

"Don't worry," said Zoe. "The cage is secure, and even if it weren't, I suspect Boris could take care of himself."

"Well, in that case, my darling, I'd say you've got all the bases covered. Everything's going smooth as silk."

Zoe crossed her fingers, hoping things would continue to go smoothly—and they did until dinner was over and the five of them were lingering over coffee in the peach and coral dining room, going over the script for the next day's shoot.

Brynne was unhappy with some of her dialogue in the hypnotism scene, demanding changes in every other line, lamenting some of the wording.

"Breeches is *archaic*," she complained. "Sheila would never *say* it."

"That's the idea, sweetie. This is where great-great-grandmama Hester's character starts to sneak in."

Cora's explanation didn't seem to register with Brynne, nor did Sam Kellogg's comment that he considered the scene "meaty."

"It ought to play like a dream," he said. "It's terribly spooky, even on the page. I swear, it made the hair on the back of my neck stand on end."

"That's *another* thing." Brynne pouted, appealing to Cosmo. "Have you seen the wig I have to wear when I'm playing Hester? It's *brown* and *frumpy*. It's positively *hideous*! No one will recognize me."

"You're overreacting, my dear," Cosmo replied. "It would take more than a wig to hide your beauty."

Brynne blushed a flattering shade of pink and favored Cosmo with her patented dimpled smile. "Do you really think so?" she cooed.

"Word of honor."

Brynne admired her reflection in the window glass, somewhat mollified by the compliment, and the discussion turned to other aspects of the hypnotism scene, with Cosmo fielding questions and offering suggestions that would heighten the effect of the segment without cheapening it with melodrama.

But Brynne liked to be the center of attention. She began fidgeting in her chair and drawing designs on the tablecloth with the tines of her dessert fork. The atmosphere in the dining room fairly crackled with tension, and Zoe didn't have to be a mind reader to sense that a storm was brewing.

Before the evening's over, she thought, *Brynne's going to throw a tantrum.* But before that happens, Ethan Quinn should arrive and help her make a getaway.

A rumble of thunder drew Zoe's attention to the window, to the expanse of lowering sky just visible beyond Brynne Loringer's reflection.

An early twilight had fallen. A mass of clouds on the horizon blended into the slate-blue sea. The rising wind threatened rain and sent whitecaps scudding across the water.

A storm was brewing outside as well, Zoe realized, and she wondered which tempest would break first.

THE HOUSE WAS DARK when Ethan arrived; the deluge was at its peak. He parked beneath the porte cochere, next to a sleek gunmetal-gray limousine that seemed half a block long, and made a dash for the front door.

The woman who answered his knock was wearing a chalk-striped designer suit that proclaimed her importance, boots with four-inch heels that did not compensate for her lack of height, and a hawklike expression that marked her as someone to be reckoned with. She scowled at him and held up the candelabra she carried, trying to get a better look at his face.

Ethan coughed to cover a laugh. In spite of the woman's high heels, he towered over her, and with her arm upraised and the candles extended, she reminded him of a miniature Statue of Liberty. He permitted himself a smile as he introduced himself, and added, "I believe Miss Piper is expecting me."

A look of gratitude softened the sternness on the woman's face. She motioned him into the foyer with an airy flap of her hand. "Come in, Mr. Quinn. I'm Cora Piper, Zoe's aunt. My niece is expecting you—and if you know anything at all about fuse boxes, you'll be my hero for life!"

"I can find my way around a fuse box," he allowed, "but I'm afraid it'll take LILCO to repair the lights."

"LILCO?"

"The Long Island Light Company. The power usually goes off in weather like this, but service should be restored by morning."

"Then we'll have to make do with candles—which, come to think of it, may not be entirely bad." After testing the latch on the front door, Cora led the way through the foyer. "I suppose Zoe told you we're in East Hampton to tape some location sequences for *Passion's Children*."

"No, she didn't, but the local paper ran an article on your visit."

"Well, one of the scenes on our schedule for tomorrow has been the cause of some dissension, so we've decided to rework the staging, and candlelight fits the mood of hypnosis, don't you think?"

The question was obviously rhetorical. Without giving him the chance to respond, Cora led him into the solarium, where the rest of the house party was assembled.

The dusk in the room was relieved by the glow of a dozen flickering candles, and as he strode toward the circle of light, Ethan recognized the actor and actress who played Rafe and Sheila Gentry on *Passion's Children*, although he didn't remember their names until Cora introduced them.

Sam Kellogg shook Ethan's hand, Brynne stopped pouting and gave him a sultry smile, Zoe saw him and waved a greeting, and Cosmo DiSantis grinned.

"Good to see you again, Ethan. Zoe was about to help me with an experiment, but I know how eager she is to see your uncle's library—"

"There's no rush," Ethan broke in. "The power's off at my uncle's house, too." Turning to Zoe, he continued, "I'd have telephoned earlier to let you know we have to postpone our meeting till tomorrow, but McClellan has an unlisted number."

"I'll make a note of it for you," Zoe replied. She brushed past him on her way to the writing desk that occupied a corner of the room, and he caught the subtle scent of lilacs.

"If you don't have to rush off, perhaps you'd like to watch my demonstration," said Cosmo. "You might find it interesting."

"Do stay," Cora urged in a wheedling undertone. "I'd appreciate having an unbiased opinion, and if you're here, Brynne's apt to remain on her best behavior."

"I'd like to stay, if you're sure it's all right, but exactly what sort of demonstration are you planning?"

"Hypnotism," said Cora. "Cosmo's going to hypnotize Zoe."

A flash of lightning punctuated her answer. The wind rattled the French doors, and in the same instant, a crack of thunder launched a fresh torrent of rain.

Cora shivered and sidled closer to the fireplace, and Sam Kellogg called, "Great special effects, chief."

"Yes," she agreed. "They were very effective. I'll have to keep them in mind for tomorrow."

The springtime fragrance announced Zoe's nearness.

"I like your perfume," Ethan said. "Lilac, isn't it?"

Zoe looked vaguely troubled. The slip of notepaper on which she had written McClellan's phone number trembled in her hand.

"That's a nice compliment," she replied, "but I'm not wearing perfume."

Cosmo placed a single candle at the center of an occasional table and aligned the chairs on either side so that they faced each other. He crisscrossed the room, extinguishing the remaining candles, then returned to the chairs and seated himself.

"Ready?" he asked.

Zoe sat in the chair opposite his. "Ready," she said.

Cosmo looked at the others. "If you'll all make yourselves comfortable, we're ready to begin."

There was some milling about as Ethan and Cora, Brynne and Sam found seats. Boris whistled and hopped onto his perch, the better to watch the proceedings.

Ethan glanced in the direction of the mynah and rose. "Should I cover the cage?"

Zoe shook her head. "That would probably irritate him."

Ethan settled back on the sofa, and Merlin crept out from beneath a wicker love seat and curled up on his lap. Cosmo hitched his chair closer to the table, claiming Zoe's attention.

"The first thing I have to do," he said, "is find out whether you're susceptible to hypnosis."

Zoe shifted slightly and folded her hands tightly in her lap. "Yes," she said. "I understand."

"I can see that you're uneasy, but I promise you have nothing to be nervous about. I have no intention of making either of us look foolish. Just do as I ask and try not to resist me."

Cosmo smiled at her encouragingly, then turned to Cora and began discussing the theatrical possibilities of hypnotism. As he talked he got to his feet and paced back and forth. His steps were slow and measured, and he spoke in a monotone, as if he were speaking to himself. He had used the word "regression" several times before it dawned on Zoe that he intended to revive her memories of previous lives.

At that point she might have protested, but her mouth had gone cottony with alarm and her tongue seemed permanently stuck to the roof of her mouth.

Yet moments later she wondered why she should be apprehensive. Certainly there was nothing frightening about Cosmo DiSantis. He was her employer, her mentor, her guide to the arcane. He had opened her eyes to the limitless vistas of astrology, and the least she could do was cooperate.

She inhaled deeply and rested her head against the upholstery so that she could watch the progress of his shadow as it moved across the vaulted ceiling. Occasionally he emphasized something he said by gesturing with his hands, and the candle flame magnified the movements and projected them onto the wall above the fireplace hood, casting images that looked now like a dog, now like a rooster or a dragon.

This isn't working, she thought. *Poor Cosmo will be so disappointed.*

The quartet of onlookers was so still that she might have been alone with him. Not the rustle of a script nor the shuffling of feet nor the creak of a chair had interrupted the even flow of DiSantis's explanation.

His voice was beautifully modulated, strangely soothing, and she wondered if he had mesmerized everyone in the room.

Everyone but her—

Or had her focus of concentration become so narrow that she saw only his shadow? Heard only his voice?

But no. Cosmo's voice was not all she heard. As the homey patter of rain on the roof grew increasingly distant, she became acutely aware of the sound of her own heartbeat, the sound of her own respirations growing quieter, slower, deeper. Just these and the rhythmic flow of Cosmo's shadow across the wall, like a charcoal drawing come to life.

She stared at the shadow, unblinking, until her eyes smarted and grew so heavy that she could no longer keep them open. And in the instant her eyelids drifted shut, they felt as if they had been glued together.

"Zoe," said DiSantis, "would you like to raise your arm?"

She tried to comply with this suggestion, but couldn't. Her arm felt leaden, and she could not unclasp her hands.

"Can you hear me, Zoe?"

"Yes. I hear you."

"Doesn't your arm feel very light, as if it would like to float above your head?"

As soon as he asked this question, Zoe loosened her fingers and lifted her arm to shoulder level. She held it there steadily, without a sign of fatigue, for a full two minutes.

"Excellent, my dear. You may want to lower it now."

A collective sigh echoed in the stillness of the room, but Zoe scarcely heard it. She wondered why Cosmo was praising her for doing something so simple. Why didn't he ask her to do something really difficult, such as opening her eyes?

"I would like you to imagine that you're in a special place. A place where you feel secure and at peace." DiSantis paused, and as if he'd read her mind, said, "By the way, you may open your eyes or keep them closed, whichever is most comfortable for you."

Only a moment ago she would not have been able to open her eyes, but now, with no conscious effort on her part, they opened wide.

"Can you tell me what you see, my dear?"

"The meadow," she answered tonelessly.

"Ah, yes. You are strolling through the meadow and it's exceedingly pleasant, the most tranquil spot you have ever seen. You can feel the sun warming your back, the trees that surround the clearing are stirring in the breeze, the grass is lush and green and the sky is clear and blue— Can you see it, Zoe?"

"Yes, I see it."

She saw all that he had described and more. She saw wild asters and the honeybees that darted among them. She saw the scarlet plumage of a cardinal perched on a lily frond and heard the fluting notes of his song. She saw the grass sway and bend as the wind moved over it, and then she felt the breeze caress her cheek and ruffle her hair and she inhaled the fragrance of new-mown hay—

"Tell me, Zoe, what time of year is it?"

"It's summer."

"Summer? Are you sure?"

"*Yeesss*. That is, I think it is. It's June, isn't it?"

"Look at the trees, Zoe."

Silence, and a hint of confusion on her face.

"The foliage on the maples would not be red in June, would it?"

This suggestion prompted another silence, longer than before, and then, hesitantly, she said, "No."

"Then what season is it?"

"Fall?" she answered tentatively. "Yes, it must be fall."

"That's correct, Zoe, and do you see the brook?"

For long moments she saw only the wash of candlelight across the lenses of Cosmo DiSantis's bifocals, and then she did see the brook, and she heard it as well, gurgling along its rocky bed.

"Yes, I see it."

"Good! Very good." Satisfied that her trance was deep and genuine, DiSantis returned to his chair and rearranged the candle so that it shone fully on her face while he blended into the gloom. "Now, my dear, I want you to picture yourself walking toward the stream, and for every step you take, you will count backward one year."

She tilted her face toward the disembodied voice, peering into the shadows beyond the wavering light of the candle as if she must confirm Cosmo's instructions by seeing him. He leaned forward, allowing her a reassuring glimpse of his face.

"Do you understand what I'm saying, Zoe? For every step you take, you will become one year younger. And one more thing. From time to time I will ask you to stop along the way and tell me what you are experiencing."

"Yes," she replied. "I understand."

Cora was having second thoughts about her niece being the guinea pig in this demonstration. Now that she'd seen mesmerism firsthand, it seemed closely akin to voodoo or some other pagan mumbo jumbo. But before she could speak out, Zoe began counting.

"Twenty-five...twenty-four...twenty-three..."

With each succeeding number, Cora inched closer to Ethan, but her eyes never strayed from Zoe's face, and at first it wasn't so bad. In fact, she discovered she was fascinated by the prospect of where her niece's reminiscences might lead.

Zoe recreated her high school graduation, a dance recital, a Fourth of July picnic, the Christmas Cora had taken her to a performance of *The Nutcracker* ballet. And the eerie thing was, as she retreated further into the past, her voice took on the clear piping treble of childhood. As she relived her first day in kindergarten, she even looked younger. Her features seemed smoother, rounder, less well-defined, as if the delicate bones of her face were still blurred by a little girl's plumpness.

And then Zoe was counting again. In a dreamy, uninflected voice she said, "Four...three...two..."

She had reached the brook. One more step would take her off the grassy embankment and into the water. But even as the toe of her sandal moved toward the shimmering surface of the stream, time seemed to telescope. The brilliant colors of the meadow faded, the light darkened, and a new scene sprang into focus.

Autumn had turned to winter. Instead of a carpet of green, snow covered the ground. Instead of the brook, she stood at the edge of a frozen pond, ringed with bonfires and dotted with skaters who were dressed in funny, old-fashioned costumes.

Most of the men sported luxuriant facial hair—muttonchop whiskers and handlebar mustaches seemed the predominant choice—and the ladies' skirts swirled about their ankles as they went skimming over the ice.

And she herself was wearing skates attached to high-button boots that pinched her toes and a wasp-waisted corset that nipped in her midriff and woolen stockings that itched. Her hair was piled on top of her head, except for a few beau-catcher strands that curled about her cheeks, and she was wearing a long plaid cape whose hood was trimmed with fur.

As she moved along the edge of the pond, picking her way toward the closest bonfire with wobbly, mincing steps, the hem of her cloak swept the snow behind her, erasing her footprints.

She was only a few yards from the fire when the figure of a man separated itself from the cluster of skaters at the center of the pond and came racing after her, skidding to halt at her side so swiftly that he might have materialized from a dream.

"I've been waiting for you, Vangie. I thought you'd never get here."

Her step faltered. She confronted the man, at a loss. His rugged shoulders and lanky frame gave him a strong resemblance to Ethan Quinn. But his hair, combed back from a widow's peak, was darker than Ethan's and his eyes were blue—

"Vangie? Is something wrong?"

She knitted her brows. She recognized his voice. Some secret part of herself realized she had met this man before, but she could not remember where.

"I'm sorry," she replied. "My name isn't Vangie. It's—"

"Evangeline. Evangeline Bliss—but not for long. In another two weeks you'll be my wife." He smiled and held out his hands to her, beckoning her onto the ice. "Come with me, sweetheart. Skate with me. I want to hold you in my arms."

Her heart skipped a beat. The frisson of awareness that leaped along her nerve ends told her she wanted that, too, more than she had ever wanted anything. Every fiber of her being yearned for this man—to be in his arms, hold him close, feel his touch—

But she was not Evangeline.

"Th-there's been some mistake," she stammered. "I'm not who you think I am."

He leaned closer, appraising her features as if he were seeing her for the first time. "There's no mistake," he insisted. "You're the woman I'm going to marry."

"But you don't know me—"

"I love you more than life itself. That's all I need to know."

Although he made this declaration simply, his expression was exalted, and when he removed her cloak and tossed it down by the bonfire, she hadn't the will to resist.

His arm circled her waist as he helped her negotiate the snowy embankment. She felt a twinge of anxiety when he drew her onto the ice, but the fear was fleeting, gone before she could identify its source.

He swung her into a waltz, and instinct took over. She followed his steps without stopping to think, without questioning how it could happen that she, who had never skated before, should be able to skate so beautifully.

They danced across the pond, their movements perfectly synchronized; turning, gliding, swaying as if they had been skating together for years, and even while she marveled at their expertise, she attributed it to her partner.

One of his hands cradled hers in an all-encompassing grasp, the other spanned the small of her back and allowed her to anticipate his lead.

Turn, two, three...glide, two, three... The tempo of their steps quickened.

Sway, two, three...spin, two, three... The wind stung her cheeks and stole her breath away.

As they glided and twirled in tandem, an intoxicating feeling of freedom blossomed inside her. She had never been so carefree, so happy, so content. The pleasure of the moment must have gone to her head. Or it might have been youthful exuberance or some imp of mischief that made her throw back her head and laugh.

Her partner laughed with her, and she surrendered to impulse and looped her arms about his neck.

"I envy Evangeline," she confessed.

He skated to a stop. "You are Evangeline, my love."

He sounded so certain, so confident, so absolutely convinced that she believed him. She smoothed her palms over his shoulders and along his lapels, savoring the taut bunching of muscles beneath his fine worsted jacket. Her voice broke as she said, "I think I'm dreaming."

"If this is a dream, I pray we never wake up."

He folded her close, claiming her lips as if he were starving for the taste of her, as if he would never have enough of her. And as he deepened his possession of her mouth, she abandoned herself to the wonder of being Evangeline, to the rapture of being young and in love and desired by this man.

She did not recall his name, but she knew she had been searching for him all her life. He was her soul mate, her destiny, her soon-to-be husband. He was the missing part of herself—the best part, the loving part, her very heart and soul. Without him she would never know fulfillment, but in the haven of his arms she found completion, belonging, a sense of homecoming.

Surely, in a world where they could be reunited, *anything* was possible.

Her elation was so great that she could not contain it. She flitted across the pond in a series of dainty pirouettes, and when he skated after her, she playfully eluded him. Again he pursued, and again she spun away, trailing effervescent laughter on the frosty night air, enticing him to join her in a romantic game of tag.

In a rare, reckless mood, she darted this way and that, flying past other skaters who seemed dim shadow figures. Although she slowed her pace, straining to see their faces, they remained featureless, without substance, as if they existed only in her imagination.

Perplexed, she stared back at the figures, even as the blades of her skates carried her on.

A weathered signpost whizzed by on her right. From the corner of her eye she caught a glimpse of stark black lettering partially hidden by snow, but she did not recognize the sign's significance until her lover's shout alerted her to impending danger.

She tried to reverse direction, tried to stop, but momentum propelled her forward, and her joy turned to terror when the ice gave way beneath her, plunging her from a world of tenderness and warmth into a glacial oblivion, where everything was dark and cold and lonely, where her restless soul would find no peace . . .

Chapter Four

Cosmo DiSantis was not prepared for the change that came over Zoe. One moment she was smiling at him, peeking through her lashes with a fey, fawnlike charm, and humming the "Skater's Waltz." And the next moment her eyes took on the fixed, unseeing stare of a shock victim.

The bloom of color drained from her cheeks, leaving her face as waxen as the candle on the table. Even the sprinkling of freckles across the bridge of her nose had paled. She was whimpering, shivering, hugging her arms to her sides for warmth, obviously distraught, and when he felt her pulse, he found that it was thready and rapid.

Although he recognized that something had gone wrong, Cosmo was not overly concerned. He counted to five, giving the prearranged signal, assuming it would rouse her. When she did not respond, he stared at her, aghast.

He saw the tiny beads of moisture that pebbled her forehead, and a film of perspiration broke out on his own skin.

He repeated the signal, gave it again and again, but his suggestions didn't reach her, and he suddenly realized that all his years of study, all his skill and encyclopedic knowledge of the vagaries of the human psyche were useless.

"Lights, please," he called. "Somebody light the candles."

Boris had been dozing, but the hubbub that followed revived him. He hopped from his perch to the floor of his cage, splashed excitedly through his water dish, and began pelting Merlin with hard little pellets of food left from his supper. As the flurry of pellets became a downpour, Merlin sought refuge beneath the sofa.

"Is it over?" Cora asked. "Is that all there is to it?"

"No, it's not over," Cosmo answered quietly, masking his concern with professionalism. "Zoe's still in a state of altered consciousness, but I'm afraid she'll have to come out of it on her own."

Ethan glanced up from the candle he was lighting. "What do you mean, on her own?"

"I mean precisely that. As I explained to her earlier, in hypnosis, control always rests with the subject."

"I heard you," said Ethan. "Evidently Zoe didn't."

"Evidently not, but that's not essential. Whether she heard me or not, she'll snap out of this eventually."

"Eventually!" Cora gasped, white-lipped with outrage. "You're not going to leave her like this. I won't let you!"

"I wouldn't think of leaving." Cosmo placed a soothing hand on Cora's shoulder. "You can stay too, but it might be better if everyone else left the room."

"Forget it," Ethan snapped. "I'm not going anywhere till I'm sure Zoe's all right."

"If he stays, I stay," Sam Kellogg declared.

Brynne Loringer made it unanimous. "I wouldn't miss a moment of this. It's marvelous preparation for my scene."

This self-centered comment drew a scowl from Cora. "Do you think we should call a doctor?"

"That would be premature," said Cosmo. "Believe me, my dear, I wouldn't do anything to put Zoe in jeopardy, and I can assure you the state of trance is not permanent. Given time, she'll come out of it."

Cora glanced helplessly at her niece. Zoe was mute with fear, paralyzed by it. She was staring blindly into space, and her eyes were so widely dilated that the merest sliver of blue showed about the rims of the pupils. Her tormented expression was enough to make Cora cry, "Must we just sit here? There must be something we can do to help her."

"We can wait," Cosmo answered, "and try to remain calm."

"Have a drink," said Boris. "Make mine a double."

An uneasy silence greeted the mynah's suggestion. It was Sam Kellogg who broke it.

"With all due respect, that's not a bad idea." The actor sauntered toward the bar, inclining his head toward Cora. "Can I get you anything?"

"Brandy," said Cora, and then, determined to outdo Boris, "Make it a triple."

Sam raised his eyebrows at the others in the room. "Anyone else?"

Brynne requested a Perrier. "Calories, darling, calories," she intoned. "I take care of my body and my body takes care of me."

Cosmo asked for a cup of tea. "Herbal, if it's available. Otherwise any kind will do."

"I'll see what I can find in the pantry," Sam replied.

And in his turn, Ethan said, "Nothing for me, thanks."

Over the next quarter hour, Zoe's circle of supporters gradually disbanded, excusing themselves on one pretext or another, wandering off to join Sam at the bar, going upstairs to bed or drifting into the living room. Even

Merlin deserted his mistress, scampering after Cosmo in search of a midnight snack.

Ethan watched the exodus, his gaze clouded by incredulity. He couldn't believe this was happening; that these people, who claimed to care about Zoe, should allow themselves to be so easily distracted from her plight.

He listened to Sam and Brynne running through their lines for tomorrow's shoot, and wondered, *How can they be so callous? So inconsiderate? So cruel?*

He heard the actors gossiping and laughing, sometimes as themselves, sometimes as Rafe and Sheila, and as they slipped in and out of character, the line that separated the workaday world from the make-believe world of the soap opera began to blur.

By the time the other two finished their drinks and left the solarium, Ethan had succumbed to the feeling that the events of the evening might have been an illusion.

It was a disturbing feeling, not one he cared to contemplate. He needed an antidote, a dose of reality, and he considered leaving, going home, not even bothering to say good-night.

But Zoe's distress seemed genuine. How could he leave her alone?

He looked at her and caught a glimmer of awareness in her eyes. He shifted the candle, sliding it across the table closer to her, studying her intently, and a vivid rush of color suffused her cheeks.

She was awake! The hectic glide of her tongue across her bottom lip confirmed it.

He glared at her accusingly. "You've been playing possum."

"Told you so," said Boris.

"Shh!" Zoe whispered. "The others will hear."

"What if they do?" Ethan demanded. "They have a right to know you were faking."

"But I wasn't—at least not till the last few minutes."

"You expect me to believe that? What kind of rube do you think I am?"

A maniacal cackle erupted from the bird cage as Boris burst into laughter.

Ethan sprang to his feet, fists clenched as if he'd like to throttle the mynah. "What is this? Play a trick on Ethan week?" He regarded Zoe, eyes narrowed with speculation, as the tide of color receded from her face. "Bravo!" he muttered. "That's a Tony-winning performance. What do you do for an encore? Pretend you've had a cardiac arrest?"

She raised wide, stormy eyes to his, the vision of injured innocence. "I wasn't pretending."

"Oh, sure. Pull the other leg. Milk this little scene for all it's worth. I'll go along with the gag. But I'll be damned if I see the humor in it. I can take a joke as well as the next man, but this one just isn't funny."

"You're right, Ethan. It's not at all funny because it's not a joke. I really was hypnotized."

Ethan's jaw hardened. His mouth turned down at the corners. "Bull!" he growled, and with that rude comment started to leave the room.

Zoe tried to stand up. She wanted to hurry after him, but a wave of dizziness pinned her to the chair. "Please, don't leave. You've got to listen."

Ethan stopped in midstride, but didn't turn around. "Why should I stay? Give me one good reason."

"Because I'm telling the truth. Because—" Zoe rubbed her forehead, swamped by confusion.

How much of what she had witnessed tonight was based on fact? How much on fantasy? Part of her recoiled from the thought that she had regressed to a former life. Yet another part embraced the premise that in the few short hours since dinner she had experienced a timeless love, the pain of loss, the promise of redemption.

And although she tried, she could not shake off the tantalizing notion that she might have been Evangeline, that Evangeline's lover might have been Ethan in a somewhat different guise.

"Because I saw things," Zoe concluded in a voice not quite her own.

"What things?"

Things too personal to tell the others about. Things she hesitated to disclose even to Cosmo, from whom she had virtually no secrets. But for Ethan's benefit, she kept her answer brief.

"Things that might affect you."

He turned to look at her. "Go on. I'm listening."

She cleared her throat. "I found out who Vangie is."

Ethan leaned against the doorjamb, curiously unmoved.

"Her name was Evangeline. Evangeline Bliss."

Ethan pushed himself away from the door. His shrug made it clear that whoever Vangie was, she had nothing to do with him. "What else?"

"I was in East Hampton," said Zoe, "and it was winter. I saw people skating on a pond."

"Which one? Was it Hook Pond? Georgica?"

"I'm not sure. I think it was smaller."

"You didn't notice anything distinctive about it?"

"Not really." But she had heard the boom of the ice breaking and felt the shock of the water drenching her skirts, sapping her strength, chilling her flesh, clogging her nostrils—

"What makes you think the pond was anywhere near here?"

"I just *sensed* it—the way you do in dreams."

Zoe averted her gaze, focusing on the drizzle of melted wax that threaded along the side of the candle, as haltingly, but in minute detail, she recreated the events that had preceded Evangeline's death. She didn't look up, even when Ethan crossed the room and stood directly in front of her.

"You're saying you drowned."

Zoe flinched at his blunt summation of her story. She couldn't bring herself to look at him. "Not me," she protested. "Evangeline."

"And this man you described—your fiancé—"

"Evangeline's fiancé."

Ethan's hand chopped the air in a brusque, dismissive gesture. "Whoever this guy was, he wasn't much good in a crisis. He didn't lift a finger to help."

"He must have, only I didn't see him. Once I hit the water, everything went black. I could feel things. I could sense things. But I couldn't see anything."

Zoe stole a glance at Ethan. His expression was faintly troubled, but his eyes were opaque and impassive.

"You don't believe me," she murmured.

"Did you honestly think I would?"

"Yes, I suppose I did." Zoe sank her teeth into her lower lip, wondering if she dared tell him the rest.

She had only to look at Ethan's button-down collar and perfectly tailored suit to know that he preferred things neat and tidy. Nothing would disturb him more than finding some concept out of the mental pigeonhole he'd put it in, and if he mistakenly assigned a square peg to a round hole, so be it.

He seemed to live by the skeptic's creed. If a phenomenon couldn't be proven scientifically, as far as he was concerned, it didn't exist.

He already thought she was lying, and it was obvious he had suppressed his own memories of Vangie—

Zoe realized his mind was closed.

No wonder she was reluctant. What if he laughed? What if he refused to take her seriously? What if he misinterpreted the vestigial sense of intimacy that impelled her to confide in him?

But whatever Ethan thought of her, the need to share the things she had experienced forced her to go on.

She described her feeling of recognition the moment she'd seen his face, and told him how dismayed she'd been when she discovered his eyes were brown. And before Ethan could interrupt, before she could reconsider, she rushed into a description of her vision, and as she told him about the hillside, the lilacs, the nocturne drifting through the darkness, she wondered if it could have been a flashback.

"The song you mentioned," Ethan probed. "Do you recall how it went?"

"I'll never forget it." Although she had heard it only once, and then inside her head, there were times when she couldn't get the melody out of her mind, and now, at Ethan's request, she sang the opening bars in a sweet, somewhat self-conscious soprano.

"Da-dumm, da-da-dum-dumm, da-dum da-da-da-dum da-dum-dumm—"

Nodding, Ethan chimed in, making a baritone solo of the melody when she lapsed into silence.

Hopes rising, Zoe exclaimed, "You know it!"

"You betcha. It's Chopin. No. 2, Opus 9, in E-flat, I believe. When I was in junior high, I had to play it in a piano recital."

"Then it's not—"

"Not original? No. As a matter of fact, it's one of Chopin's better-known works, which explains why you're familiar with it. You've probably heard it any number of times."

Ethan sighed and sat opposite her in the chair Cosmo had vacated. "Look, Zoe, I'm flattered that you're attracted to me." *Flattered* was putting it mildly. He was astonished, even stunned, that a woman as colorful as Zoe should be interested in him.

Not that he considered himself dull. He had a busy social life, friends of both sexes, and he'd certainly never had any lack of feminine company, but he was—well, conventional, for want of a better adjective. And "conventional" was one adjective he would never apply to Zoe.

Lots of others came to mind, though. Words like "warm" and "witty," "soft" and "sexy." And despite her eccentricities, she seemed completely natural. He'd bet a month's salary that, from her small bare toes to her unruly red hair, there was nothing artificial about Zoe Piper.

Add to that an earthy laugh that went straight to his libido and the hint of vulnerability that struck a protective chord in him, and you had a composite that was damned near irresistible.

Just now, for instance, he was strongly tempted to take her in his arms and assure her everything was going to be all right. But when she stared at him with her wide, unblinking eyes, she reminded him of Merlin.

If he gave in to temptation, how would she respond? Would she, like Merlin, curl up on his lap? Or would she sink in her claws?

"I'm not sure what you expect of me," he said. "But since you've been candid, I'll be equally frank. I'll admit the attraction is mutual, but there's nothing mysterious about that. It's chemistry, pure and simple."

"But you do believe I was hypnotized? After everything I've told you, you must believe that!"

"I believe you believe it, and maybe that amounts to the same thing. But to cast me as your skating partner because there happens to be a slight physical resemblance— I'm sorry, Zoe, but that just won't track." Ethan's grin seemed forced. It didn't reach his eyes. "I'll say one thing for you, though. You've got a great imagination."

Zoe straightened her spine. Her frown told Ethan she did not appreciate his levity. "I didn't imagine drowning," she said. "I couldn't begin to imagine anything as terrifying as that. But if Evangeline died that way, if it actually happened, it could explain my fear of the water."

"Well, but you see, I have a problem with that. The ponds hereabouts are fairly shallow. Even allowing for the conditions, it'd take some doing for an adult to drown in one of them."

Zoe ran her fingertips over the arm of her chair, absently tracing the pattern of tropical flowers on the slipcover.

For every argument she came up with, Ethan had one to refute it. And the things he'd told her made good sense. He'd lived in East Hampton for several years, so it was reasonable to assume he knew more about the ponds than she did. If he said it was unlikely Evangeline had drowned, Zoe really ought to believe him.

And she might very well have heard the nocturne on the radio...at a concert...in a movie sound track.... If she'd heard it in a romantic comedy, the bittersweet nostalgia the music evoked could be a simple matter of association.

But none of this explained why Ethan had called her Vangie, nor did it explain why he denied it.

Honesty forced Zoe to acknowledge the possibility she had misunderstood him—

But she hadn't misunderstood. She knew she hadn't. Just as she knew she could not accept his arguments.

Ethan hadn't made the leap into the past. He hadn't seen the things she'd seen, felt the emotional ties she'd felt. He hadn't experienced the passion, the tenderness, the desolation— Not in this life.

Which brought them to an impasse.

Ethan did not believe, and Zoe could think of no way to convince him. Unless—

Would he agree to be hypnotized?

She leaned forward, studying his clean-cut features, then slumped back, defeated by his dark, implacable gaze.

No, she decided. He wouldn't. Not in a million years.

But perhaps there was another way. If she had more evidence, proof that Evangeline Bliss had existed—

Her nails dug into a salmon-orange hibiscus that bloomed on the arm of her chair.

She was accustomed to marching out of step, summoned by an elusive, barely perceived dream. She had pursued the dream all her adult life, since the day she'd turned eighteen, moving from town to town, from job to job, drifting, constantly driven toward some as yet unidentified goal. And with every move to every strange city she wondered, *Is this the place? Will I find what I'm looking for here?*

Her parents disapproved of her vagabond life-style. They said they wanted something better for her. Her mother thought she lacked ambition, and her father urged her to settle down. But she hadn't let them dissuade her. Even if she'd wanted to follow their advice, she couldn't abandon her quest.

Nothing could stop her. Not discouragement or derision, not all the wrong turns she'd taken, not the occasional roadblock she encountered along the way. No detour was wide enough, no delay long enough to make her lose sight of the dream.

And if Ethan thought she was chasing rainbows, if she could not enlist his support, she would pursue the dream alone—just as she always had.

She was not without resources, and now, for the first time, she had something solid to go on.

She had a name.

Evangeline Bliss.

She would begin her investigation with that.

Chapter Five

When Zoe told Ethan she intended to check out Evangeline Bliss, he accused her of being morbid. "Your imagination's slipped into overdrive," he said. "You're letting it run away with you."

"At least I have an imagination," she replied.

"Are you implying I don't?"

"If the shoe fits—"

Ethan gave her a pitying look. "The trouble with Pisces astrologers is, they're supersensitive—much too sensitive to wear shoes."

"Well, the trouble with Scorpio bankers is, they do everything by the numbers."

After a few minutes of verbal sparring, they worked out a truce. Ethan swore he wouldn't make any more cracks about astrology, and Zoe promised not to indulge in sarcasm.

From then on, Ethan was all business. He mapped out directions to his uncle's house. "If you need transportation, I can give you a ride over there before work."

"That's not necessary," she answered. "Aunt Cora said there's a bicycle in the garage I can use."

"In that case, I'll leave a key for you beneath the welcome mat."

Although Zoe thought that a most unimaginative hiding place, she managed not to say it.

Thanks to her restraint, when Ethan left the truce was still intact, but by then she was exhausted. Mentally, emotionally, and physically drained, she was in no condition to play Queen of the Nile.

She stopped by the kitchen for a sandwich and a glass of milk, postponing the confrontation with her bed. In her weariness it seemed a stroke of good fortune when she found Brynne Loringer languishing at the breakfast counter, munching on a chicken leg.

"Welcome back to the land of the *living*," said the actress.

Her choice of phrases was like the scrape of fingernails across a chalkboard. It set Zoe's teeth on edge. To forestall any questions about the hypnosis, she asked, "Where are the others?"

Brynne pointed her drumstick toward the ceiling. "In their rooms, presumably sleeping. *I* should be, too. If I don't get a *solid* eight hours sack time, I look like death warmed over on camera. But it can't be helped. I *always* have insomnia in a strange place, and my mattress is too soft. It bothers my back."

Zoe sipped her milk and tried to look solicitous. "What a shame. I prefer a soft mattress myself, and mine's quite firm."

Brynne dropped the chicken bone and daintily licked her fingers. "I don't suppose you'd consider trading?"

"Why not?" Zoe answered casually. "Anything to help the cause."

Brynne thanked her effusively and said she was "*too* generous." Almost as an afterthought, the actress added, "Some of my things are in the closet—"

"That's okay," said Zoe. "All I need is my pajamas and toothbrush. Let's worry about switching the rest of our clothes tomorrow."

"*Darling!* What a *splendid* idea!"

Brynne's gratitude was so excessive that Zoe felt guilty as she lighted a candle and climbed the back stairs, but her conscience stopped plaguing her when she walked into her room and tripped over a basin of water.

She held up her candle so that the light spilled into the corners of the room, and discovered why Brynne had been so anxious to make the exchange.

The roof leaked.

Half a dozen buckets were scattered about the floor to catch the seepage of rain through the ceiling. Several smaller pots dotted the bed, without completely protecting it. In places the pink taffeta spread was damp, in others definitely soggy.

Zoe got into her pajamas and went back downstairs, determined to view the situation philosophically. There were divans in the family room, couches in the living room, no shortage of comfortable places to sleep.

She tried the family room first. It was occupied. Sam Kellogg was sprawled on a divan, snoring. In the living room, she found that Cosmo had staked a claim to the couch. Fresh out of options, she tiptoed on to the solarium.

When she entered the room, Boris gave her a dirty look. She had forgotten to cover his cage.

"Read the instructions. Read the instructions."

Pellets of birdseed crunched beneath her bare feet as she made her way to the cage. The mynah supervised her every move as she fitted the cover in place.

"My foot has gone to sleep," he declared. "Mind if I join it?"

"Please do."

Smiling at his aggrieved tone, she made her way to the sofa. Within minutes, her candle was out and she was lying in the darkness, with a quilt tucked around her for warmth and Merlin curled into a cozy lump at her feet.

She yawned, wondering where the cat had been hiding, and how he'd known where to find her. She yawned again, listening to the patter of rain against the French doors, letting the sound soothe her, willing herself not to think about Ethan or Evangeline or the echoes of the nocturne inside her head.

Her eyelids were heavy. They closed of their own weight. She snuggled deeper into the sofa cushions, drifting in the limbo between wakefulness and sleep—

And then Boris started talking. Or not talking as much as screeching. Squawking, "Moneek monear, moneek monear, moneek monear," over and over, again and again and again. And when he'd run through his litany of nonsense, he switched to a chorus of complaints. He had a headache, a toothache, acid indigestion. His feet hurt. He was developing corns and ingrown toenails. And allergies. Hay fever. The heartbreak of psoriasis. He had arthritic elbows, dry skin. His throat was parched.

"Water," he screeched. "Gimme water."

Merlin dragged himself off Zoe's feet and stalked out of the solarium. Cosmo, normally the gentlest of souls, staggered in from the living room and shouted, "Pipe down, you overgrown magpie, or I'll give you something to complain about!"

Silence descended upon Gull Cottage. Blessed, glorious silence. But just when Zoe began to relax, Boris started mumbling. Quietly. Beneath his breath. And no matter how hard she listened, most of his mutterings were unintelligible.

She plugged her ears.

Boris muttered louder.

She unplugged them, straining to hear.

His mumbling fell to a murmur.

She pulled the quilt over her head. She burrowed under a pillow, but she could not shut out the mynah's screech.

What had possessed her, coming to East Hampton? Why hadn't she stayed in New York? Why had she agreed to this bird-sitting assignment when she'd known it wouldn't work out? She had been here less than a day, but it seemed like *forever*. How could she get through the month? How long could she last without rest?

"Pretty bird, pretty bird, pretty bird," the mynah boasted.

Zoe groaned and punched her pillow, resigned to being his captive audience.

With great satisfaction, the mynah told her, "You've made your bed. Now you have to lie in it."

Toward dawn the rain stopped. Zoe took her quilt out to the deck. She stretched out on a chaise by the pool and, lulled by the surf, serenaded by flocks of waking gulls, at last she fell asleep.

BY NINE O'CLOCK the next morning, with Boris fed and watered, groomed and tutored, napping contentedly in his cage, Zoe had reverted to her natural optimism.

Her spirits rose as she showered and got into her favorite sundress, a soft, faded madras that brought out the blue in her eyes. She tied back her hair with her "lucky" scarf—she'd been wearing it the morning she met Ethan—and by the time she finished packing a book bag with the supplies she would need, she felt positively buoyant.

The skies had cleared. The day was brilliant, the air perfumed by late-blooming lilacs. Wherever she looked, she caught glimpses of ocean, dunes or countryside that pleased her eye and sweetened her disposition.

It was true what they said about riding a bicycle. A person didn't forget how to do it. She hadn't been biking for years, but after a couple of test flights up and down the driveway, she was ready to set off for the Seymour estate.

She rode through the town, past the village green, waving at the other cyclists she saw. She turned onto a narrow residential street, and a friendly dog appeared from behind a hedge and ran along beside her.

Zoe laughed and pedaled on.

It seemed nothing could go wrong on a morning this beautiful. Admittedly, her visit to Gull Cottage had gotten off to a rocky start, but as she steered the bicycle onto a private driveway lined with trees that might have been giants a century ago, she dared to hope that the worst was behind her.

From now on, she thought, things can only get better.

She stopped pedaling when the driveway curved into a horseshoe and the Seymour residence came into view.

It was a gem of a house, set amid manicured lawns, crowned by venerable maples and anchored by chimneys. Graced by a fanlight above the front door and by the crisp green shutters that flanked its window bays, the austere Georgian facade had been mellowed by age. The stones of the front steps sloped to slight hollows at the center, and this pathway, worn by two hundred years of use, accentuated the hospitable feel of the place.

Zoe tested one of the grooves with her sandal, and found it a perfect fit. Her breath caught in her throat as she retrieved the key from under the mat.

If the inside of the house was as gracious as the outside, working here would be a treat.

The front door opened into a long central hall, with arched entries to a formal drawing room, family parlor and dining room along one side, and to the study, breakfast room and kitchen on the other.

Zoe spent the next half hour happily exploring, going from room to room, from treasure to treasure, pausing to admire parquetry floors and fruit wood wainscotting, a wide, sweeping staircase and graceful balustrade.

Some nineteenth-century Seymour must have been a seaman. She found evidence of his occupation in the study, in an antique sextant and brass telescope, and in the scale model of a whaling bark called the *Nellie T*.

Hand-painted Dutch tiles framed the parlor fireplace; a pair of Chinese vases brightened the hall. The drawing room featured a ceiling medallion, winged cherubs reposing on billowy clouds. In the dining room, Zoe came face-to-face with a portrait of Hiram T. Seymour.

From his place of honor above the mantel, Hiram's hooded black eyes scowled down at the gleaming mahogany table—sternly, somberly, with cold disapproval. But his scowl was not limited to the table. It seemed to follow her everywhere.

Zoe imagined what it must have been like for Ethan's grandmother, trying to choke down supper with her brother sitting opposite her, his expression sour enough to curdle milk. Then, with a shudder, she turned her back on the dining room and hurried on to a cheerier scene.

The breakfast-room windows overlooked a carefully tended herb garden, and beyond that a strip of velvety lawn that led to a latticework gazebo, overgrown with roses.

The library extended from the back of the house. "It used to be a music room," Ethan had explained. "Uncle Hiram had it remodeled when the collection got too big for the study. You can get to it through the rear hall that leads from the butler's pantry, or you can use the outside entrance, across the terrace from the kitchen.''

Torn between eagerness to see the library and curiosity about the rest of the house, Zoe glanced at her watch.

It was ten minutes past eleven. Since most of the morning was gone, she decided she might as well tour the rooms upstairs before she settled down to work.

She returned to the entry hall and was halfway up the stairs when, without warning, she was gripped by the certainty that she was not alone.

Someone was following her—watching her!

She spun around and leaned over the banister, hastily scanning the hallway.

It was deserted. But still the feeling persisted.

''Who's there?'' she called.

She held her breath, listening, waiting for an answer, while the casement clock in the parlor ticked off thirty seconds...forty-five...a full minute. Gradually the feeling waned.

She drew a ragged breath. Her legs gave way, and she sank down upon the stairs, hugging her knees to her chest.

If Ethan were here, he'd say her imagination was working overtime. And in this case, she was willing to admit, Ethan might very well be right. She could almost hear the laughter in his voice as he said something blunt and reassuring—something like, ''Do you think the eyes in Uncle Hiram's portrait can see through walls and follow you, even here?''

She forced a shaky smile, attempting to laugh off the incident.

''God, I wish Ethan was here!''

The words had scarcely left her mouth when the phone rang and Zoe was on her feet, racing down the stairs. She picked up the receiver on the parlor extension before it could ring again.

"Ethan! Hello! I'm so glad you called."

There was a moment of absolute silence. "How'd you know it was me?"

Good question, she thought. But if she gave an honest answer, it could lead to more discord.

"Who else would call me here?"

"No one, I guess." Ethan sounded dubious, faintly troubled. "Is everything all right, Zoe?"

"Of course. Why wouldn't it be?"

"Well, I just thought— Look, I know I should've told you about the library—"

"What's wrong with the library?"

He missed a beat. "You haven't seen it yet?"

"I haven't had the chance."

"But it's almost noon."

Zoe recalled her sleepless night and tightened her grip on the phone. "I know what time it is," she answered crossly, "but I didn't get here till after ten-thirty, and since then I've been getting acquainted with the house. It's lovely, by the way."

"Thanks," said Ethan. "I think so, too."

"Now, what were you saying about the library?"

"I don't know if I mentioned it, but my uncle was in a nursing home several months before his death, so the house was closed. Since I moved in, I've opened the rest of the rooms, but I haven't got round to the library yet. I meant to do it last night, but then the power went out."

"Will it take much work to make it habitable?"

"No. I think all you'll have to do is remove some dust-covers and air it out."

"No problem," said Zoe. "Consider it done."

"There's one more thing I have to tell you," said Ethan. "It's—well, the truth is, Uncle Hiram was kind of a pack rat. I'm afraid his personal records will have to be sorted before they can be cataloged."

"Are there quite a few?"

"Yes, you might say that. But I want you to know, I fully intend to help you get them straightened out."

"Seems fair enough to me."

"It's a date, then. I have to be in a meeting at four, but it shouldn't last more than an hour. So I'll see you around five."

Ethan hung up before Zoe could protest that she'd planned to leave early that afternoon. Sometime before the weekend, she wanted to stop by the town hall and find out how to go about searching the Suffolk County records for Evangeline Bliss's death certificate. Since this was only Thursday, she supposed the search could wait, but she couldn't help wondering if Ethan was trying to distract her.

If he is, it's working, she thought. She was dismayed to realize how well.

Ethan was rooted in reality, feet on the ground, nose to the grindstone. He had admitted he was attracted to her, and in the next breath, dismissed the attraction as chemistry. Which was a perfect example of the way he tried to impose order on perceptions he didn't understand. He either denied his instincts or reduced them to the lowest common denominator, and lived by the laws of probability.

She, on the other hand, found reality confusing. The more she tried to make sense of the seemingly senseless world around her, the less she understood it. And so she studied astrology, hoping someday to find enlightenment. But until that day arrived, she lived by instinct and intuition.

Ethan and she were polar opposites, mismatched in every way, but it didn't necessarily follow that they were incompatible. Each of them could provide strengths the other lacked. They could compromise. They could harmonize. They could complement. Intellectual differences could be stimulating, physical differences exciting.

She thought about Ethan's smile, his lean athletic body. She thought of his hands. Hands that were big enough to swallow up her hands, strong enough to offer support. Hands that were deft and sure and capable. Confident hands that knew when to be gentle and when to make demands....

Zoe shivered with anticipation. She could almost feel his touch.

Common sense counseled against becoming romantically involved with him, but intuition told her she could not escape her fate. And given the choice, she was not at all certain she would want to escape. Not as long as there was a chance that their romance could become more intimate, more profound, more abiding.

And, however remote, there was such a chance. She knew it existed whenever she saw the dreams in Ethan's eyes.

ETHAN'S FOUR O'CLOCK appointment was with Haines Randolph, vice president in charge of everything at Merchants Bank. Randolph was an autocrat and a bit of a snob. He wasn't terribly knowledgeable about banking, but he knew how to delegate authority, and as a member of one of the Hamptons' most influential families, he had excellent contacts. He'd gone to the right schools, wore the right clothes, belonged to the right clubs, knew the right people. He'd come to work at the bank directly from college, and risen to the vice presidency the old-fashioned way. He'd married the boss's daughter.

In the parlance of Ethan's grandmother, Randolph was "an operator."

Lydia Quinn had suffered a heart attack shortly after Ethan applied for a transfer to the Long Island branch, and during a visit to the hospital, Ethan happened to mention the vice president's name.

"If Slick gives you any grief, let me know."

Ethan had stared at his grandmother, surprised by the discovery that East Hampton had been her girlhood home, and even more surprised by her familiarity with Haines Randolph. Astonishment had left him slow on the uptake.

"Slick?" he'd repeated incredulously.

"That was my nickname for him."

"You called Haines Randolph 'Slick'?"

Lydia nodded complacently and tapped the backs of her fingers against Ethan's chin, prompting him to close his mouth.

"Haines always was a smoothy, from the time he was a little boy. And he used to have an eye for the ladies— Well, suffice it to say, I could tell you stories about Haines Randolph that would curl your hair."

Lydia gave Ethan's chin a more affectionate pat, then lay back against her pillows. "Funny how things seem to go in cycles," she mused. "I haven't seen Haines since his marriage. Haven't even thought of him for years. I wonder if he's reformed."

At the time of this discussion, Ethan hadn't known the answer to his grandmother's question. But before her death, he'd learned enough to tell her that Haines Randolph hadn't mended his ways.

"Then my nickname still suits him?"

"I don't know about that," Ethan replied. "His 'Slick' days may be over."

"But he still has an eye for the ladies?"

"More than an eye, Grandmother. My secretary informs me the women at the bank call him Handy Randy."

In spite of her failing health, Lydia had laughed as merrily as a young girl, and Ethan had left the hospital thanking Haines Randolph for providing this momentary diversion.

Two years later, Ethan was still grateful. Under ordinary circumstances he wouldn't have worried about the summons to the vice president's office. But the months since Hiram Seymour's death had been far from ordinary, and with Zoe Piper's advent, Ethan's circumstances had begun to flirt with the paranormal.

All that business about Evangeline, for instance. And the way Zoe looked at him, as if she were reading his soul. As if she knew things about him that he didn't know about himself. As if she could anticipate his actions—

How the devil had she known it was him on the phone?

"Who else would call me here?" she'd asked. Which was eminently practical, extremely logical, and totally out of character for Zoe.

At three forty-five that afternoon, Ethan sat at his desk, dreading the meeting with Randolph.

The vice president would ask for a departmental report, just as he did every Thursday. With the utmost diplomacy, he would guide the conversation toward the Seymour estate, and once the subject was broached, he'd invite Ethan to tell him how probate was coming along. And although Randolph would never be crass enough to say it, at that point he would expect a detailed outline of Ethan's plans for disposing of the library.

And how, Ethan wondered, *am I going to explain Zoe?*

If he claimed he'd been impressed by her credentials, he'd be lying.

If he said he'd hired her to help organize the auction because he wanted to get to know her, he'd sound like an idiot.

If he admitted, from the instant he saw her, he'd felt drawn to her, he'd sound like a flake.

If he confessed he'd been bewitched by red hair, a smile like sunshine, and eyes the color of forget-me-nots, he was likely to find himself out of a job.

So what was he to tell Haines Randolph?

Four o'clock found Ethan without a solution to his quandary. He presented himself at the vice president's office as if he were on his way to the guillotine. But his interview with Randolph did not go as he had imagined it would. No explanations were required because Zoe's reputation had preceded her.

"She's the young woman who predicted the fall in stock prices last October," Randolph said.

With some reluctance, Ethan allowed that she had.

"Remarkable," said Randolph.

"Yes," said Ethan. But a fluke, nonetheless.

"I understand that wasn't an isolated occurrence. Her clients swear by her ability to forecast trends. Not that any of them are willing to sing her praises in public, mind you. They're very closemouthed about their connection with her."

Ethan studied the toes of his wing tips. "Who are her clients?"

"That, my boy, is a jealously guarded secret. I've been trying to crack it for months, and even with my contacts, I've only come up with one individual who admits to consulting her."

"Perhaps her clients move in less prominent circles than you."

"Not at all," said Randolph. "My informant happens to be very highly placed. Top drawer, if you know what I mean. If I told you his name, you'd recognize it, and his brokerage house is listed on the big board. But for obvious reasons, he's concerned about privacy. Just consider what might happen if it were bruited about that his investment tips have been influenced by an astrologer. No, my boy! That wouldn't do. It wouldn't do at all. It would, in fact, be disastrous, both for him and for his firm."

And rightly so, thought Ethan. The idea of a major brokerage house interpreting planetary movements instead of hard data made him feel queasy. He wondered if Haines Randolph had made any investments on the recommendation of Zoe's client, but before he could inquire, the vice president favored him with a conspiratorial grin.

"So, my boy, we arrive at the sixty-four-dollar question— In strictest confidence, you understand."

Ethan nodded. "Of course, sir. That goes without saying."

"Good, good!" Randolph spread his hands on his desk top and leaned forward, lowering his voice to a whisper. "I'd like very much to meet the young lady. Do you think you could arrange an introduction?"

Chapter Six

A pack rat. That's what Ethan had called Hiram Seymour. But had she paid attention? No! Not until she saw the evidence with her own eyes.

A stack of banker's boxes, labeled *Records, Uncle H.*, partitioned one end of the library and all but barricaded the door. Zoe had to walk sideways to get around them into the musty half-light that pervaded the room. Once inside, before her eyes grew accustomed to the dusk, she barked her shins against a smaller carton that blocked the path to the fireplace.

She opened one of the boxes, then a second and a third.

Each was full of papers, a hodgepodge of bills and invoices, household accounts, letters and circulars, greeting cards, newspaper articles, even old grocery lists. Not filed. Not alphabetized or arranged chronologically. Not segregated by greater or lesser importance. Just bundled into the box like a paper booby trap. And she was the unsuspecting boob who'd walked into the trap.

Zoe dropped her book bag on one of the cartons and made a brief inventory of her find. She counted eleven boxes—twelve including the one she'd stumbled over. Hiram Seymour must have saved every scrap of paper that passed through his hands.

She sighed and turned away from the cartons. Her gaze skimmed over the ghostly forms of sheet-shrouded furniture to the bookshelves that lined two walls of the room. A third wall, elaborately paneled, held the fireplace, and the fourth, banks of windows covered by heavy velvet draperies.

She crossed to the windows and opened the curtains, and after unlatching the windows to admit the fresh air, began removing the dust shrouds, exposing a pedestal table and deacon's bench, a pair of burgundy leather wing chairs, a matching sofa.

A grand piano occupied a niche near the windows, its boxy lines attesting to its age. She lifted the fall board and touched middle C, then tapped out a one-fingered scale, surprised to find the instrument in tune, at least to her inexpert ear.

She stood at the keyboard, absently testing the keys, until it dawned on her she was picking out the notes of the nocturne. With an uneasy start, she swung away from the piano.

"That's enough wasting time," she murmured. "Better set up shop."

She hastened toward a rolltop desk at the far end of the room and was disappointed to find it locked until, beneath one of the remaining dustcovers, she found an L-shaped steno desk, equipped with an electric typewriter.

As she transferred the supplies from her book bag to the desk drawers she decided, while the rolltop was handsome and loaded with character, a modern desk would be more efficient.

And efficiency mattered. It mattered a lot, considering that the portion of the library on which she would focus filled ten four-foot shelves, which meant she had to catalog approximately four hundred books.

Zoe tried out the steno chair, made minor adjustments to the back, and pulled the last two items from her book bag: the sandwich and thermos of coffee her aunt's caterer had packed for lunch.

The sandwich was spectacular—shrimp salad with a whisper of curry on pita bread—and the coffee was a special grind, rich and aromatic. But she scarcely tasted the gourmet blend.

Organizing the Seymour Collection was going to be a formidable task, and although she'd have much preferred to spend a leisurely hour or two leafing through the works that were the heart of the collection, she knew she couldn't give the books the appreciation they deserved until she'd dealt with Hiram Seymour's papers.

She drank the last of the coffee, eyeing the stack of banker's boxes. She first step, obviously, was to separate the wheat from the chaff, and the only way to tackle that project was to kick off her shoes, choose a box at random and dive in.

The first box contained canceled checks, most of them decades old. The second held more of the same. She found little of interest, except for monthly payments to G. Quinn, Custom Gardening, which began in 1931 and stopped abruptly in '34.

Zoe set these checks aside to ask Ethan about, and went on to a third box.

This one contained copies of tax returns, along with some financial records that might be pertinent to the collection. It also held correspondence, including a series of postcards dating from the thirties that bore the salutation "Dear Hi," and were signed by someone named Lydia.

In spite of the casual greeting, the tone of the cards was dutiful. They described days spent sightseeing in London, Paris, and Rome, but the details they offered were impersonal. With one exception. A card postmarked Venice, written in July 1934, requested Hiram to send more money.

So Lydia must have been Hiram's sister.

Ethan confirmed this when he got home. "She was my grandmother. And Gerald Quinn was my granddad. His family operated greenhouses upstate. They grew flowers, nursery stock, and supplied them wholesale to florists. Then the depression came along and their customers couldn't pay their bills, so to help his parents make ends meet, Granddad came to work here."

"Is that how he met your grandmother?"

"That's how," said Ethan, riffling through the canceled checks. "He came by once a week to mow the lawns and take care of the grounds, but he was responsible for more than maintenance work. He designed the terrace out back and put in the fountain. Take a look at it, Zoe. He did a beautiful job."

Zoe dusted off her hands and moved to the windows, which offered a view of the terrace and fountain, and in the distance a brick pathway winding over the gently rising lawn to a knoll that marked the western boundary of the property.

"Uncle Hiram approved of Granddad's work," Ethan continued, "but he didn't approve of his sister making friends with a gardener. And that's all they were in the beginning. Friends. In 1931, when my grandfather started working here, Grandma was only thirteen."

"How old was your grandfather?"

"Twenty-nine. Almost thirty."

"Old enough to be her father."

Ethan shrugged. "I think that was part of the attraction. Her father was killed in World War I, just days before the armistice, and her mother never had much time for her or Uncle Hiram. Until they were old enough to pack off to boarding school, she left most of their day-to-day care to her housekeeper. But that might have been just as well. It seems Great-granddad had some sort of ill-fated love affair before he met Great-grandma. He never got over his first love, and naturally enough, this tended to put a crimp on his marriage.''

''His wife must have resented it.''

''Yes, she did, and from comments my grandmother made, I got the impression that her resentment spilled over onto her children. She was also something of a social climber. Her greatest concern was that her son and daughter should do nothing to sully the Seymour name, and in that respect at least, Uncle Hiram was in total agreement. So when his mother died and he became his sister's guardian, and the first thing Grandma did was to develop an interest in the gardener— Well, you can imagine his reaction.''

Zoe could imagine it. Vividly.

She stared out the window, at the sun-splashed fountain, but it was the obsidian eyes in Hiram's portrait she saw. She thought about his miserly hoarding of paper, and wondered if he had been as frugal with his affection.

Yes, she decided, he must have been.

And his younger sister must have been starved for approval, ripe for the attentions of an older man. Perhaps about her brother's age?

''Uncle Hiram was only seven years older than my grandmother,'' Ethan went on, answering Zoe's unspoken question. ''But you're probably right. She may have been looking for a surrogate. And when her brother tried to put a stop to the friendship, she would have seen my grandfather in a different light.''

''And the more Hiram opposed her, the more she persisted.''

Ethan set aside the checks and picked up the postcards. "So he fired Granddad, and packed Grandma off to Europe."

"What happened when she got back?" asked Zoe.

"More of the same, I suppose. My grandparents never talked much about their courtship, but I know they were married the day Grandma turned eighteen."

"Not with Hiram's blessings?"

"No," Ethan said. "They eloped. And knowing Granddad, he wouldn't have been a party to that if he'd thought there was any chance Uncle Hiram would come around."

Not an auspicious start to a marriage, thought Zoe. She wondered whether his grandparents had been happy together.

"They were happy," said Ethan.

Zoe turned away from the window and intercepted Ethan's gaze. He seemed not to have noticed that, for the second time in the space of a minute, he had divined her thoughts.

"I'm sure of it," he insisted, as if she had argued the point. "I'm not saying they didn't have their share of problems. They had it rough financially the first few years, but after the war things got easier. And they were married forty years. There's no way they could've lasted that long if either of them had any regrets."

"They must've been content," Zoe agreed huskily. "You're living proof of that."

"Me and two more grandsons."

Ethan's grin made his eyes light up. How could she ever have found blue eyes more entrancing than midnight-brown eyes starred with gold? Her throat felt tight. She swallowed to ease the constriction.

"You have brothers?"

Ethan nodded.

"Are they older? Younger?"

"Older." He glanced at her quizzically, amusement shining in his eyes, and in a flash of inspiration, she sensed what he would say next.

She looked at him, and the insight grew stronger. It became more than a hunch, more than a premonition. She tingled with certainty, as if her consciousness had fused with his.

Didn't you see them in my horoscope?

The words were almost audible. She was so attuned to his thoughts that she could hear the mockery in his voice.

Then his eyes darkened and the certainty ebbed. Instead of teasing her, he tossed the canceled checks into the box she was using for discards and said, "You've accomplished quite a bit this afternoon."

"It looks that way, but it's slow going. I don't want to throw away anything that might be important."

"You're conscientious," said Ethan. "I appreciate that. But if you want to stay sharp, you ought to take a break. How about knocking off for dinner?"

Zoe knelt beside the records she had been sorting and gathered up a handful of documents. "I can't quit now. It's barely five-thirty. As it is, I won't get to the cataloging before Saturday."

"Those records have already waited fifty years. What difference does one more day make?"

"None, I guess, but I'd like to get started on the library as soon as possible. Besides, I'm not used to keeping bankers' hours."

Ethan frowned. "I told you I'd help clean up this mess and I will. First thing tomorrow morning."

Zoe hesitated. Ethan's tight-lipped expression urged her to change her mind. "You're the boss," she replied slowly. "I'll just finish going through this box before I leave."

Ethan sat on his heels beside her. "Do you have to get home right away?"

"Not right this minute, but I do have to check on Boris, and I want to do some reading."

He caught hold of her wrist and she lapsed into silence, electrified by the glowing warmth that spiraled out from his fingers, heating her skin, seeping into the marrow of her bones, coursing through her bloodstream like feathers of fire. And before she could pull away, she was enveloped by the conflagration.

An image sprang to mind of Ethan drawing her into his arms, kissing her. Nibbling. Sampling. Brushing her lips with his lips slowly, repetitively. Learning their sweetness. Savoring their softness. Tracing their contours with bold little sweeps of his tongue. And when she was tantalized beyond endurance by his sensuous game of advance and retreat, he deepened his invasion, shaping his mouth to hers as if he were memorizing every taste, every texture. Searching. Exploring. Lingering, as if he might absorb her very essence....

Her heart was pounding. Her pulses raced. Her lips felt tender, swollen. She dug her nails into her palms, struggling against the vision.

It seemed so real! As real as the sheaf of papers in her hand. As tangible as the rug beneath her feet, the books on the shelves—and infinitely more exciting.

Was it precognition? Was it some sort of telepathy? Had Ethan experienced it, too?

She studied him surreptitiously, watching his lips move. No matter how she tried, she could not tear her gaze away from his mouth. She heard the rumble of his voice, and realized he was speaking to her.

"P-pardon me?"

He scowled as if she were deliberately being obtuse, and relinquished his grip on her wrist. "Look, Zoe, if you'd rather spend the evening with Boris than have dinner with me, all you have to do is say so. There's no need to spare my feelings."

Hiram Seymour's papers fell from her nerveless fingers. "Dinner?" she murmured. "You're inviting me to dinner?"

"I realize it's a big favor to ask, but assuming we can find a restaurant that doesn't require shoes, yes, I am."

Overcome by self-consciousness and determined not to show it, she curled her bare toes into the carpet. "If the food's good, I don't mind wearing shoes, but why do you call it a favor?"

"Well, as I was saying, it wasn't actually my idea. Haines Randolph wants to meet you."

"Haines Randolph?"

"One of the VPs at the bank."

"Is he interested in your uncle's collection?"

"No. He's interested in consulting you about investments."

"Where did he get my name?"

"From the newspapers. Apparently he read about your Wall Street prediction last fall."

A shadow of distaste clouded Zoe's features. "That was not my finest hour."

"Haines seemed to think it was."

"Well, he's wrong."

"You got a lot of publicity."

"Notoriety's more like it," she countered tartly, "and it was totally without my consent. I never intended to go public with that prediction."

"If that's true, how'd the papers get wind of it?"

She shook her head. "All I can tell you is, they didn't hear about it from me."

Ethan studied her with dawning comprehension. "Then it must've been your client."

Zoe offered grudging confirmation. "That's why I'm careful about who I advise," she said. "I don't usually see clients without a referral from someone I know—"

"Enough said," Ethan broke in. "I understand your caution."

The hell of it was, he did. Seeing herself quoted in the papers couldn't have been pleasant for Zoe, especially since her Wall Street prognostication had been a shot in the dark. An accurate shot, he'd give her that much, but blind luck, nonetheless.

Although Randolph had assured him the stock market caper wasn't an isolated incident, Ethan found it hard to believe that many of Zoe's forecasts had come so close to the target.

How could she duplicate that initial success when she was not a financial analyst? He doubted she'd ever heard of Adam Smith or John Kenneth Galbraith or supply-side economics. She probably thought GNP was an abbreviation for Gemini, Neptune and Pluto. Given her limitations, it'd be a miracle if she guessed right more than ten percent of the time. So he respected her concern for privacy, and applauded her wariness about taking on new clients.

And luckily for him, he had foreseen the possibility that she might be less than thrilled about meeting Haines Randolph.

"Don't get your hopes up," he'd warned the vice president. "Zoe's kind of quirky. It's hard to predict how she'll react. She might agree to an introduction, but she could just as easily refuse."

"She'll see me," said Randolph. "Once you've explained who I am, she'll realize the prestige alone would be worth a fortune."

Still dubious, Ethan had replied, "I don't think Zoe cares about money."

"That's nonsense, my boy. Sheer blasphemy! *Everyone* cares about money. But on the off chance the unthinkable happens, and Ms. Piper does refuse, I'm relying on you to establish her price."

Haines Randolph was greedy. He made no effort to hide it. But like his other qualities, his streak of avarice only ran skin deep. And because he seemed relatively harmless, Ethan agreed to try and arrange the introduction to Zoe.

"No guarantees," he'd told Randolph, "but I'll see what I can work out."

And he'd kept his word. He had delivered Randolph's invitation. And as he'd anticipated, Zoe had turned it down. But he had no intention of sweetening the pot with promises of prestige, and he certainly wouldn't insult Zoe by offering her money. For all her quirkiness, one of the nicest things about her was that she wasn't materialistic. If she had a price, Ethan suspected it would not be one Randolph could pay.

She had made her decision, and all things considered, Ethan could think of no incentive that would persuade her to change her mind.

Of course, it didn't help that his mind refused to function when she was near. Whenever he tried to reason things through, he found himself wondering whether her skin owed its silkiness to cosmetics or if it was naturally that creamy and fine grained. Was her body perfectly proportioned, or was it his imagination? Was her waist as small as it looked, the curve of her hips as sweet? Were her breasts that ripe and yielding?

The straps of her sundress fastened over her shoulders in perky little bows, and his fingers itched to untie the straps and uncover the beauty the faded cotton concealed.

Zoe stirred uneasily, lifting her hand to her shoulder and fidgeting with the streamers on the bow as if she sensed his musings. He watched, spellbound, as with languid delicacy she slipped one finger beneath the strap and inched it higher on her shoulder.

Ethan held his breath, arrested by the frictionless glide of her finger beneath the strap. He saw her slightest movement, heard the slightest sound—the erotic sibilance of the narrow cotton strap against her skin, the fluttering pulse in the hollow of her throat....

Was that her heart racing, or his own?

Do you know what I'm thinking, sweetheart? Can you feel how much I want to touch you...hold you...kiss you? Do you want me as desperately as I want you? What would you do if I—?

Zoe withdrew her hand from her shoulder and the spell was broken.

Ethan sucked in a breath; the scent of lilacs filled his nostrils. His head was reeling. He felt dizzy, vaguely disoriented.

Damn! What was happening to him? He'd never experienced anything like this before.

Or had he?

Wasn't there something familiar about his fantasy? A feeling of nostalgia? Had his imaginings been a memory or a daydream?

That's crazy! he told himself. *Hold it right there. Don't be any more ridiculous than you already are.*

He hauled himself erect and paced the length of the room and back, forcing himself not to look at Zoe. Within seconds, he began to feel clearer, more in control, and as sanity returned he remembered her resolve to say no to favors.

He stopped in midstride and clapped his hand to his forehead.

Was that what this was all about? Was she going through the motions, waiting for a bit of coaxing?

Could be, he thought. At least it was worth a try.

"I've worked with Haines Randolph for several years," he said. "My grandmother knew him when he was a boy. Based on things she told me and my own observations, I wouldn't trust him with my daughter, but I think you could trust him not to give away any trade secrets, and if he consulted you in a professional capacity, it'd be in his own best interest to keep it quiet."

"So you recommend I have dinner with him?"

He felt Zoe watching him and sensed that she was depending on the truthfulness of his answer. "Not unless you're comfortable about it, but except for a few hours of your time, I honestly don't see that you've got anything to lose."

"And you'll be there?"

He glanced in her direction, and she caught and held his gaze. His voice was not entirely steady as he replied, "Oh, yes, I'll be there. I wouldn't leave you unchaperoned with Haines Randolph if he offered to make me president of Merchants Bank."

Chapter Seven

Brynne Loringer was not a happy camper. Indignation oozed from her voice, as palpably as fog rising off the sea.

And Cora's mood was not much better.

Zoe heard them quarreling as soon as she walked into the foyer, and bypassed the living room, heading for the stairs. She found Sam Kellogg sitting on the third step from the bottom, shamelessly eavesdropping on the battle.

"I see I'm not the only one who wants to stay out of the cross fire," she said.

"My mama did not raise a fool," Sam replied. "There are occasions when retreat is the better part of valor, and one of those occasions is when Brynne's on the warpath."

"What set her off?"

"Who knows? She's been griping about the leaks in the roof damaging her wardrobe, but if you ask me, that's only the tip of the iceberg."

"Was it a bad day on the set?"

"Yes, and it's not just today. Things have been generally putrid since the writers walked out. We've been limping along with free-lancers—some good, some bad—so there's no consistency. Cora's done her best for us, and believe me, that's a lot. She has more tricks up her sleeve than anyone else in the business. But tricks are tricks and gimmicks are gimmicks. They'll carry us for a while, but none of us feels good about it.''

"Have the ratings been falling?"

"McClellan's guest shots gave us a boost. Turns out he's the nasty-nice kind of character the viewers love to hate.''

Tongue firmly in cheek, Zoe remarked, "I guess it's true what they say. There really is no accounting for tastes.''

"That's the truth," said Sam. "And Laurence's ego would get even bigger if he knew what a hit he was. The amount of viewer mail that singles him out has been nothing short of phenomenal. I've never seen anything quite like it.''

"Well, at least the show's holding its audience."

"It seems to be so far, but the strain's getting to the whole crew, and Brynne's been feeling more than her share.''

"Then maybe it'll help her to blow off steam."

"Let's hope so," Sam muttered. He rolled his eyes toward the ceiling as the pitch of voices from the living room reached a new crescendo.

"I am *not* accustomed to *roughing* it!" Brynne wailed.

"Darling," Cora replied with equal shrillness, "Gull Cottage is hardly roughing it.''

Sam grinned at Zoe and shook his head, and she sank down on the stair beside him.

"This may not accomplish anything," he whispered, "but I must confess it's diverting.''

"How long have they been at it?"

"Most of the afternoon, although things have really heated up in the last ten minutes. I'd say you've arrived in time for the curtain." Sam put his forefinger to his lips. "That's enough chitchat now. I don't want to miss a word of this.''

Indeed, the finale seemed to be upon them. "You can tell that to the marines!" Brynne was shrieking. "You can *stuff* it where the *moon* don't shine. *Look* at this dress. Just *look* at it! It's *ruined*."

"By that tiny little water spot? It's practically invisible."

"*Tiny! Invisible!* It's big as bloody Texas."

"You're exaggerating, sweetie. It'll never show on camera."

"Right on, Cora baby, because *I* won't wear it!"

Brynne underscored this declaration by flinging the garment in question into the hall. It sailed toward the stairway and settled about Zoe's shoulders in a cloud of amethyst silk.

"That's a great color on you," Sam observed.

"Do you really think so?"

"Yes, really. Stand up. Let's have a closer look."

Zoe rose, holding the dress in front of her, just as Brynne flounced out of the living room and marched toward the stairs. She stopped with one hand poised above the newel post, narrowing her eyes at Zoe.

"What d'you think?" Sam inquired. "Was this little number made for Zoe or not?"

Brynne tossed her head disdainfully. "Better her than me."

"Are you serious?" asked Zoe.

"Deadly," said Cora, tottering after the actress. "Brynne, sweetie, if you feel that strongly about it, we'll find you another outfit."

Brynne's mouth hardened. "Before tomorrow."

"You drive a hard bargain—"

"Tomorrow," said Brynne. "Or you can find yourself another Sheila."

Cora sighed. "All right. Consider it done."

Brynne's petulance vanished. She turned to Cora, widening her eyes, her smile all sweetness and light. "Thanks, chief. I appreciate it, and I want you to know, I wouldn't have hassled you about the stain if I weren't concerned about the show."

Zoe smoothed her hand over the skirt of the dress, trying to locate the water mark. "What'll happen to this dress?"

"For all I care you can *burn* it," said Brynne. "I never want to see it again."

Zoe glanced at Cora. "Would you mind if I borrow it for tonight?"

A V-shaped furrow appeared between Cora's brows. "It's not that I mind, but I'm a wee bit curious—"

"I'm having dinner with Ethan and one of the vice presidents from his bank."

"Well, that explains it," said Cora.

But it didn't. Not really.

Zoe's taste in clothing ran more to loose-fitting, casual cotton than it did to violet silk, and she wasn't the type who would change her style to attract a man. She seldom dated, and then no one worth mentioning. Now and again Cora arranged for her to meet some worthy eligible, but none of the candidates had sparked Zoe's interest, and when Cora had pressed her about this, she'd insisted she was in no hurry to settle down.

"I've got nothing against marriage," she'd said. "If it happens, it happens. If it doesn't, it doesn't. But there's no need to panic. I'm only twenty-six. I've got plenty of time."

Cora knew better. Experience had taught her time was one commodity there was never plenty of. It didn't seem that long ago since she was Zoe's age, yet here she was pushing sixty, and she had no idea where the years between had gone. One day she'd looked in the mirror and a pert, young face had looked back at her; the next time she'd looked, a middle-aged woman had taken the young girl's place.

She had traded her youth for a career, and she knew, if given the chance, she would do it all again. But while the choices she had made were the right ones for her, they were not the ones she would wish for her niece.

Even so, it was perturbing that Ethan Quinn seemed to have succeeded when her own attempts at matchmaking had failed.

"Tell me, darling," she said, "where is Ethan taking you this evening?"

Zoe recalled Ethan's remark about a restaurant that served barefoot patrons, and flushed a telltale pink. "I'm not sure. He didn't say."

"What about this vice president?"

"Mr. Randolph? What about him?"

"Will Mrs. Randolph be joining you?"

Zoe shook out the folds in the dress, then draped it across her arm. "I think it'll just be the three of us."

Three's no good, thought Cora. A budding romance needs privacy. I'll have to find this Randolph fellow a dinner partner. Someone to keep him occupied while Zoe and Ethan get properly acquainted. Someone attractive and personable—

Brynne!

Would she do it?

She will, thought Cora. Not only does she know which side her bread's buttered on; she also owes me one for letting her win the fracas about the dress.

But could she be trusted not to come on to Ethan?

Not a chance, thought Cora. Brynne was a natural born vamp. She couldn't control her tendency to make a play for anything in pants any more than she could stop breathing. But the evidence seemed to indicate that Ethan was not susceptible to her charms. Last night, for instance, Brynne had uncorked her ingenue-sexpot routine, and Ethan had responded with friendliness, clearly underwhelmed.

Which might be too good to be true. And as Cora quickly reminded herself, when something seemed too good to be true, more often than not it was.

She acknowledged the possibility that Ethan was putting on an act, that in reality he was as wily an operator as Brynne. But somehow she didn't think so. Good men were hard to find, but Cosmo and Sam were proof they still existed. And if, please God, Ethan Quinn could be numbered among the good guys, he might be the man for Zoe.

What it all came down to, Cora concluded, was that she couldn't trust Brynne, so she had to trust Ethan. And she fervently hoped tonight's test would prove that he was deserving of her trust.

WHEN ZOE THOUGHT ABOUT IT later, she was never quite sure how that Thursday dinner for three became a foursome, but that was what happened.

At eight o'clock that evening, costumed in amethyst silk, she found herself seated in one of the Hamptons' most popular eateries with Ethan, Haines Randolph and—wonder of wonders—Brynne Loringer.

When Ethan realized Brynne was crashing the dinner party, he'd been the perfect gentleman. "Randolph will be delighted," he'd assured Zoe. "I should have thought to invite her myself."

Haines Randolph was more than delighted. He seemed taken aback when Ethan walked into the dining room with a lady on either arm, but in the seconds it took his trio of guests to reach his table, his expression ran the gamut from wonderment to adoration.

Although it was Zoe who had incited his promotion of this get-together, he had eyes only for Brynne, and when she gave him her dimpled smile, he bowed over her hand and spoke in hushed, worshipful tones.

"I am your most devoted fan, Miss Loringer. You must sit here, next to me."

Zoe sat next to the window, but she ignored the view of the sunset and concentrated on Ethan.

Had he noticed her Sheila getup, and if so, did he approve? Merlin hadn't recognized her in her high-heeled sandals, with her hair sleeked into a Psyche knot, but then Merlin was unusually perceptive, much more sensitive to her feelings than most humans. He might have sensed her hesitation about appearing in public in disguise.

But as she studied her dinner companions, she realized she needn't be concerned.

Ethan was a banker. He was wearing banker's garb. But his air of bemusement and dreamer's eyes made him seem more like a poet.

Haines Randolph was also a banker, and like Ethan, conservatively dressed. But there was a dapperness about his clothing, a hint of lechery in his smile that revealed the aging Don Juan.

And Brynne was ever the actress, always playing a role. Tonight she was playing the coquette, Josephine to Randolph's Bonaparte.

Even the restaurant had a split personality. On the outside, it looked like a windmill; on the inside it resembled Le Petit Trianon.

On further reflection, it occurred to Zoe that she had no cause to worry about her own pretenses. Nothing was what it seemed to be, and that being the case, she might as well relax and enjoy the show.

And what a show it was! The setting was opulent, the food lavish, and the leading characters glamorous. Act One began with Brynne and Randolph occupying center stage, gossiping about mutual acquaintances:

> Randolph *(astonished)*
> You know the Buffington Ritzes?

> Brynne
> But of course, Haines. I was maid of honor at their wedding. Suzy and Buffy are such a darling couple.

> Randolph *(sadly)*
> Not anymore. It seems old Buffy's run afoul of the law...insider trading or some such thing. Anyway, Suzy's filed for divorce.

> Brynne *(gasping)*
> No! I don't believe it.

> Randolph
> I'm sorry to say it's true. I have it on the best authority.

> Brynne
> Who told you?

> Randolph *(smugly)*
> Chi-chi Waldorf. He's acting as Buffy's lawyer.

> Brynne *(not to be outdone)*
> Well, I always knew it wouldn't last.
> *(Pauses. Bats her lashes. Wets her lips.)*
> You know Chi-chi Waldorf?

The second act was more of the same, and despite the flawless delivery, by the third act the dialog had begun to lose its punch. When the waiter came around to take their orders for after-dinner drinks, Ethan was restless and Zoe couldn't stop yawning.

In the midst of one yawn, she turned to Ethan, just as Ethan leaned closer to her. "Would you mind if we skipped the coffee?" she murmured, and in the same moment Ethan whispered, "Let's get out of here."

The next thing she knew, Ethan had thanked Haines for the dinner, made their excuses and was guiding her out of the dining room.

"Thank God that's over," he muttered as he handed her into his car.

"Amen," said Zoe. Ethan circled the car and climbed behind the wheel. As they drove away from the restaurant she added, "If I were Laurence McClellan, I'd say that performance was marred by protagonists who are less than three-dimensional."

"Meow," said Ethan, and then, holding back a grin, "Two-faced."

"Single-minded."

"Half-witted."

They looked at each other and laughed.

"It was fun while it lasted," said Zoe, "but I can't top that."

Ethan sobered. "It's just as well. If we'd kept it up, we might've descended to their level."

Zoe bit her lip, conscience-stricken. "You're right. We're as bad as they are."

"Never!" said Ethan. "Lord, I hate that scene. All that bogus crap."

"But you have to admit the macaroni au gratin was good."

He gave her a scoffing glance. "Do you think anyone there tonight cared about the food?"

"Obviously you don't."

"No. I think most of the people who go to places like that are running with the pack. It happens to be 'in' with a certain crowd, so it's the place to be seen."

"I suppose the same holds true for most of the summer people."

"Most of them, yes. They claim they want a change of pace, but any fundamental change might threaten their identities, so instead of getting away from it all, they come out here and bring it all with them—the traffic, the parties, the cliques, the fads, the wheeling and dealing, the headaches."

"In other words, all the phoniness."

"Exactly. They never see the real East Hampton. If they did, they wouldn't recognize it. Most of 'em wouldn't know the genuine article if it bit them on the behind."

"Then again, they might," Zoe replied. "They might know more than you realize. Maybe they see the truth from a different angle, but that doesn't make it any less valid. I mean, it's easy to feel superior if you know what you want out of life, but if you're still looking for answers, if all you have is questions, people accuse you of rationalizing or being irresponsible or running away or not knowing when you're well off—"

"Or being superficial," said Ethan. "Not knowing your own mind. Not knowing the difference between illusion and reality."

"Yes, that too."

"And you resent it."

"Wouldn't you, if you were expected to settle for second best?"

"I'm sorry, Zoe. I seem to have struck a nerve, but as long as the subject's come up, why don't you tell me what you want?"

She drew in a shaky breath, already regretting her outburst. If she were completely honest with Ethan, if she told the whole truth, it would lead to a rehash of last night's argument, and so she responded with a partial truth.

"What I'd like more than anything is not to talk about this any more, at least for tonight."

"You've got it. Any other requests?"

"Just one," she answered. "I'd like to go someplace you consider 'real.'"

ETHAN TOOK HER to the beach, which shouldn't have come as a surprise, but did. What was more surprising was how easily Ethan helped her to overcome her fear of the ocean. All it required was a smile from him, and her apprehension seemed foolish.

They left the car at the end of an unpaved road that cut across the dunes. Ethan dug a flashlight out of the glove box, but they didn't need it. A three-quarter moon lighted their path through thick clumps of marsh grass, down a steep wooden stairway to the shore.

At the foot of the stairs, Zoe stopped to take off her shoes. Ethan said he'd known all along she wouldn't make it through an entire evening wearing them, and she made a face at him. He slipped her sandals into the side pockets of his jacket, and tucked her hand into his as they walked along the hard-packed sand at the edge of the tide line.

The beach went on for miles, and appeared to be totally deserted. With rare exceptions, the cottages they passed were dark. "A few of the owners may come out this weekend," Ethan explained, "but they'll only stay till Sunday. The season won't get underway for several weeks."

Zoe had no clear idea of their precise location or whether the beach was public or private, but with Ethan beside her, with her hand warm in his, she didn't care.

Sometimes they talked. Sometimes they were companionably quiet. Once or twice they broke into a run to avoid the breakers; then Ethan pulled off his own shoes and rolled up his pant legs, and after that, more often than not they didn't race the waves.

They kept to a leisurely pace, letting the surf wash over their feet, and Ethan told her about his widowed mother and his brothers, who were the fourth generation of Quinns to operate the family business.

"My grandfather managed to hang on to one nursery and greenhouse," Ethan said. "My father invested in land and built new greenhouses. Under his management the business really expanded. And now that Dad's gone, Sean's taken over management of the farms and Clayton handles distribution and sales. Before the two of them pass the business on to their sons, Quinn's will probably go nationwide."

"That's quite a tradition," Zoe remarked.

"It's a lot to live up to." Ethan bent down to pick up a smooth, flat stone and with a deft sidearm toss, sent it skipping over the water. "There was a time I might have joined the firm if I'd thought it would work out."

"Why didn't you think it would work?"

"Because of the age difference. Sean and Clay were only eighteen months apart. I came along ten years later, and since they were both so much older than me, when I was growing up I always felt as if I was in their shadow. So after high school I decided to go away to college to declare my independence. And after I got my degree, I had enough confidence in my own ability to go home, but it seemed to me my brothers didn't see me as an equal. I was still the kid brother, and they treated me accordingly."

"So you went into banking."

Ethan nodded. "As it turned out, I'm good at what I do, and by the time I'd gotten some successes under my belt, I'd realized two things. The first was that I didn't have to prove anything to anyone but myself. The second was that I didn't want to go into the nursery business."

"Then you're happy with the way things turned out."

"Yes, I'm reasonably content." Only lately he'd had the nagging feeling that there ought to be more to life than career satisfaction. He bent down and scooped up another rock and weighed it in his palm. "How about you, Zoe? Are you happy working for Cosmo?"

"I must be. I've been at The Second Story more than three times longer than I've stayed at any other job. I've even unpacked my suitcase."

"So you're not planning to leave New York?"

"Not as long as I'm making progress."

"Toward what?"

"I don't know yet, but I will. Soon, I hope. And in the meantime, I'm learning as much as I can."

Ethan threw the rock into the air and batted it along the beach with the sole of his shoe. "I'm in favor of learning. They say knowledge is power, and I think it's true, but I'm not sure whether there's much future in astrology."

"The future is *now*, Ethan. Don't you see?"

"I see that we're talking about two different things. You're way off in the stratosphere and I'm suggesting it might be prudent to keep some money in the bank and one foot on the ground."

Zoe dug both feet into the sand and watched a wave foam around her ankles. "My mother's a great believer in nest eggs. Also in adages. 'You should set something aside for a rainy day,' she says. 'A person has to eat.'"

"And what do you say to your mother?"

"I tell her I'll get by. I may not be able to afford macaroni au gratin at twenty dollars a serving, but macaroni and cheese tastes almost as good, and costs considerably less."

Another wave washed in, and Zoe lifted the hem of her skirt as the water rose to her knees. When the water rushed out, her sandy foothold crumbled and she stumbled backward—into Ethan's arms.

His hands closed about her rib cage, fingers splayed to steady her, and before she could regain her equilibrium, his lips grazed her temple, the corner of her eyelid, her cheek.

In a small voice, breathless with anticipation, she murmured, "So much for keeping my feet on the ground."

She felt his mouth curve into a smile as he turned her to face him, and it seemed completely right, completely natural to twine her arms around his shoulders and stroke the back of his neck, to test the crisp, springy hair at his nape and lift her mouth for his kiss.

His lips tasted salty, then delectably sweet; cool, then desirous and hot. His hands moved over her back, exploring the fine bones of her spine, measuring the span of her waist and the swell of her hips, arching her closer to him, and his embrace was more tantalizing than she had imagined, more passionate than she could have dreamed.

He touched the tip of his tongue to hers, and her lips softened and opened beneath the rough urgency of his. An involuntary shiver of excitement rippled through her, and as one kiss blended into another, she clung to him, awash with sensation, caught in a spiral of pleasure that had no beginning and no end.

The rest of the world seemed to spin away. She was aware only of Ethan; the taste of his kisses, the silky friction of his hands caressing her through her dress, the strength of his arms, the proud length of his body pressed to hers.

She didn't notice the succession of waves rolling farther and farther onto the shore. Neither did Ethan, until the crest of the breakers hit him at midthigh. His muffled outcry alerted her and, startled, they broke apart.

Ethan met her eyes and smiled. He looked earnest, crestfallen, and utterly appealing. "This certainly puts a damper on things."

"It may be just as well. We have plenty of time—"

His grin widened, and she left the rest of the thought unspoken. And shaken, but laughing, holding hands, they splashed through the surf to higher ground.

Chapter Eight

Ethan spent most of Friday helping Zoe sort his uncle's papers.

At least, that's what he called it.

Every time she looked up, he was watching her. And every few minutes he came across something he had to ask her opinion about, and he took advantage of the opportunities presented by these consultations by propping a hand at either side of her on the desktop, so that his shirt sleeve tickled the back of her neck or ruffled her hair as he bent over her chair, putting his head so close to hers that his breath fanned her cheek.

He seemed to be fascinated by the straps on her sun top. Once, when one of the straps had slipped off her shoulder, he broke off in the middle of a question and made a great show of replacing it. After that, while they were in the midst of a discussion, he would toy with the loops on the bows, alternately loosening and retying one. Or he would draw the end of a streamer over her collarbone, or run a lazy forefinger along the strap, tracing the narrow strand up over her shoulder blade, then down to the rise of her breast, then back to her shoulder and down the other side.

The most unsettling thing about this was that his fingertip never strayed from the strap.

Not once.

He never touched her skin.

It was frustrating. It was maddening. It drove her to distraction.

Why was he tormenting her this way? Didn't he realize how disturbing it was? Couldn't he see that he was shattering her concentration, making it difficult for her to get any work done?

She sat at the steno desk, going through a stack of receipts, weeding out the ones that were not pertinent to the library, but by midday, because of Ethan's teasing, she had barely made a dent in the pile.

She was already off schedule; if he kept this up, she'd fall further behind. It would take an extra week to sort Hiram's records.

Do something, she told herself. *If you want him to stop, all you have to do is say so.*

If she wanted him to stop.

The next time he approached she offered no objection, even though he charted the course of a strap half a dozen times.

Obviously she wanted more than idle teasing, more than indolent touches and butterfly caresses. But what did Ethan want?

Last night she had responded to his kisses with unqualified enthusiasm, and how had he reacted?

He'd grinned—

No, he'd laughed! And then he'd hauled her out of the water, half carried her up the beach, found a few sticks of driftwood and built a fire. After that, he'd helped her look for her shoes—they'd fallen out of his pockets when the wave struck.

They hadn't found the sandals, but Ethan's shoes were safe, dangling by their laces around his neck, and they'd joked about that. He'd said, "After my visit to your apartment, I've made it a rule to protect my shoes when I'm with you or Merlin."

By the time their clothes were dry it was very late and she was tired. She'd told him about Boris's chatter keeping her awake the night before. They'd returned to the car and during the drive to Gull Cottage she'd dozed off. She had only the haziest recollection of what happened after that, but she remembered, when Ethan walked her to the door, he had offered to pay the dry cleaning bill for her dress.

He'd said, "If it can't be salvaged, I'll replace it."

"Don't worry about the dress," she'd answered, only half awake. "Sometime, when you have a few hours to spare, I might tell you how I came to borrow it."

"It's borrowed?" For some reason that seemed to trouble him. He'd fingered one end of the sash, studying the fabric with a strange intensity. "It's silk, isn't it?"

"Yes," she'd said, "it is."

Still he'd studied the sash. "What would you call this color?"

"Amethyst, orchid, lavender—"

"Lilac?"

"Yes, I guess you could call it that."

She'd been puzzled by his behavior last night, and was even more puzzled now. Except for those few minutes when he'd kissed her, and his odd question about the color of her dress, Ethan had been cordial, attentive, but not particularly amorous.

So what does he want? Zoe wondered.

As that Friday dragged on, she found herself dreading his next foray—and longing for it.

When she thought about his ritual tracing of her shoulder strap, her nipples tightened with expectation, and she silently acknowledged that she wanted greater intimacies. But how could she entice him to vary the ritual?

She could take a page from Brynne Loringer's book and flutter her lashes at him, but even if she managed not to look hokey, she didn't think coyness would work with Ethan. Whatever enticement she chose shouldn't seem staged. She had to demonstrate her receptiveness subtly, by some small movement.

Perhaps she should turn to the right or to the left. Then again, she could lean forward a fraction of an inch. Or it might seem more natural if she leaned back.

She could stretch or shrug or sit up straighter.

Or what if she inhaled at an opportune moment, and the backs of his fingers grazed her breast? Would he know that she'd willed it to happen? Would he think it was an accident, or—

No. It was too big a gamble. What if he didn't notice? What if he noticed, but didn't care? How could she bear the rejection?

By five o'clock that afternoon, the two of them working together had gone through less than half as many cartons as she would have working alone. Clearly, if she ever hoped to catalog the library, she would have to put in overtime—but not here at the Seymour estate.

She gathered up a batch of receipts and found the corresponding titles on the shelves. After making notations for her accession log, she began loading the books into her carryall.

"Calling it a day?" Ethan inquired.

"Yes, except that I thought I'd do a little reading tonight."

"Looks like a lot of reading to me." He glanced thoughtfully at her supply of books, then got to his feet and stretched. "Want a lift home?"

"No, thanks," she answered firmly, clutching the handles of the carryall. Riding the bicycle back to Gull Cottage might help clear her head. "Will you be here tomorrow?"

"Sure. Wouldn't miss it."

Which meant a change of strategy most definitely was in order.

AFTER ZOE LEFT, Ethan sat on the corner of her desk, surveying the array of library supplies she had brought. Glues and tapes, bottles of Liquid Paper, index cards, labels, pencils and pens, a paper punch. And then, of course, there were her reference books.

He thumbed through one of them, absorbed in thought.

Something was going on with Zoe and him. Something portentous. Something that signaled a major upheaval in his life.

What had started as a completely normal man-woman attraction was turning into something more serious and much more complicated, and after the peculiar happenings of the last few days, Ethan had to admit, their relationship had him stumped.

Relationship.

When applied to the way he felt about Zoe, the word struck him as hollow and meaningless, but for the time being it would have to do.

To say that he was drawn to her didn't begin to express his feelings.

To say that he desired her didn't express his needs.

To call her his "significant other" was stretching it a bit, and to call his feelings infatuation diminished them somehow. It made his involvement with Zoe seem childish and temporary.

Yet he hesitated to call it love.

He'd always thought of love as a gentle emotion, like the boundless calm at the eye of a hurricane. But his feelings for Zoe were anything but tranquil. They were more akin to the storm itself. Consuming. Uncontrollable. Defying reason. With an otherwordly aspect that scared the hell out of him.

The story about Evangeline, for instance.

If any other woman had told him a tale like that, he would have run, not walked, to the nearest exit. With Zoe, he had wanted to run. His instincts had warned him to keep his distance, but in spite of his better judgment, he couldn't stay away.

Three hundred years ago he might have said, "The woman has bewitched me."

Nowadays, witchcraft being less widely accepted, it might be more appropriate to say that he was developing a fixation.

The way their thoughts coincided was downright eerie. And why did he associate Zoe with lilacs? The fragrance . . . the flowers . . . even the color?

Yesterday she'd worn a sundress of faded violet blue. Last night, a cocktail dress of lavender silk. And today an eyelet camisole, the color of heather. And in each case, it was all he could do to keep his hands off her.

Was it the lady he found irresistible, or was it the shades of lilac she wore? Should he blame the unseasonably warm weather that kept her lovely shoulders bare?

"Damn!" Ethan muttered. It wasn't like him to notice women's fashions, nor was he in the habit of waxing lyrical about shoulders. In a sudden burst of impatience, he shoved away from the desk and slammed out of the library.

THAT EVENING he went to a charity gala at a nearby country club, and instead of merely putting in an appearance, he stayed till after midnight, talking with friends, listening to the jazz combo, even sitting in at the piano for a number or two.

The combo was just finishing the set when he noticed a willowy blonde who was giving him the eye. She was tall, long legged and pampered looking, sultry and sexy and smart. And, he discovered when they danced together, she was available.

With her arms around his neck and her mouth close to his ear, she purred, "I hope you realize my intentions are strictly dishonorable."

Ethan was flattered by her interest, but unmoved. He held her at arm's length and replied, "As long as you're being honest, will you respect me in the morning?"

"Darling," said the blonde, "who cares?"

I do, Ethan realized. He bade the blonde good-night and wished her happy hunting, mystified by his reaction. She was the physical type he often dated and had always found attractive—

But she wasn't a redhead, and she wasn't Zoe.

A few minutes later he left the party and made his way home alone, unable to shake the feeling that something spooky was going on.

ON SATURDAY Zoe wore a lettuce-green shirtwaist, long-sleeved, high-necked, buttoned primly to the collar. She was crisp, efficient, businesslike, but her starchy dress and circumspect demeanor did little to cool Ethan's ardor.

He thought of what it would be like if he unbuckled the belt and unbuttoned every button. He imagined kissing each millimeter of creamy flesh as it was exposed, and by the end of the day he knew that Zoe's allure had little to do with the color lilac or the witchery of naked shoulders.

It was the lady herself he found seductive.

So what was he to do?

Some women took offense if a guy made a pass; others were insulted if he didn't. He didn't know Zoe well enough to say whether she fell into one of these extremes, but in either case, doubted he could be objective. He saw her in a romantic light that tended to cloud his vision, but his gut feeling was that she couldn't be categorized.

He glanced at her obliquely, and found that he could study her at his leisure. She was moving back and forth along the bookshelves, looking for specific titles, pausing now and again to consult the document she held, and while he watched she climbed onto the step stool and reached for a volume on one of the upper shelves.

Ethan's breath came short as he admired the lissome grace of her body, the sweet curving perfection of waist and hips and thighs.

Oh, yes! he thought. *She's in a class by herself.*

And he wanted her so much that he was tempted to forgo the niceties of courtship and simply sweep her off her feet, carry her upstairs to his bedroom and immerse himself in her splendors.

But another part of him, some previously unsuspected chivalrous streak, looked forward to the wooing, and promised that if he resisted temptation for only a few hours, the ultimate pleasures of making love to Zoe would be increased tenfold.

Besides, although her back was to him, he could sense that she was engrossed with her book.

She had told him she took her work seriously, and from what he'd seen, this was true. And the other night, when they were soaked by the wave, she had suggested they bow to the forces of nature.

"It may be just as well," she'd said. "We have plenty of time."

In other words, don't rush things.

So why not take Zoe at her word, and let nature take its course?

And while he was at it, why not bite the bullet and finish sorting these blasted records?

Ethan checked his watch. It was already after five. Another day was shot, and three banker's boxes remained.

His throat felt tight. He swallowed to clear it. "A few more hours should wrap this up," he said.

Zoe nodded and reached for another book. She didn't turn around.

"If you want to keep working, I'm willing," he said.

For a moment she froze, as if she couldn't believe her ears, and then she swung around to look at him. "That would clear the decks for Monday," was her noncommittal reply.

"Yes, it would," he agreed. "You could start right in with the cataloging."

She hugged the book to her bosom. "That'd be wonderful, if you're sure you don't mind."

"Honestly. It'll be my pleasure. The truth is, I'll be glad to see the end of Uncle Hiram's papers."

"Me too."

Her smile was radiant, her gratitude so transparent that he felt a twinge of guilt. His offer was not unselfish. He had an ulterior motive. He hoped to trade a few hours of work for Zoe's undivided attention.

"Tell you what," he said lightly, as if the idea had just occurred to him. "After we finish up here, we'll go somewhere for dinner."

Zoe sobered. "I'd like that, Ethan. Really I would. But I don't think we'd better."

Somehow he hid his consternation. "Well, if you have other plans—"

"I don't," she said. "It isn't that."

"Then would you mind telling me what the problem is?"

Zoe ducked her head and brushed at a smudge of dust on her skirt. "It's Aunt Cora."

"What about her?"

"If we see too much of each other, she'll think there's something more than your uncle's library between us."

"And?"

"And if she thinks there's something personal between us, you're liable to wind up as a character on *Passion's Children*."

"Is that all?" Relief threaded his voice. He sounded upbeat, lighthearted, and when Zoe looked up and met his gaze, he grinned.

"It's not funny," she said.

"Isn't it? Come on, Zoe, lighten up. You can't be speaking from personal experience."

She averted her face and did not answer. She looked acutely uncomfortable.

"Okay," said Ethan. "I assume that means you are. So tell me, which character are you?"

"Sheila," Zoe mumbled beneath her breath.

Ethan did a double take, not sure he'd heard her correctly, and then he chuckled. "I'm sorry," he apologized. "It's just, I could've sworn you said Sheila."

"I did," said Zoe. "And believe me, Ethan, if we see each other socially, you'll be written into the show."

Now he laughed outright. "If you're Sheila, I suppose I'll get to be Rafe."

"I don't know who you'll be, but I do know Aunt Cora will use you. I'm not saying you'll be readily identifiable. You'll be exaggerated, impossibly heroic, larger than life—"

"That doesn't sound half bad."

"It is, though. Take my word for it. It's easy to dismiss as a joke until it happens to you, but once it does, you'll see it as an invasion of privacy. You'll begin to feel self-conscious whenever you're with me, because the most innocent things we do could be dramatized out of proportion, set to 'Hearts and Flowers,' and telecast coast to coast."

Zoe's fingers were tensed about the spine of the book so that her knuckles blanched, and somewhat belatedly it dawned on Ethan that this was no hoax.

"My God, you're telling the truth! This has actually happened to men you've dated."

"Yes, but not lately. Not since I've started issuing warnings whenever I'm asked out."

"That must play hob with your social life."

"You might say that." Zoe loosened her grip on the book and gave him a wry smile. "The topper is, Aunt Cora can't figure out why I don't go out more."

"She's not aware that she's responsible?"

"She is and she isn't. She admits she looks to me for inspiration, but I don't think she's aware that her scrutiny spills over onto the men I date."

"And you haven't told her?"

"No, although there's been a time or two when her adaptations have become too intrusive. I've complained about that."

"But she hasn't taken the hint?"

"She would if I made an issue of it. Frankly, it hasn't seemed worth it."

Ethan frowned. "You're more forgiving than I am."

"It's not a matter of forgiveness," said Zoe. "Aunt Cora's done a lot for me. She's always been there, the one person I could count on. And it's not as if she does this maliciously. It's not as if it's planned. It's a habit she's gotten into, practically a conditioned reflex."

"The show must be awfully important to her."

"It's her *life*, and that makes it more important to me than a casual date."

"Ah, but what if the date weren't so casual?"

Zoe shrugged. "A man who genuinely cared about me wouldn't ask me to choose between him and my aunt."

"He might not ask, but would you do it?"

"That would depend on my feelings for him."

"I see what you mean," said Ethan. And he did understand. Perfectly.

The threat of *Passion's Children* provided a ready-made litmus test of sincerity, not unlike the challenge faced by the knight in the fairy tale who had to slay a dragon before he could storm the gates of the enchanted castle and rescue the beautiful maiden.

Zoe's castle was The Second Story. She had erected a moat with her scholarly pursuit of astrology. And if Cora Piper was the dragon, that made him the hapless suitor who was stranded on the drawbridge. He could turn around and hightail it back to safety or proceed at his own risk.

The choice, he recognized, was up to him.

But when he looked at Zoe, he realized that his decision was already made. It had been from the moment they met.

"I appreciate your leveling with me," he said, "but I have nothing to hide. My invitation is still open."

Zoe's smile told him he had survived the first obstacle. "In that case, I accept."

ETHAN ACCOMPLISHED MORE in the next two hours than he had in the previous two days. Zoe was astonished at how industrious he could be, especially since she was in a festive mood and found it hard to settle down.

Ethan urged her to take a break. "Consider it time off for good behavior. You've earned it."

"I should be working," she insisted. "That's why you're paying me."

"Right you are," he said. "It's my nickel, so if you want to make yourself useful, you can decide where you'd like to go for dinner."

Laughing, Zoe agreed, and while Ethan was up to his elbows in musty old records, she concentrated on the list of restaurants in the yellow pages. She debated the merits of seafood versus prime rib, Szechuan versus Italian, home-style cooking versus haute cuisine, and finally decided on a place in Sag Harbor that advertised a view of the waterfront and incomparable paella.

"Good choice," said Ethan.

With his approval, she called the restaurant and made reservations for two at eight-thirty.

By seven o'clock, Ethan was rooting about in the last carton and she was at her desk, puzzling over a letter to Hiram from a Viennese psychic.

Ethan looked up and caught her scowling. "Uh-oh. What's the matter?"

She held up the fragile sheet of foolscap. "Nothing that a few years of German wouldn't fix. At least, I think this is written in German."

"I'm no help there," said Ethan. "French was all I studied."

Zoe spread the letter on the desktop. "I'll ask Cosmo to take a look at this. He should be able to translate it."

"Is it something important?"

"Could be. I can't make out enough of it to be sure, but it seems to refer to your uncle's corresponding with Carl Jung."

"*The* Carl Jung?"

"I assume so. Jung was a lifelong proponent of astrology. He also believed in the collective unconscious. In fact, he coined the term—" Zoe broke off in midsentence, aware that her digression was straying into areas that held little of interest for Ethan. "Anyway," she finished, "I haven't found the correspondence."

"Maybe it got mixed in with the general library."

Zoe glanced around the room, surveying the crowded bookshelves. "That's possible, I suppose."

"But you doubt it?"

"Yes, I do. You'd never guess it from the way he handled his records, but your uncle was quite fastidious in his treatment of the Seymour Collection."

Ethan stretched out on the floor, using the wall as a backrest, his head propped on one hand. "I know the collection meant a great deal to Uncle Hiram. He told me more than once he regarded it as a trust, so if he did receive letters from Carl Jung, I'm sure they'll turn up."

"Yes, of course they will. I'll just have to make a thorough search." Zoe sighed and shoved an errant curl away from her forehead.

"You don't seem reassured," said Ethan.

"Maybe I'm borrowing trouble, but this isn't the first indication I've seen that part of the collection might be missing. There are items mentioned in various letters that I can't seem to locate."

"Can you tell me what they are?"

Zoe drew a file folder toward her and switched on the desk lamp, scanning the notes she had taken. "There's an early monograph by J. B. Rhine, Eugène Osty's *Supernormal Faculties in Man*, and a book by W. J. Dunne. It's not mentioned by name, but it's probably *An Experiment with Time*."

"You're familiar with it?"

"Yes, I'm familiar with all three. Each of them is a valuable work, although not particularly rare. But there is a reference to one title I've only heard about. Something called *World of the Spirit*. It created quite a stir when it was published, and it's mentioned in some of the earliest studies on psychical research, but I don't know of anyone who's seen an actual copy of the book."

"Not even Cosmo?"

"No. Not even him."

"Can you tell from the reference when this book was acquired?"

"Not exactly, but I did get the impression it was purchased before your uncle's time."

Ethan levered himself to a sitting position, mulling this over. "When was it published?"

"Over a hundred years ago. Maybe as early as 1850. It was a pioneer work on spiritualism. You know—life after death, communication beyond the grave, that sort of thing."

"So it would be rare."

"And important," said Zoe. "It would be a major find."

"Well, if it's here, you'll find it," Ethan replied quietly. "There's no doubt about that. You said yourself my uncle was fastidious—about everything but his records."

With a mock-ferocious grimace that coaxed a smile from Zoe, Ethan went back to his sorting, and she went back to making notations about the documents he had unearthed.

Three-quarters of an hour later he held triumphant fists above his head, and announced the box was empty.

"Hallelujah!" said Zoe.

Ethan had shredded some discarded sheets of paper, and he tossed the scraps into the air, surprising her with a blizzard of confetti.

"We'll finish this celebration at the restaurant," he said. "Give me five minutes to wash up and change my shirt, and then we ought to leave."

While Ethan was changing, Zoe stepped into the powder room to freshen her lipstick and comb the confetti out of her hair. By the time he came downstairs, she had collected her carryall and was waiting for him in the entry hall.

They were on their way out the door when the phone rang. Ethan hesitated.

"Better answer it," she said.

She lingered in the open door while he returned to the parlor to pick up the phone. Within seconds, he called, "Zoe, it's for you."

There was an urgency in his tone that made her heart leap into her throat. "Who is it?" she asked, hurrying to join him.

"It's Cora. She sounds upset."

Hysterical was more like it, Zoe discovered. Her aunt was wailing, frantic, babbling a mile a minute, and all but incoherent.

"Slow down," Zoe pleaded. "You're not making any sense."

Cora inhaled, a long shuddering breath. When she spoke again, her voice was less shrill, and this time her message was clear.

"You've got to come home, Zoe. I need you. The dining room's been stolen."

"It's what?"

"It's been stolen."

"B-but who—what—?"

"I don't know!" Cora howled. "I went for a walk on the beach, and when I got back the furniture was gone."

"All of it?"

"Every stick. The table and chairs, the china cabinet and hutch, the paintings, the dishes—even the rug! The only thing left is that papier-mâché shark with the map of the world on his belly. And what's worse—I mean the absolute dregs of it all—is that the caterer's threatening to quit!"

Chapter Nine

Instead of taking Zoe to dinner, Ethan drove her home. When they turned onto Frigate Alley, the caterer's van careened by them, headed for town. Evidently, Cora had not been able to persuade the cook to stay.

The grounds about Gull Cottage were ablaze with light. Cora was waiting at the end of the drive, looking harried, apprehensive, forlorn and furious all at once.

Ethan braked to a stop, and she piled into the front seat. "I'm not going back in there," she declared. "For all I know, whoever robbed the place is still inside."

Zoe put a comforting arm about her aunt. "Where are the others?"

"They've gone to the city for the weekend." With a brave parody of a smile, Cora added, "I don't mind admitting, I wish I'd gone with them."

Ethan parked near the front door and climbed out of the car, leaving the key in the ignition. "No signs of a break-in," he observed. He bent down to peer at Cora through the driver's side window. "Have the police been informed?"

"Not by me. When I saw what had happened, I called your place. After that I got the hell out."

"You told Zoe you'd gone for a walk."

"That's right. Just down the beach. I couldn't have been gone much more than an hour."

"Was the caterer here while you were gone?"

"He might've been. He really didn't say. All I can tell you for sure is that he almost trampled me on his way to the door."

"Did you happen to get a look inside his van?"

Cora stared at Ethan, saucer-eyed. "You can't think *he* stole the dining room? Oh, my, no! The way he over-charges is a crime. I suspect he's been padding the bills and taking kickbacks, but he's not capable of burglary."

Apparently satisfied with Cora's assessment, Ethan straightened. "You two wait here," he said, starting toward the house.

Zoe watched him walk away, wavering between the urge to go with him and the need to stay with her aunt.

In the end, duty overcame desire. Cora was still quite shaken, clinging to her hand, and so Zoe remained in the car until Ethan reported that, aside from the dining room, the contents of Gull Cottage appeared to be in order.

Zoe guided her aunt into the living room and left her in Ethan's care while she made a pot of tea. By the time the tea was ready, Cora had regained her composure and was more concerned about hiring another cook than finding the missing furniture.

"A television crew is like an army," she explained. "A very hungry army. And a caterer's crucial to the success of a remote production. If I don't find someone to supply meals for the cast and crew before Monday morning, I might as well cancel the location shoot and go on back to the studio."

"Haines Randolph may be able to recommend a re-placement," said Ethan. "As soon as I've called the po-lice, I'll get in touch with him."

"I appreciate your help," Cora told him, "But it might be better if we held off contacting the police till I've had a chance to talk with the rental agent. I'm not absolutely certain that Larry's not behind this."

"Why would McClellan steal his own furniture?"

"I'm not saying he personally loaded the stuff on a truck and hauled it away, but it's possible he sold it to cover his gambling debts. If that's the case, I wouldn't want to embarrass him."

Ethan glanced at Zoe, who nodded agreement. "Okay," he allowed. "If that's the way you want it, I won't call the police. But I don't like the idea of you two being out here alone—"

"You could stay with us," Cora said.

Zoe frowned at this suggestion. "That's hardly necessary, is it, Aunt Cora? Sam and Cosmo will be back tomorrow, and this neighborhood must be well patrolled. We wouldn't want to be a nuisance."

Cora turned to Ethan, a disarming twinkle in her eyes. "Would spending the night here be terribly inconvenient?"

"Not at all," he replied. "I'd be happy to stay."

Zoe bit her lip, forcing back an objection. Ethan's presence in Gull Cottage would bring him under her aunt's surveillance, which was just the sort of situation she had hoped to prevent.

But she had done her best. She had warned Ethan. If she lodged further protests, she might arouse Cora's suspicion, and short of pushing him bodily out the door, there was nothing more she could do.

Her only recourse was to avoid being alone with him and watch helplessly while, with a smile at Cora and a befuddled look at her, Ethan went off to phone Haines Randolph.

THAT EVENING went more smoothly than Zoe had anticipated. Contrary to her fears, Ethan did not seek her out.
While he was busy making arrangements for a substitute
caterer, she closeted herself in the kitchen and began
preparations for dinner, and in the hour it took her to bake
potatoes, toss a salad and slide some lamb chops under the
broiler, neither he nor Cora made any move to offer assis-
tance.

They didn't help with the cleanup either, and when she
excused herself and went upstairs to bed, Cora was running tapes of *Passion's Children* and offering pithy comments about the trials of being the executive producer of
a top-rated soap.

Ethan seemed vastly entertained by her company.

Alone in her room, Zoe made every effort to ignore the
laughter that drifted up from the solarium. She plugged
her ears and told herself that she would rather read herself to sleep than join the revelry downstairs.

But, she thought, even so, they might've asked her to
stay.

The following morning she was up with the sun, and the
house was quiet. She climbed into cut-off jogging pants
and an old T-shirt and took Merlin for a romp on the
beach.

When she got back, it was after nine. Ethan and her
aunt were still sleeping, but Boris was awake, demanding
his breakfast.

In the solarium she found evidence of last night's diver-
sions: empty beer and soda cans, and a bowl that obviously had held popcorn. Video cassettes littered the
coffee table, and the television had been left on, tuned to
a channel that was running cartoons.

She fed and watered Boris before she did anything else,
and he looked on with his usual air of malignity while she

replaced the cassettes in their holders, fluffed sofa pillows and generally tidied up the room.

When Merlin wandered in from the deck, the mynah fluttered to the uppermost reaches of his cage.

"Thufferin' thuccotash! I tawt I taw a puddy tat."

Zoe hastened to turn off the cartoons.

"I *did*! I taw a puddy tat."

Zoe shooed Merlin into the living room and closed the sliding doors after him.

"Utterly dethpicable," Boris lisped.

Zoe dumped the empty cans into the popcorn bowl and sighed as she carried the remnants of Saturday's refreshments along the deck to the kitchen.

Next thing, she supposed, Boris would be doing his impression of Pepe LePew, which was just what she needed to make her life complete.

It was after eleven before Zoe heard Cora stirring, and almost noon before Ethan put in an appearance. She was lying in the sun beside the pool when he came out of the kitchen, balancing a tray laden with carafes of coffee and orange juice and plates filled with scrambled eggs, sausages and croissants.

She studied him from behind the smoked lenses of her sunglasses as he laid a place for himself at a poolside table. "Want to share my breakfast? There's plenty."

"No, thank you," she answered stiffly. "I had breakfast *hours* ago."

"Then maybe you should have some of this for lunch." Ethan grinned. She did not.

"Late night?" she inquired.

"Uh-huh. Cora and I talked till half-past two."

Zoe pushed the sunglasses to the top of her head, the better to stare at him. "I noticed the two of you seemed to hit it off."

"She's quite a woman." Ethan bit into a croissant before he went on. "I had no idea of the complexities involved in producing a soap—not to mention the creativity it requires."

"And now you do?"

"Well, I'm no expert, but from Cora's description, I'm beginning to grasp a bit more of the picture."

"How nice for you."

Ethan sampled his sausages and eggs, ignoring her sour-grapes tone. But Zoe heard it, and it grated so much that she winced.

It dawned on her that she was jealous; out of sorts because Ethan had paid her aunt more attention than he had paid her. Or maybe it was because he respected Cora's accomplishments and considered astrology trivial. But it was silly of her to be envious. Cora wasn't her rival, and chances were Ethan was just being pleasant—

He's always pleasant, thought Zoe. *And that makes it difficult to guess what's going on in his mind.*

At the moment, however, he must think that she was behaving like a bratty two-year-old. If he weren't so polite, he'd probably tell her to grow up.

Trying to sound more congenial, she asked, "What else did you talk about?"

"Lot's of things. My work at the bank. Laurence McClellan. You. She told me Laurence was the client who gave your Wall Street prediction to the press and we also talked about the experiment with hypnosis the other night—"

Zoe bolted to a sitting position. "You didn't tell her about Evangeline?"

"I didn't have to," Ethan replied.

An awful sinking feeling washed over Zoe. "What do you mean, you didn't have to?"

"Cora already knew about her, only she calls Evangeline by a different name. She told me all about Sheila's being possessed by the spirit of great-great-grandmother Hester."

"That's not the same."

"Sure it is. The names may be different, but a ghost is a ghost is a ghost."

"But Hester's fictional!"

"So's Evangeline."

"She's not. She *existed*. She was as real as you and I."

"Hester's real to Sheila, too."

"In a soap opera! Look, Ethan, I told you yesterday, Aunt Cora looks to me for inspiration. Didn't you hear anything I said?"

Ethan shrugged. "I heard you, Zoe, and I noticed the parallels. So you tell me, who's borrowing from whom? Is this a case of art imitating life, or are you imitating Cora's script?"

Zoe shot to her feet. "I— You— Of all the— You can't—"

His effrontery left her gasping . . . inarticulate . . . all but speechless. Unable to verbalize her outrage, she spun on her heel and marched into the house, up the stairs to her room.

The slam of her door reverberated all the way to the swimming pool, and Ethan hunched over his plate, his appetite suddenly gone.

Smart guy, he told himself. Thought you had things all figured out. You might've kept your mouth shut and your theories to yourself, but you couldn't leave well enough alone. You had to show off.

Whether his theories were right or wrong, he'd taken his chance and blown it.

Zoe was steamed, and he didn't blame her. If someone tried to poke holes in his pet daydream, he'd be steamed, too.

The trouble was, he wasn't sure Zoe knew she was dreaming. If she didn't, that made his offense even worse, at least in her eyes. He shouldn't have blurted out the truth. Not without more preparation. He should have handled the situation with more delicacy, more tact. And he'd tell her so—as soon as she had cooled off enough to listen.

He glanced up at Zoe's bedroom window, wondering how long this would take.

Although according to her aunt, she had yet to forgive Laurence McClellan, she didn't strike him as the kind who would hold a grudge.

Did what he'd done put him in McClellan's league? Would Zoe see it as a personal betrayal?

"God, I hope not," Ethan murmured.

But to be on the safe side, it wouldn't hurt to find a way of letting her know that however awkward his execution, he had acted with the very best intentions.

ZOE SPENT THE AFTERNOON in the haven of her pink-canopied bed, going through the ephemeris, plotting the alignment of planets on her own chart and Ethan's, trying to detect where she had gone wrong and what had made her think they had anything in common.

She checked her original calculations, and when she found no mistakes, checked them again. But there weren't any changes. Not only were their suns complementary, but her moon was compatible with Ethan's. His Venus was conjunct her Mars. All the aspects were harmonious, with the exception of Mercury, which would continue to be retrograde until the middle of next week.

The inescapable conclusion was that this was not a good day for her to make snap judgments, and the more she thought about the planetary configuration, the more she realized its guidance coincided with her feelings.

Now that she had recovered from the first flush of anger, she didn't want to believe that Ethan had deliberately set out to hurt her. She wanted to give him the benefit of the doubt.

On Monday morning, when she arrived at the library, she found that Ethan had left a nosegay of violets on her desk. Touched by the gesture, she decided she had been right to adopt a wait and see attitude.

Late that afternoon, when Ethan got home from work, Zoe was gone, but so were the flowers. He considered that a favorable sign.

On Tuesday he left gardenias, on Wednesday roses, and on Thursday a bouquet of lilacs. When he got home that evening, Zoe's bicycle was propped against the doorstep.

He didn't bother pulling into the garage. Instead, he parked at the end of the walk and hurried into the house, along the back hallway to the library. He had taken several steps into the room before he saw that Zoe was standing on the terrace, holding a sprig of lilac.

His gaze swept over her, from her bright tousled curls to her slender bare feet. A tender light leaped into his eyes when he registered the muted plum cotton of her halter dress. The fine gauzy fabric clung to her breasts and floated about her legs as she turned toward him.

"Zoe."

He spoke her name softly and held his hands out to her, palms up, silently beckoning her into his arms. It was all she could do to resist his appeal, but she contented herself with slipping her hands into his.

"You don't seem surprised to see me," she said.

"No, I'm not. After you showed up for work Monday, I knew it was only a matter of time till you'd forgive me. But I can't begin to tell you how happy I am that you waited for me today."

The eagerness in his eyes and the hungry way he looked at her offered confirmation of his delight. He raised her hands to his mouth and pressed a kiss into each palm, then lifted her hands to his shoulders.

She brushed the sprig of lilac against her mouth, then held the blossoms to his lips. "Thank you for the flowers," she murmured. "When you put your mind to it, you certainly know how to make a woman feel welcome."

"I aim to please."

His arms circled her waist, folding her close as he scattered fervent kisses across her eyelids, her cheeks, her temples. He nuzzled her earlobe and rubbed his cheek against hers, evoking delicious shivery sensations that spread in an erotic chain reaction from every point of contact with him.

He stroked her hair, the nape of her neck, caressing her as if he never wanted to stop. His touch was seductive, and at the same time it was as if the pleasure he derived from the silky warmth of her skin, from the simple act of molding his hands to the curve of her breasts, her waist, her hips, was an end in itself.

"God, you feel good," he growled. "Do you have any idea how much I've missed you?"

"I missed you, too."

His mouth was only a whisper away, and when they kissed, she tasted the nectar of the lilacs that lingered on his lips. His embrace tightened possessively, so that he felt the soft imprint of her breasts against his chest and she felt the passionate surge of his arousal. Both of them were trembling when the kiss ended.

Secure in the shelter of his arms, Zoe outlined his mouth with questioning fingertips.

"I've wanted to do that ever since we met," she confessed.

Ethan grinned. "If there's anything else you'd like to touch, be my guest."

Her eyes shied away from his. Just thinking of the parts of him she would like to touch made her feel as if she were blushing all over. "Thanks, anyway," she replied, "but I think I'll wait till later."

"Later," he repeated solemnly, as if they were sealing a pact.

THEY FINALLY GOT their dinner out that night, but Ethan seemed more interested in her than in the paella. They held hands beneath the table while she brought him up to date on developments at Gull Cottage.

She told him her aunt had found a new caterer. "He's the Randolphs' cook, and he's working out very well."

Ethan offered her a morsel of shrimp and followed it with a kiss. His lips coasted across her cheek to the delicate hollow at the angle of her jaw.

"What's the latest on the dining room?" he whispered against her ear. "Did Cora speak to the rental agent?"

"On Sunday," Zoe replied breathlessly. "Just after you left."

"What did she find out?"

"About what she expected. Laurence phoned last week from Monte Carlo and instructed the agent to send a house key to a Mr. Smith, care of General Delivery, East—"

A soft gasp of ecstasy interrupted her answer as Ethan began probing the sensitive recesses of her ear with the tip of his tongue.

Her body went slack; her head lolled to the side. She buried her face against the warm column of his neck.

"—Hampton," she finished on a sigh.

She did not see the waiter's approach, but she sensed it when Ethan sat more erect.

"Is everything satisfactory, sir?"

"Perfect," said Ethan. "Delicious."

There was a faint chink of glassware as the waiter removed their dinner plates and refilled their champagne flutes.

"For dessert we have a superlative pineapple flan, or if you'd prefer to make your selection from the pastry cart—"

"The flan will be fine," Ethan broke in.

"For two?"

"Yes, please."

"An excellent choice, sir."

With a conspicuous glance at Zoe, the waiter turned and left the table, and Ethan hugged her close and kissed the top of her head.

"He's gone, Zoe. You can come out now."

The laughter in his voice vibrated against her cheek and restored a semblance of sanity.

Over the flan they discussed the latest chapter in the saga of the disappearing furniture. On Monday, she told him, the contents of the solarium had vanished.

"Everything?" asked Ethan.

"Not quite," she said. "Whoever took the furniture left Laurence's pictures and his reviews, and of course, they didn't take Boris."

"I imagine Boris had a few choice words to say about that."

"He did," said Zoe, "but I'd rather not repeat them."

"Poor McClellan."

Zoe assumed Ethan was sympathizing with Laurence's failure to unload the mynah, until he added, "He must be on a losing streak."

"I'm afraid so," Zoe answered.

"How's Cora taking it?"

"I think she has mixed feelings. She's upset this is happening. She wants to change the locks, but Laurence won't give his permission. And she's worried about him. She's afraid he'll gamble away his last penny, but she can't help taking notes for future reference. That part's second nature to her."

"What about the rest of you?"

Zoe hesitated. "You'll think we're heartless—"

"No, I'd never think that."

Ethan touched a strand of hair that curled against her temple, twining it about his forefinger with a gentleness that made her heart race. His smile encouraged her to confide in him.

"Well, we're laying bets about which room will go next."

His smile became a chuckle. "I'd put my money on the master bedroom. That gold-inlaid bed alone must be worth a small fortune."

"Maybe," said Zoe, "but I'm not sure it's humanly possible to get that bed out of the house."

On that note, they left the restaurant, and during the drive from Sag Harbor to East Hampton, Zoe gave Ethan a progress report about her work on the library.

"The cataloging's going well," she said. "In fact, it's going better than I'd hoped, but I still haven't found those missing books."

"Have you had the chance to search the shelves?"

"Yes, as thoroughly as I can without removing all the books and looking behind them."

"That'd be a job."

Zoe agreed. "It may come to that, though, unless—"

"Unless what?"

"Well, I wondered if you have a key to the rolltop desk."

"Probably. Uncle Hiram left a drawerful of keys, most of them unlabeled. If you think the missing stuff's in the desk, it might be easiest to call in a locksmith." Ethan glanced at her quizzically, but before she could answer, he continued. "Was Cosmo able to translate the Austrian's letter?"

"Yes, and I was right about the reference to Carl Jung. Evidently he and your uncle corresponded over a period of several years."

"The letters from Jung should make interesting reading."

"Yes, they should—if I ever manage to locate them."

With this bit of coaxing, she had hoped Ethan would make a definite commitment to see about unlocking the rolltop, but his response left something to be desired.

"I wouldn't be too concerned," he said. "If Uncle Hiram ran true to form, Jung's letters are bound to turn up."

His easy dismissal of papers that could be of inestimable importance reminded Zoe of his refusal to accept the influence of the occult.

If Ethan didn't believe in astrology, how could he believe in her? And if he didn't take her seriously, how could she share her last piece of news with him?

The answer was, she couldn't. So she kept it to herself.

She didn't tell Ethan about the spur of the moment side trip she had taken on her way home from work last Monday, nor did she tell him that her detour had taken her across the village green and over an old-fashioned stile to the historic South End Burying Ground, where she had spent a quiet hour strolling among the monuments.

The most impressive of these, a statue of a knight surmounted by a Gothic Revival arch, belonged to Lion Gardiner, who, according to Zoe's guidebook, had settled Gardiners Island. Other members of the Gardiner clan were buried nearby, and they included a New York state senator and the wife of a United States president.

Not all the markers were as impressive as the Gardiners', however. Some were quite modest, and as she was leaving the cemetery a simple square of sandstone shaded by sycamores caught her eye.

She was standing beside the marker, studying the moss-covered stone, when a breeze rustled the tree leaves and a momentary shifting of the shadows threw the carving into relief.

Bliss.

The name sprang out at her, and as she knelt beside the stone, another breeze allowed her to decipher the rest of the epitaph.

Evadne, beloved wife of Hershel. Died May 15, 1888. Age 17 years.

For the next fifteen minutes Zoe had scurried back and forth, reading the other monuments. She'd found Buells and Isaacs and a multitude of Mulfords, but Evadne's was the only marker with the surname Bliss.

On Tuesday she had stopped by the offices of the *East Hampton Star*, and with the help of a clerk, located a microfilm containing Evadne's obituary.

The death notice was brief—as brief as the seventeen-year-old's life. It offered little more information than her gravestone had. But Zoe left the newspaper office armed with the knowledge that Evadne Bliss had been survived by a daughter, Evangeline.

Now that Zoe had proof of Evangeline's existence, she was eager to share it with Ethan, and when he delivered her to Gull Cottage that Thursday and they kissed good-night at the door, she was tempted to tell him about her discovery. The words trembled on the tip of her tongue until it occurred to her that as long as Ethan had so little faith in the value of her work, she had no reason to assume he would accept her evidence.

Pride kept her silent and the evening ended, not with intimacy, but with secrecy. Neither of them mentioned Evangeline.

Chapter Ten

A clap of thunder rattled the library windows, and at the distraction, Zoe glanced up from the data she was entering on an index card and reached for another tissue.

Cataloging a library was a grubby job. Constant exposure to dust and molds made her nose itch, and just now she felt a sneeze coming on.

For half a minute or longer she sat, eyes watering, Kleenex poised, then gradually the feeling receded.

She put down her pen and flexed cramped fingers, arched her back first to one side, then the other, and rubbed at a kink in her neck with a slightly inky hand.

"Ready to knock off for the day?" Ethan inquired from the doorway to the hall.

Zoe turned to him and smiled. "I might as well keep working till this rain lets up."

"I'd be happy to give you a ride home."

She shook her head. "I'll need the bicycle to get here tomorrow."

"We could load it in the trunk."

"I appreciate the offer, but I'd just as soon catalog a few more books."

"That's what you said an hour ago."

Ethan strode into the library and set tall glasses of iced tea on the corner of her desk. Then, taking a firm grip on either side of her steno chair, he wheeled her across the carpet toward the hearth with a swiftness that made her head swim.

As he handed her one of the glasses, he declared, "If you won't quit working, you can at least take a break."

The determined set of his jaw told her it was pointless to argue. "Thank you," she said, trying a sip of tea. "This is very good."

Ethan sat in a wing chair facing her, wishing she were less preoccupied. Last Thursday he had thought they'd resolved their differences; since then, he hadn't seen nearly enough of Zoe.

Or rather he'd seen her, yet he hadn't.

Between the cataloging and the goings-on at Gull Cottage, she had little time for him. He had to negotiate every minute they spent together, and even when he managed to get her alone, they usually wound up talking about the library.

Zoe seemed to eat, breathe and sleep her work. He imagined she cataloged books in her dreams, and although he stood to benefit from her professionalism, there were occasions when he thought she got carried away.

This evening was a perfect example.

He had left the bank in the midst of a rainstorm, hoping the power would fail so that Zoe would be forced to take the night off. When he arrived home, he'd found he'd gotten half of what he'd hoped for. The power had failed, but Zoe was working by candlelight.

"It's dark in here," he'd remarked, when he'd discovered her bent over her note cards. "Aren't you afraid you'll ruin your eyes?"

She had spared him an absent smile and the answer, "People got along without electricity until the last hundred years."

Sometimes he wondered if she was consciously evading him. And sometimes she looked at him with a kind of sadness. At times like those, he knew that she was watching for some sort of sign from him, and he'd feel totally bewildered, as if he were grappling with shadows.

More than once he'd started to ask exactly what she expected of him. "If only you'll tell me," he wanted to say, "whatever it is, I'll move heaven and earth to give it to you."

But natural caution prevented his making this pledge.

He had never signed a contract without reading the fine print. He'd never endorsed a blank check, and the banker in him resisted the idea of giving Zoe an emotional carte blanche.

Ethan stretched his legs toward the hearth and crossed one ankle over the other, thinking how much the candlelight suited her.

Especially tonight.

It had been an oppressively hot day, and despite the rain, the air in the library was muggy and close, heavy with the scent of the fading lilacs on the steno desk. But Zoe looked delectably cool—and oddly out of place.

Ethan thought it might be a trick of the subdued lighting that gave her the appearance of having wandered in from the turn of the century. Or perhaps it was her clothes.

She was wearing a white peasant dress with a soft gathered skirt, a dropped waist, and an elasticized ruffle that dipped off the shoulder, exposing the delicate line of her throat. Her hair was swept back from a center parting and held in place with combs, so that a cascade of curls spilled from the crown of her head, and with every movement of her head, her glossy curls caught the candle glow, and her hair magnified and reflected the radiance so that the red seemed shot with gold.

More than a little dazzled, Ethan tore his gaze away from Zoe and scowled at the empty hearth.

Here he was, along with an entrancing, desirable woman—a woman he just might be falling in love with—and he felt inept, clumsy, uncertain what to do next.

If he had felt more confident, or if Zoe had seemed more approachable, he would have kissed her. He still might, if he could work up his nerve.

If the weather were cooler, he could have built a fire. That might have broken the ice.

If the power hadn't failed, he could have tuned the stereo to the FM station that played the big-band music from the forties. Those sentimental old ballads were perfect for dancing, and dancing would give him the ideal excuse to hold Zoe in his arms.

If he were a poet, he would have told her how adorable she looked with a smudge of ink on her cheek, how enchanted he was by the mystery in her eyes.

But there was no electricity, the evening was sticky, and he was too tongue-tied to spin pretty compliments. Furthermore, Zoe had almost finished her iced tea. Any second now she would go back to work, and this opportunity would be lost.

There was only one thing left for him to do; he hoped it would please her.

He fished a small brass key out of his shirt pocket and dropped it into her lap. "It's to the rolltop," he said.

Her startled gaze met his above the rim of her glass. "Where did you find it?"

"I had it made. The locksmith came by last night."

Zoe didn't thank him. She didn't have to. Her expression told him she was delighted, and she was already on her feet, all but running toward the desk.

Ethan followed with one of the hurricane lamps, holding the candle in its glass-mantled holder so that the light fell on the rolltop. Zoe leaned down to fit the key in the lock, then looked up at him and smiled as if he had given her the world's greatest treasure.

"This is wonderful!" she said.

He cleared his throat. "I'm glad you like it."

The lock was stiff from years of disuse and difficult to turn. Zoe tried it twice, encountered resistance, jiggled the key and tried again. On the fourth attempt the lock opened.

She closed her eyes; her lips moved as if she were saying a prayer. When she opened her eyes, Ethan held up crossed fingers.

"Here goes nothing," he said.

She mimicked his gesture, then drew in a breath and carefully raised the cover.

A few inches of the writing surface came into view, along with the edges of a stained green blotter, and then he saw an assortment of papers, yellow with age, nibs and penholders and an inkwell, its contents long since evaporated, its glassy sides mottled iridescent purple.

Zoe had slid the cover a quarter of the way up its track when it stuck. She lowered it, then lifted again. It stopped in the same place.

"It seems to be jammed," she said.

Ethan bent down and lowered the lamp, peering through the opening.

"Can you see what's hanging it up?" she asked.

"Not enough light. Hold the cover steady while I see what I can find."

He reached one hand beneath the lid and felt his way along the slatted underside to the edge, then traced the wooden groove to the top.

"Anything?" asked Zoe.

"Not yet."

He felt a profusion of cubbyholes as he slid his hand from left to right along the upper track, where the cover joined the case. It occurred to him that these dark, boxy squares would provide an ideal breeding ground for mice. Then he thought of mousetraps and spindles and letter openers and God knew what other snares might be lurking in the desk, and he was careful to keep his fingers flat, so that they swept aside any protruding papers without extending into the openings.

When he was halfway across, he set the hurricane lamp on the floor and held the cover open with his free hand, allowing Zoe to shift her grip before he continued.

He had almost reached the top right-hand corner when his hand was stopped by something solid.

"Hello . . . what's this?"

Zoe leaned closer. "What've you found?"

He explored the obstacle warily, identifying a smooth, rounded shape with the hardness of stone. "Feels like a paperweight. Either that or a bar of soap."

He tried to nudge the obstacle deeper into its cubbyhole, but some barrier behind it wedged it tightly in place. He slid his hand beneath the object and along the next bank of cubbyholes to the other side.

"Can't budge it," he said. "Let's see what happens if you slide the cover down an inch or two."

While Zoe lowered the cover a hairsbreadth at a time, he pressed outward against the slats, lifting them over the obstacle. After the first inch, he felt something give.

"Just a little more slack, but take it easy."

After another fraction of an inch, the object began to slant downward.

"Hand me a pencil," he said to Zoe. "If I can slide it out a little farther, the cover should rock it free."

But in the seconds it took Zoe to collect a pencil from the steno desk, Ethan decided to take a different tack.

"Tell you what," he said. "I'll push the slats out with both hands, while you try working whatever's jamming it loose."

"But the lid—"

"It'll be okay. We can use some books to prop it open."

He held the lid until Zoe had positioned her reference books at either corner of the cover, then, with a slight lift of his elbow, he signaled her to duck under his arm.

She knelt in front of him, nose pressed to the narrow opening between the writing surface and the cover, pencil at the ready, eraser end up.

Ethan felt her warmth, her softness, and his surface calm deserted him. He leaned forward, swaying closer to her, and her hair brushed his chin. He could almost taste its fragrance. He leaned back, and found himself staring at lustrous skin stretched to pearly translucence by the delicate ridge of her spine. He bit back a groan, wrestling with the urge to plant kisses in the vulnerable hollows where the base of her neck met her shoulders.

His heart was doing wild flip-flops against his rib cage. His throat ached with wanting her.

"Ready?" he inquired in a thick, unrecognizable voice.

Zoe looked from side to side, studying the angle at which his forearms disappeared beneath the cover. She scanned the outside of the lid, tipping back her head until it was cushioned by his shoulder.

Ethan reacted to this new torment by tackling the job at hand. With all the strength he could muster, he pressed his palms against the slats at either side of the obstacle, and a barely perceptible bowing in the wood enabled Zoe to plan her movements.

Reaching beneath the cover, she located the object with the pencil, then rested her cheek against the rolltop and poked the tip of her tongue between her teeth, concentrating for all she was worth on exploring the unseen article's hard, smooth curves until the eraser skipped behind a slight roughening and found a purchase.

"Ready," she said.

"All right, then. On the count of three."

Ethan counted, then strained forward, pressing the slats again, while Zoe worked at the object with the eraser. Seconds ticked past, then half a minute. The muscles in his shoulders and arms began to twitch with exertion.

"Hold on," Zoe pleaded. "I think I've got it."

He gritted his teeth and held. A few seconds later he felt something give, and in the next instant he heard something fall inside the desk and roll across the blotter toward the gap in the lid.

Zoe made a reflexive grab and managed to stop the object before it rolled off the writing surface. She hesitated briefly; Ethan felt her tense, and then she seemed to recoil.

She pushed against his arm, scrambling to her feet and turning away a moment before the object rolled beneath the opening in the cover and dropped into Ethan's hand.

Whatever the thing was, it was decorative; shaped like a powder box, and so small that when he set it on its filigreed silver feet, it stood on his palm with room to spare. The rounded sides were enameled with a winter motif: holly wreaths and mistletoe, a stag and a snowshoe hare, even a pair of skaters picked out in intricate detail.

The top attached to the sides with silver hinges, and was a polished circle of lapis lazuli, handsomely wrought, deep azure veined with gold.

Ethan touched the stone, admiring the craftsmanship. "What in the world—"

"It's a music box," said Zoe.

He opened the lid, casting a troubled glance at her as Chopin's Nocturne in E-flat tinkled out.

She had retreated as far as the windows, and was staring out at the rain.

How had she guessed it was a music box when she hadn't seen it?

SHE WAS STANDING on a hillside, surrounded by darkness and by the fragrance of lilacs. And somewhere, someone was playing a piano....

It's Ethan, thought Zoe.

The moment the vision recurred, she knew that the piano player was Ethan, just as she had known that the object inside the desk was a music box from the moment she touched it.

So she wasn't surprised when Ethan sat at the piano and began playing.

The notes of the nocturne filtered through the shadows, twinkling like fireflies before the breeze snatched them away.

She could interpret the vision now.

She knew that the music box had some connection to Evangeline, and although she could not put a name to Evangeline's fiancé, she understood the significance of the lilacs and the nocturne. She had recognized the hillside, and finally, inexplicably, she knew why the melody seemed so ephemeral—so poignant.

THE NOCTURNE was seductively melodic and, it seemed to Ethan, deeply personal. He played it through to the end, astonished that he remembered it after all these years.

He had reached the coda when the sound of a door closing told him Zoe had left the house.

He hurried after her, puzzled by her strange behavior and more than a little disturbed.

His uneasiness grew when he stepped onto the terrace and found she was nowhere in sight.

The rain was coming down harder than ever, pouring off the eaves of the roof and streaming across the flagstones.

Surely she hadn't decided to ride the bicycle back to Gull Cottage before the storm let up? But if she hadn't gone home, where was she?

He cupped his hands to his mouth and shouted her name, then made his way across the terrace. By the time he reached the fountain, his shoes were wet and his shirt was plastered to his back. He stopped, hands on hips, wondering if he should go back to the house for a raincoat, but a faint rustling noise from the shrubbery ahead of him drove this consideration from his mind.

He called Zoe's name again and cocked his head to one side, listening. The only sounds he heard were the pelting rain and driving wind, whipping the branches of the trees.

He shielded his eyes, frowning into the darkness, and caught a glimpse of movement.

"Zoe, is that you? Wait up!" he called.

Again there was no reply, but a split second later, a flash of lightning illuminated a slight figure dressed in white, rushing along the brick pathway that wound through the garden.

Ethan growled an oath and ran after her.

The rain had pooled in the dips in the path, and the bricks were slippery and treacherous. In places he almost lost his footing, but he didn't slow down. By the time the path ended, he had gained on Zoe. She was close enough that he could see her climbing the grassy incline, heading toward the knoll at the western border of the property.

He shouted her name again, and again she didn't answer. She didn't pause, didn't give him a backward glance, didn't seem to hear him.

He continued across the lawn, lengthening his stride, hoping to catch her before she reached the thicket of lilacs at the top of the knoll. He was afraid, if he lost sight of her, he wouldn't be able to find her again in the darkness—unless she wanted to be found.

Near the top of the hill the going got rougher. Mist rose like steam from the thick growth of grasses, disguising the uneven terrain. He stumbled into a chuckhole and before he could stop his skid, fell to his hands and knees.

He sat on the ground, clasping a badly bruised knee to his chest, and when he discovered a three-cornered tear in his pants, seriously contemplated going back to the house.

What the hell am I doing? he wondered, irritated by the fall. If Zoe wanted to go slogging through the rain, it was no skin off his nose. He'd shouted himself hoarse, and she didn't respond, which made it fairly obvious she didn't want his company. He'd already ruined his slacks, and chances were, if he caught up with her, she wouldn't listen to reason. So why should be risk his neck trying to stop her?

He had dragged himself to his feet, resolving to give up the chase, when lightning erupted directly overhead, and permitted another glimpse of her pale, wraithlike figure.

She was standing at the edge of the thicket less than thirty feet away, arms folded across her bosom, utterly still.

"Zoe?" he said quizzically. "Want to tell me what's going on?"

She didn't reply, didn't acknowledge his presence with so much as the flicker of an eye.

He limped toward her, then paused and looked downhill, trying to figure out what she was staring at. Was it his uncle's house she found so absorbing?

He closed the gap between them, favoring his bruised knee. "What's gotten into you? Why don't you answer me?"

The questions seemed to startle her, or perhaps it was his harsh expression.

She lifted her chin and watched his approach, eyeing him gravely as he drew near. He saw her throat work, saw that she was shivering, and put his arms around her. She went limp against his chest, letting him warm her, leaning her head against his shoulder as if her neck could not support its weight.

"This is where she's buried."

The mutter of thunder drowned out her voice. He wasn't sure he'd heard her correctly.

"What was that?" he demanded. "What did you say?"

"This is where she's buried."

The words sent a chill down his spine. He didn't have to ask whom they referred to. He knew Zoe was talking about Evangeline, and the knowledge made his mind reel.

The earth seemed to quake on its foundations. Only later did he recall the sudden raging thunder that broke around them. He acted with a certain no-nonsense authority, yet he felt as if he were in a stupor as he guided Zoe down the slope through the violence of the storm.

When they reached the house he wrapped a blanket around her and bundled her into his car. Less than an hour after they had found the music box, he delivered her to Gull Cottage.

"Listen to me," he said, as he walked Zoe to the door, "I want you to take tomorrow off. Take Friday, too. Have a long weekend."

"But the cataloging—"

"Can wait," he declared. "You've been working too hard. You're not yourself."

Zoe's laughter had a brittle edge. "I'm myself now, Ethan. But I must admit, for a while tonight things were touch and go."

Chapter Eleven

Shortly after daybreak the following morning, Ethan made another trek to the hill behind the Seymour house, hoping against hope that he would find nothing out of the ordinary.

The weather had cleared and the air was fresh and cool, lush with bird song, enriched by the scents of the burgeoning earth. The sun was rising when he reached the knoll, and he sat on his haunches, studying the lay of the land.

The storm had washed away most of the evidence of last night's events. A casual observer might have thought no one had visited the knoll for weeks. But Ethan was not a casual observer. Far from it. And as the sun climbed higher in the sky, he saw a sliver of gray flannel torn from his pants, traces of footprints, an occasional trampled place in the rolling green grass, a few white threads tangled in the underbrush.

And just beyond that, what looked like a slight depression in the ground, shallow enough that it would be imperceptible when the sun hit it. But now, shadowed by the thicket, partially hidden by brambles and lilacs, the distinctive rectangular shape of the swale was unmistakable.

Was that where Zoe had stood?

Ethan rose and crossed to the swale, glancing back at the house, comparing the view of the library windows to the view he'd seen last night. When it seemed the same, he stopped.

On a fine night, with the windows brightened by electric lights, the interior of the library would be easily visible.

Only it used to be the music room, he reminded himself, turning to survey the thicket.

A red-gold hair caught on a twig an inch or so lower than his chin convinced him that this was the spot to begin his search.

He doubled over, hands on his knees, peering into the underbrush.

The dense branches and thick carpet of leaves obscured his view of the ground, and he dropped to his knees, shoving some of the branches aside, reaching into the brush to a point he estimated would mark the perimeter of the depression, and digging his hand into the layer of humus to scoop it away.

When he had cleared an area about two feet square, his fingernails scraped against stone.

He plunged both hands into the brush, tunneling beneath the spongy humus, pulling out roots and clumps of weeds, clearing the way along the smooth chunk of granite to an edge, then working his way along that edge until he encountered what felt like a number carved into the stone.

Dragging out a last handful of turf, he sank back on his heels, breathing hard as he appraised his find. Droplets of sweat rolled off his forehead and into his eyes; he blinked to clear his vision.

Had he uncovered a date, or was he imagining things?

He tossed the humus aside and wiped his forehead with his shirt sleeve, then stood and started down the hill.

If he were to do this right, he'd need tools to clear the underbrush: pruning shears, a hatchet, a shovel, a scythe. And while he was at it, he should phone his secretary and arrange for her to cancel his morning appointments. Maybe this afternoon's, too.

From the little he'd seen so far, this looked like an all-day job.

AT EIGHT-THIRTY that morning, Ethan returned to the hilltop with a wheelbarrow loaded with gardening tools, and for the next six hours he worked without stopping, pruning, digging, hauling away branches.

He hadn't had breakfast—hadn't even had coffee—and he didn't break for lunch.

The sun was hot, the sky cloudless. By ten o'clock, with the temperature in the nineties, his shirt was soaked with sweat.

He peeled it off and renewed his labors, working like a man possessed.

The tools raised blisters on his palms. When they broke, they burned like fire. A cross-hatching of scratches covered his hands and forearms. Nettles made welts on his skin. His mouth was dry as cotton batting, but he put off stopping for a drink.

Just five more minutes, he told himself. I'll have some water as soon as I've trimmed these branches.

But when the branches were cut, he threw them toward the growing accumulation of greenery and kept working.

His mood seemed to shift with the shadows.

Sometimes he'd find himself pulling weeds and tilling the soil as if he were tending a formal garden, and he'd wonder why he was taking such pains when he should be focusing on the bigger task of cutting the lilacs down to size.

Then for no good reason, his spirits would lift and he'd catch himself whistling, tunelessly, almost silently, because his lips were too parched to produce a proper whistle. But inside his head he'd be whistling the nocturne.

And once or twice, when he was hacking his way through a jungle of branches, he wondered why he was doing this at all.

This is pointless, he'd think. A waste of energy. Zoe went off the deep end, but that doesn't mean I'm going to find anything unusual. I'm busting my rump, working like a dog, and when everything's said and done, all I'm going to have to show for my trouble is an aching back and some hunks of rock.

But an hour after the sun had passed its zenith, he unearthed a slab of granite inscribed with the letters *ANGEL*, and beneath that, in smaller characters, *om tw*.

Ethan redoubled his efforts, no longer doubting that his work would be rewarded. But other, more dismaying questions buzzed through his mind.

Who had planted the lilacs around the grave? Why had they been neglected? And how in the name of heaven had Zoe known the grave was here? Was it possible there was some connection between her and Evangeline?

By midafternoon he had found other parts of the tombstone and pieced them together, and although some of the letters were missing, he had assembled enough of them that he could fill in the blanks.

The full inscription was bordered by constellations of stars. It read, *EVANGELINE BLISS, born May 15, 1888, died December 23, 1907. From two, one. From one, the infinite.*

Fatigue set in while Ethan tried to figure out what the inscription meant. He groaned and fell back upon the grass, aware of a terrible thirst, of blisters and stiff muscles, cuts and scrapes, and the prickly sting of sunburn on his shoulders and the back of his neck.

Too exhausted to think, barely able to move, he loaded the gardening tools into the wheelbarrow and trundled it down the hill.

When he got to the house, the first thing he did was drink two glasses of water. Then he stepped out of his grimy jeans into a hot tub. He followed the bath with a cold shower and two more glasses of water, and by the time he settled in the kitchen with a ham and cheese sandwich and an icy schooner of beer, he felt almost human.

A second sandwich and a tall glass of milk completed the transformation.

As he carried his dishes to the sink and rinsed them, it occurred to him that there was something else he had to take care of.

Before the evening was over, he had to see Zoe.

GULL COTTAGE was in chaos. The living room had vanished, and whoever took the furniture had let Boris out of his cage.

This development went undetected until Cora got home from the afternoon's shoot and walked unsuspecting into the foyer, where she was greeted by a dive-bombing mynah.

Her scream brought Sam to the rescue; he alerted the others, and for the next two hours, Zoe and Sam, Cosmo and Brynne mounted a counterattack. Armed with badminton rackets and butterfly nets, they pursued the swooping mynah from room to room, upstairs and down, trying to herd him into the solarium, but their efforts were unsuccessful until, tired of the game, Boris made one last strafing run and flew back to his perch.

At eight that evening, when Ethan stopped by to see Zoe, a morose Cora was pacing beside a mound of luggage in the porte cochere, while the chauffeur loaded suitcases into the network limousine.

"This is it," she told Ethan. "I've had all I can take. I'm going back to New York."

"What'll you do about the show?"

"Where I go, it goes. We've got enough East Hampton footage to get us through, and my assistants can wrap things up here tomorrow. We'll have to do some rewrite, but now that we've lost the solarium, we'd have to do that anyway."

Ethan watched the chauffeur transfer a Vuitton tote and matching wardrobe to the limousine's trunk. He was almost afraid to ask his next question.

"Is everyone going with you?"

"Everyone but Zoe. Someone has to baby-sit Boris, and since she has your library to contend with, she volunteered to stay." Cora managed a harried smile. "She's around here somewhere, if you'd like to see her."

Ethan nodded. "If you've no objection, I think I'll go inside and look for her."

"Suit yourself," said Cora, "as long as you don't expect me to come with you. Gull Cottage isn't big enough for that bird and me. I refuse to set foot in the house again."

His footsteps echoed through the vast emptiness of the living room and solarium as he crossed the slate floor of the foyer. He tried the kitchen wing first, then made his way back to the dusky living room, and eventually found Zoe outside the French doors, trying to coax Merlin from beneath the deck.

Ethan called "Hello," and at the sound of his voice, the cat slunk out of his hiding place. After a cautious look around, he made a beeline for Ethan, bounded up his pant leg and into his arms.

"It's okay, fella." Ethan scratched the cat behind the ears, glancing at Zoe. "What's happened to the terror of Columbus Avenue?"

"It seems he's met his Waterloo. Boris has *him* terrified."

"I gather he's not the only one."

"If you're referring to my aunt, she's simply annoyed. Not that I blame her. It's humiliating to think you've been outwitted by a bird, and what makes it more humiliating is knowing that the bird thinks so, too."

Ethan cradled Merlin against his chest, relieved that Zoe seemed none the worse for her experience of last night.

"You obviously didn't come all the way out here to talk about my cat," she remarked, giving him a measuring look. "What's on your mind?"

"I wanted to talk about Evangeline, but if you're busy—"

Zoe ran her hand over Merlin's ruffled fur, wondering what had prompted this about-face. "This is as good a time as any," she said. "Everyone else is packing, so it's not likely we'll be interrupted."

Ethan hesitated, uncertain where to begin. After a long, uncomfortable silence, he decided to start with an apology, and once that was out of the way, he went on to describe the discoveries he had made.

Zoe listened quietly, her face solemn and intent, and as the story unfolded Merlin began purring, lulled by the sound of Ethan's voice.

"This has been a revelation," he admitted at last. "All along I thought you were imagining things, but it turns out Evangeline's grave is up on the knoll."

Ethan's scowl told Zoe how perplexing he found this. "So now you don't know what to think," she said.

"No, I don't," he replied. "Unless you found a record of the grave among my uncle's papers."

"I didn't," said Zoe. In her mind Ethan's acceptance of the truth about Evangeline was synonymous with belief in her work, and so she went on to tell him what she had learned about Evadne.

When she finished, Ethan let out a long, low whistle. "Wow!" he exclaimed softly. "That's quite a story."

"Yes, it is," she replied. "And what impresses me most about it is the date. Evadne died on May 15, 1888, the day Evangeline was born."

"That's sad, of course, but I don't see the significance—"

"Do you recall the day we met?"

Ethan shook his head. "I remember it was a Sunday."

"It was the 15th of May."

"Was it?" For a moment, Zoe thought Ethan might try to pass this off as yet another coincidence, but at last he said, "Frankly, I don't know what to make of that."

He looked so miserable that her first impulse was to comfort him. She threw her arm across his back, intending to give his shoulder a consoling pat, and felt him wince and shrink away from her.

"I'm sorry," she said stiffly. "I realize this is difficult for you—"

"Don't, Zoe," he protested, biting back an oath when her withdrawing hand dragged the collar of his polo shirt against his neck. "I'm the one who's sorry. It's just my lousy sense of timing and this blasted sunburn."

He turned away, concealing a grimace, but she saw that he was in pain. She lifted the cat out of his arms and took him by the hand.

"Come with me," she said.

He eyed her suspiciously. "Where are we going?"

"Inside, where the light's better. I'm going to put something on that burn."

He dug in his heels, offering momentary resistance, and she tugged at his wrist.

"Come along," she directed in the same fond, coaxing tone she'd used with Merlin. "I give you my word, this won't hurt a bit."

She led him to the kitchen and aimed him toward the breakfast counter. "Have a seat," she told him.

Sighing with resignation, he sat. "Now what?"

"I have to get a jar of aloe cream from my bathroom, but it'll only take a minute. In the meantime, you can take off your shirt and make yourself comfortable."

He realized the last two instructions contradicted each other mere seconds after Zoe left. He hiked his shirt tail up to his shoulders, and tried to work one arm out of the sleeve, but the brief attempt hurt so much that he gave it up as a lost cause. He turned his head as far as he was able, wondering if the sunburn looked as hot as it felt, but discomfort put a stop to that effort, too.

"I'm stuck in this shirt for the duration," he muttered.

Discouraged by this prospect, he slumped forward, resting his head on his forearms, crossed on the counter.

When Zoe returned and found him half in, half out of his shirt, she started to make some teasing comment about how long it must take him to undress, but after one look at his back, his slowness seemed less than amusing.

"Here, let me help you," she said.

As gently as she could, she pulled the shirt over his head. She wanted to weep when she saw the livid skin across his shoulders.

"Oh, Ethan. What've you done to yourself?"

"I'm scorched," he mumbled. "Parboiled."

Getting out of the shirt seemed to exhaust his bravado and use up his last ounce of energy. As soon as he was out of it, he slouched over and closed his eyes.

"Do your thing," he told her.

She scooped out a generous dollop of cream, then paused with her hand poised a fraction of an inch away from his back. Without even touching him, she could feel the heat of the burn.

"I'll be very careful," she said.

Ethan's mouth quirked up at the corners. He didn't open his eyes. "I know you will, Zoe, but don't ask me to watch."

She drew in a breath, steeling herself to do what had to be done. Her voice broke as she said, "This may feel cold."

The warning preceded the chill of the cream by less than a second. She consciously kept her touch light, scarcely touching him at all as she applied the soothing emollient to his back, gingerly stroking the cream upward to his shoulders and finally to the areas on his neck, where the skin was such an angry red that she knew the gentlest touch must hurt.

Ethan shivered. By the time she finished, his teeth were chattering. But he didn't complain. Not once. And he didn't flinch from her.

Zoe saw this as a symbol of his confidence, and was moved by it.

He believes me, she thought, and she rejoiced.

Before the network limousine left for the city, Sam Kellogg helped her get Ethan to the sofa bed in the family room.

"You'd better stay here tonight," she said as she tucked a sheet around him. "I don't think you should be alone."

"Whatever you say, Zoe. I wouldn't want to worry you." Ethan opened one bleary eye long enough to wink at her, then fell asleep as soon as his head touched the pillow.

The aloe cream seemed to have given him some relief, but she couldn't help worrying. Outside in the hall she solicited Sam's opinion. "Do you think he's all right? Maybe I should phone a doctor."

"I don't see why he'd need a doctor when he's resting comfortably, and he's got you to take care of him. I'd say he's in very good hands."

By ten-thirty that evening the others had left. Even Merlin had gone back to the city with Cora. "He'll be happier with me, my darling," Cora had argued. "He hasn't been himself since he got here. If I were you, I'd ship him out of here before Boris destroys the little ego he has left."

Brynne left a message for Haines Randolph with Zoe. "Tell him I won't be able to keep our dinner date this Saturday, and that I'll expect him to let me know the next time he's going to be in New York."

Cosmo promised he'd be in touch. He assured Zoe, "If any problems arise with the library, I'm only a phone call away."

Zoe stood in the driveway, watching the limousine pull away, and when the chauffeur made the turn onto Frigate Alley, she hurried back to the family room to check on Ethan.

He was still sleeping, but for a long time she sat in the family room, marveling at how much she had learned in the few short weeks since she'd met him. She thought about Evangeline and the music box and the revelations Ethan had uncovered today, and she wondered about the meaning of her vision.

Now that the gravestone had been discovered, would Evangeline find peace?

ETHAN DIDN'T GO to work on Friday morning. At Zoe's insistence, he called in sick. By that evening, after several more applications of the aloe cream, his sunburn had begun to heal, but neither he nor Zoe suggested he leave Gull Cottage.

Instead they grilled steaks by the pool and opened a split of champagne, and when the steaks were done to juicy perfection, they turned off the underwater lights and ate supper on the deck, under a skyful of stars. And after dinner they walked for miles along the beach, holding hands, stopping now and again to exchange a languorous glance, a kiss, a sigh, always touching but seldom talking. Communicating without words, they were content just being together.

On Saturday morning when Ethan woke, Zoe was showering him with quarters.

"What's all this?" he demanded, pulling her down on top of him.

"You know the slot machine in the master bath?"

Eyes alight with a mixture of deviltry and passion, he ran his hands along her back, fitting her hips to his. "Yes," he replied, "what about it?"

"I hit the jackpot!"

"Mmm. So did I," he answered, nibbling delicately at her earlobe.

He tried to steal a kiss, but she playfully wriggled away from him. Mounds of quarters rained off the sofa bed as he rolled after her, pinning her beneath him.

With mock sternness, she said, "If you behave yourself and help me count my winnings, I'll take you to brunch."

He smiled into her eyes, considering her invitation. "How about breakfast in bed?" he countered, making another try for her lips.

She fended him off with gentle fingertips against his mouth, and swung her feet off the sofa bed. He made one last lunge for her, but twinges of pain from his sunburn pulled him back against the pillow.

Zoe confronted him breathlessly, folding the lapels of her robe higher across her breasts. "How about Madame Makarova's Deli?"

He sobered. "Is that your final offer?"

"That's it," she said firmly, and in a softer tone added, "for now—"

It was the promise of the "for now" that got Ethan out of bed.

They collected the quarters, showered and dressed and drove into town, stopping by his house so that he could get a change of clothes. And then they drove on to the Russian fast-food deli, fighting the weekend traffic.

Madame Makarova's was crowded. While they waited for a table they browsed through the gift shop, pricing babushka dolls and lacquered boxes, replicas of icons and Fabergé eggs.

Zoe tried on gingham kaftans, and Ethan disappeared into the changing room and came out wearing baggy trousers stuffed into top boots, a tunic and vest and embroidered sash. Zoe topped off his ensemble with an astrakhan cap, then stepped back to admire the effect.

"You look dashing," she said. "Very romantic and Count Vronsky."

He clicked his heels together and executed a wide, sweeping bow, returning her appraisal with an intensity that made her blush.

"And you look lovely, Zoe."

It was almost noon before they were seated, and trying on clothes had whetted their appetites. They had delicate smoked salmon, blintzes and piroshki filled with beef, mushrooms and onions, the pastry light enough to melt in the mouth. They finished their brunch with portions of charlotte russe and were on their way out of the deli when their path was blocked by a waiter with a bristling mustache and sad, drooping eyes, who proudly displayed a bottle of Stolichnaya frozen in ice.

"Is this not a work of art?" he inquired, pointing out the circlet of daisies and baby's breath that wreathed the bottle. He insisted they try some. "Guaranteed Russian," he said.

The waiter poured the liquor into ruby-banded liqueur glasses, and looked on approvingly while Ethan and Zoe downed the shots. The vodka went down easily enough, but for the next half hour, whenever Ethan wasn't looking, Zoe surreptitiously fanned her mouth.

They were window-shopping on Main Street when he caught her at it. She pretended to be covering a yawn, but he wasn't fooled.

He grinned and swung her hand and admitted he felt as if he could breathe fire, too. "Now I know how the cossacks do those wild dances," he said.

They saw a poster for a kite festival in the bookstore window, and talked about driving to Bridgehampton to see what the festival was like.

"The kites'll be expensive," Ethan remarked. "Exclusive silk jobs that sell for hundreds of dollars a throw. But there'll be too many people. The roads will be a nightmare."

"I'll take your word for it," said Zoe.

Although she was already convinced, Ethan added, "Besides, I'd rather be alone with you."

Instead of making the trip to Bridgehampton, they returned to Gull Cottage and spent a quiet afternoon beside the pool, occasionally dancing to music that came from a cruiser anchored offshore.

Early that evening a sports car pulled into the driveway. Ethan's face fell when he saw the man at the wheel. "It's Haines Randolph," he muttered. "I wonder what he wants."

"Brynne was supposed to have dinner with him," Zoe replied contritely. "She left a message, only I forgot to deliver it."

Ethan stayed by the pool while Zoe went off to answer the doorbell. In less than ten minutes Randolph had departed, and she was back.

"That was quick," said Ethan.

"That's one advantage of not having furniture in the living room. I invited Mr. Randolph in, but there was no place for him to sit down."

Ethan frowned. "Seriously, Zoe. What did you say to him?"

"I apologized for my oversight, with special emphasis on the part about calling Brynne the next time he's in New York. And I also agreed to schedule him for a consultation this fall."

If Ethan had pressed her, Zoe might have admitted that agreeing to advise Randolph seemed a small price to pay for preserving their evening together.

They prepared a simple supper—an omelet, a salad, a tray of cheese and fruit—and after the meal they adjourned to the pool. Ethan swam laps while Zoe sat on the top step at the shallow end, paddling her feet in the water.

She watched him do a surface dive and approach underwater. When he reached the steps, he flipped into a turn and swam toward the deep end. He finished two lengths of the pool before he came up for air.

"The water's great," he told her. "You should find a suit and come on in."

She shook her head. Her toes curled around the rim of the step.

"You'd be safe with me, Zoe. I wouldn't let anything happen to you."

She looked at him, and almost cried out that it was too late for promises of safety. Something had already happened to her. At some time in the last few weeks she had taken an emotional plunge. She had ventured into uncharted depths, and now she was in over her head. She was floundering, and Ethan was directly responsible.

I'm in love with him, she thought, and in the moment she made this admission, Zoe realized how consuming love could be—and how confusing.

Is he the soul mate I've been searching for? she wondered. *If he is, what happens next? Where do we go from here? Should I tell him how I feel? Should I say nothing?*

Ethan had acknowledged he was attracted to her. He seemed to enjoy her company. But how could she be sure his feelings went beyond attraction? What if they didn't? What if he didn't care for her? How could she trust him? How could she trust *herself*?

The answer was, she couldn't. Her judgment was clouded. She saw Ethan through a romantic haze, and as long as the haze persisted, she couldn't be objective.

But none of that made any difference. Whether Ethan cared for her or not, whether she could trust him or not, her feelings would remain the same, and so would the outcome.

Fatalist that she was, Zoe believed that certain things were predestined; however much she anguished over her fate, however much she resisted it, there was nothing she could do to change it.

And she couldn't resist Ethan. The truth was, she didn't want to.

When she went upstairs to bed that night, he climbed the stairs with her, and in the starlit sweetness of that warm summer night they became lovers.

They made love tenderly, fiercely, with exquisite slowness, then slept for a while in each other's arms and woke to make love again.

Toward morning, Ethan roused her with kisses. "Zoe, sweetheart, I've been thinking—"

"Hmm," she answered in a drowsy murmur. "What about?"

"There are five bedrooms in this house, and before this weekend's over, I intend to make love to you in every single one of them."

She gasped, pretending consternation. "Does that include Cleopatra's barge?"

Ethan hauled her tightly against him. "You bet your asp it does."

Throughout that long lazy Sunday, he never lost sight of this ambition, and Zoe reveled in his achievements.

That night, passion sated, spent and utterly content, she lay in the Egyptian bed, cradled by the hard curve of his body. She was about to doze off when Ethan cried out in his sleep, and she knew that her odyssey was not yet over.

He had called out a name, in a sharp, urgent voice. And the name that he called was Vangie.

Chapter Twelve

The music box was where Ethan had left it Wednesday night, on top of the piano. Zoe approached it with some reluctance. Prepared for a rush of images, she kept her gaze fixed on the library windows as she reached out to touch the box.

Nothing happened.

Her concept of time never wavered. Outside on the terrace, the spray of the fountain created rainbows. No visions clouded the unbroken blue of the Monday morning sky.

She picked up the music box.

Still nothing.

She opened the lid, and the nocturne began to play. The melody evoked feelings of loss and loneliness, but her sense of identity, of who she was and where she was, remained intact.

Still holding the music box, she moved closer to the windows and stood there, studying the hillside while the nocturne continued to play. She listened to the melody once...twice...three times. On the fourth repetition the tinkling notes slowed; in the midst of the fifth, they whirred to a stop.

She set the box on the windowsill, bending down to rewind the mechanism, and noticed the engraving inside the lid.

"For T.S. My love, my heart, my life. From E.B. Christmas, 1907."

Zoe touched the initials with marveling fingers.

"E.B.," obviously, was Evangeline Bliss, and "T.S." her fianceé. The nocturne must have had some special significance for them, and so Evangeline had bought the music box and had the message engraved. Had she anticipated the holiday and given her fiancé his gift before the skating accident, or had T.S. received the present after her death?

Did the *S* stand for Seymour?

Zoe left the box on the windowsill and crossed to the rolltop, wondering what other secrets it might divulge. When she raised the cover, the first thing she saw was the stack of books at the back corner of the desktop. A quick inspection of the titles told her she had found several volumes of importance to the library.

With the exception of the Jung correspondence, all the missing works were there, including a first edition of *World of the Spirit*.

One by one, she shifted the books to the steno desk, and at the bottom of the stack she found two items of even greater interest. The first was a packet of letters, bearing postmarks from the years 1906 and 1907, addressed to Mr. Thomas Seymour; the second, a slim, cloth-bound journal.

As recently as last Wednesday, the rare first edition would have commanded her attention, but now she set the book aside and glanced through the letters, arranging the envelopes by date. The earliest, written in the spring of 1906, had been mailed from Philadelphia.

Carefully, feeling all thumbs with eagerness, Zoe withdrew a sheet of notepaper from the envelope and spread it on the desktop, focusing on the signature at the bottom of the page.

The note was signed "Fondly, Evangeline."

This is it, Zoe thought. *The key I've been looking for.*

If Thomas Seymour was Evangeline's fiancé, it would answer many questions.

Her gaze flew to the top of the page.

Dear Thomas,

How pleasant to find your flowers in my dressing room when I arrived yesterday! Did you know that lilacs are my favorite? They always remind me of home and of loyal friends like you, who are generous with praise and never think to criticize my talent. Thanks in no small part to your bouquet, last night's performance was a triumph. The audience called me back for three encores, and the impresario tells me tonight's concert is sold out. My father also seems pleased, and joins me in wishing you well.

That ended the first note, and without looking up, Zoe reached for the next envelope. This one was fatter, mailed from Providence, Rhode Island. When she removed the note, she found a newspaper clipping tucked into its folds.

Heart skipping with excitement, she switched on the desk lamp and settled back to read.

Over the next few hours, as her picture of Evangeline and Thomas grew clearer, she was able to separate the letters into two distinct categories. In the first group were the half dozen notes written during the spring and early summer of 1906.

From the reviews and concert programs enclosed with these notes, Zoe concluded that Evangeline had been a prodigy at the piano, and under her father's management was developing a reputation as a virtuoso.

She wrote to Thomas about the cities she visited, about current events and mutual acquaintances, and for the most part her tone was breezy, chatty, as if she had dashed off the notes in spare minutes between rehearsals or while she was en route to the next stop on her tour. Now and again, however, a hint of homesickness came through.

In one note, in reference to a comment Thomas had made, she replied:

> You say you envy the opportunity I've had to travel, yet I would gladly trade places with you. I miss my friends, the ocean, having my own things about me. But most of all I miss the privacy of East Hampton, where everyone knows me as plain Vangie Bliss, and nobody gives a bean if I've forgotten my hat or if my gloves don't match. I can't tell you how horrid it is, having to be "on stage," the "dignified artiste" every minute of every day!

Soon after this note, there was a three-month gap in the letters, and when the correspondence resumed, it became apparent to Zoe that Evangeline had spent that time in East Hampton, much of it with Thomas.

A new affection and gradually a deeper intimacy crept into Evangeline's tone. In a letter from Saint Louis, dated October 4, 1906, she addressed Thomas as "My Dear." By November, she had progressed to "Dearest Thomas," and in January, 1907, she called him simply, "Dearest."

By the following spring, with a bit of reading between the lines, it was obvious that Evangeline had fallen head over heels in love with Thomas Seymour. Her letters had become longer, more thoughtful, with less focus on herself and more on him.

She spoke of the places they had gone together the previous summer, of the fun they'd had, the people they'd seen. She began pouring out her heart to him, and often spoke of missing him.

In May she confided how much she regretted that she would not be able to make it home before September. "My father has arranged a series of guest appearances for me on the West Coast," she wrote.

Thomas's reaction to this announcement must have been scathing. In her next letter, Evangeline was conciliatory.

My darling,
   If I had only myself to consider, I would not have agreed to extend this tour. My fondest wish is to be with you. You must believe that. But I must also think of my father, and how important these appearances are to him. After all the sacrifices Daddy has made to launch my career, I feel that I owe him this much. Please, my love, my dearest love, try to understand.

Her plea for understanding and her protestations of love seemed to have won Thomas over. In July, Evangeline had written him from Seattle. This note was brief, only two short lines, and Zoe didn't have to read between them to interpret their meaning.

"Yes, my darling! Yes, yes, yes! I would be honored to be your wife."

The letters that followed were ebullient with happiness, full of plans. When should they announce their engagement and how? Should they wait till the tour was over? Should they have a traditional party, or should they simply tell their families, friends and neighbors, and rely on word of mouth? And what about the wedding? Should it be formal or quiet, big or small? Should they have the ceremony in church or at the house Thomas had bought for them?

Evangeline was firm about one detail. She didn't want a wedding trip. "I've had enough traveling to last the rest of my life. Once I come home to you, dearest Thomas, I shall never leave you again."

In a letter dated August 8, 1907, in the course of setting the wedding date, Evangeline revealed a blossoming interest in numerology.

I have met the most remarkable woman. She left a message at the hotel before Sunday's performance, advising me to have an extra piano backstage, because one of the strings on my Steinway was going to break! My father, as you might expect, told me to forget the warning. He said anyone who would leave such a message had to be crazy, and anyone who would take it seriously, a fool. I hope you will not judge me so harshly, my darling, but I found I could not ignore the prediction. And lo and behold, the string broke in the midst of the Chopin—the very nocturne you are so fond of—so as it turned out, the clairvoyant stranger saved the day! I asked her to tea yesterday so that I could thank her, and came away from our meeting convinced that she has the ability to see the future.

My dearest doubting, yet doting Thomas, I'm sure by now you are wondering what all this is leading up to. I can only hope you will be patient with me, but I

must confess to a certain uneasiness about the dates
you have suggested for our wedding. After talking
with my newfound friend, I would much prefer that
we take our vows on the second day of the New Year.
As it was explained to me, the numbers of this date
total twenty-one, which has the most fortunate vi-
bration of karmic reward.

The last envelope, different from the others, contained
a wedding invitation. On January 2, 1908, if she had lived
that long, Evangeline Bliss would have become Mrs.
Thomas Seymour.

Zoe rested her elbows on the desktop and cupped her
palms to her eyes, imagining Thomas's despair.

Evangeline's death was tragic, but her fiancé's lot
seemed the greater tragedy. Instead of honeymooning with
his bride in their new home, he had buried Evangeline on
the knoll, surrounded her grave with lilacs, and confronted life without her.

It was possible Thomas had never stopped mourning
Evangeline, but eventually he must have recovered from
his grief. Zoe wondered if he had ever married. Was
Thomas Hiram's father? Ethan's great-grandfather?

She was lost in thought, deep in the past, when Ethan's
touch on her shoulder brought her back to the present. She
looked up at him, faintly misty-eyed, and he dropped a
light kiss on her lips.

"How's it going?"

"All right, I guess." She blinked and shook her head,
still making the eighty-year transition. "I didn't hear you
come in— What time is it?"

He glanced at his wristwatch. "Twelve-thirty."

"What are you doing home so early?"

"Playing hooky. I thought we could do lunch."

She blinked again, and ran her hand over her eyes. "Could I have a rain check? There's a lot of reading I'd like to get through today."

Ethan grinned and lounged across the corner of her desk, swinging one leg over the side. "I figured you'd be busy, so I brought lunch home. What do you say to a picnic?"

"This is awfully nice of you, but I—"

"Can I tempt you with clams casino? Cold roast chicken? Potato salad? Strawberries?"

She licked her lips and his grin widened. "You've gotta eat, Zoe. We can have our picnic just outside on the terrace."

"Well, I—"

He put an end to her arguments with another quick kiss, then slid to his feet and headed toward the hall. "I knew you wouldn't turn me down," he said. "Give me five minutes to set things up, then come on out."

Zoe slipped the wedding invitation into its envelope, aware that she had been steamrollered. In the nicest possible way, of course, but steamrollered, nevertheless.

Still, there was a good deal of truth in what Ethan said. She did have to eat. And a picnic with him would be ever so much more pleasant than a peanut butter sandwich at her desk.

Although she couldn't pinpoint exactly what made her decide in Ethan's favor, she found herself on her way to the powder room to wash up for lunch.

Besides, she thought, as she dried her hands, this picnic would present an ideal opportunity to tell him about Evangeline's letters.

WITH THE SUN glaring down on it, the terrace was too hot for comfort, so Ethan had spread their picnic on a patch of lawn shaded by maples.

Half an hour after she joined him, Zoe realized how badly she had miscalculated. She broached the subject of the letters while Ethan was serving the chicken, and by the time he handed her her plate, she sensed that he did not share her excitement.

In fact, as she rushed on, giving him a capsule summary of the information she had gleaned from the letters, Ethan seemed more interested in the food than in Evangeline. When Zoe revealed the fiancé's name, Ethan confirmed that Thomas Seymour had indeed been his great-grandfather, then added a careless, "What of it?"

"What of it?" Zoe sputtered, stunned by his indifference.

"That's what I said," was Ethan's comeback. "What of it?"

He speared a forkful of potato salad, chewed and swallowed, then washed down the salad with a sip of white wine.

"Look," she said, deciding to try another tack, "maybe I'm not telling this very well."

"Nope," said Ethan. "You're doing fine."

"I can't be. If I were doing this right, you'd be more enthusiastic. Maybe you'd better read the letters yourself."

"Thanks anyway, Zoe, but I can't get too worked up about reading other people's mail. If it's all the same to you, I think I'll pass."

She stared at him, openmouthed with disbelief. Was she mistaken, or had he just insinuated she was a snoop? Testing him, she replied, "Aren't you the least bit curious? I mean, these people were your relatives—"

"Thomas was. Not Evangeline."

"Very well," Zoe allowed. "I stand corrected. But Thomas loved Evangeline. They were engaged. If she'd lived, she would have been your great-grandmother."

Ethan helped himself to another slice of chicken. "Even if she had married Thomas, we're talking about a couple who've been dead for three-quarters of a century."

"But you're too high-principled to read their mail! Come on, Ethan, you can't have it both ways."

Zoe leaped to her feet, too agitated to sit still. She turned on her heel and was about to march back to the house, when Ethan's hand snaked out and fastened about her ankle.

If he had tried to use force, she would have broken free, but he held her with gentleness, with the sensuous touch of the fingers he trailed over her calf to the bend of her knee. His thumb dipped beneath the hem of her skirt to cherish the silken warmth of her thigh before his hand retreated to her ankle.

His voice was as soft and persuasive as his touch as he said, "Listen, honey, I'm sorry I don't much care about reading a bunch of old letters. I wish I could be more enthusiastic, if only for your sake. If you want me to act as if I'm interested, I will."

He was stroking her instep, and she felt the erogenous sweetness of the caress in every part of her body. "No," she answered, her breath catching in her throat as his caresses inched higher. "No, of course I don't want you to put on an act."

"That's good, because right now I've got other things on my mind."

His hand made a skin-tingling foray along her shin, and her knees turned to jelly. She collapsed on the grass beside him.

"Such as?"

"Dessert," he said, reaching for a handful of strawberries.

Her jaw dropped, and grinning wickedly, he popped a berry into her mouth.

His teasing mood was infectious, and she was not immune. When she sank her teeth into the fruit, she nipped his finger as well, and Ethan retaliated by toppling her backward onto the ground, cushioning her landing with his arms. She clung to his shoulders, pulling him after her as she fell, molding her body to his, and suddenly neither of them was teasing.

She arched closer and kissed him, and with quick little darts of her tongue licked the berry juice off his lips.

"Is there anything else you'd like?" she inquired in a throaty murmur.

"Oh, yes," he replied, and with an ardor that took her breath away, proceeded to show her what he wanted.

IT WAS AFTER THREE before Ethan returned to the bank and Zoe got back to the library. Since the morning had been devoted to the letters, she had fallen further behind with the cataloging. That being the case, it seemed only fair to make some effort to catch up, but the romantic interlude with Ethan had broken her concentration. She found it hard to think about anything but their picnic—and Evangeline's letters.

They had no place in the Seymour Collection, but she couldn't throw them away. She couldn't keep them, either; not without Ethan's consent.

Before Zoe left that afternoon, she filled her carryall with the books she had found in the rolltop. She debated taking the letters, too, but at the last minute chose another option. Bundling the letters together, she left them on the music rack, with a note explaining her quandary and asking Ethan to read them.

"You've stated your objections, and I accept them," she wrote, "but properly speaking, these letters belong to you. Therefore, you'll have to decide what should be done with them."

On Tuesday she asked if he'd had a chance to look the letters over. "No," he answered. "Maybe tomorrow." On Wednesday he said, "I swear I'll get to them as soon as I have the time."

He claimed he didn't have a free moment, but as the week wore on, Zoe noticed that he had time to take her dancing, time for a walk on the beach, time for ball games and band concerts and moonlight swims.

It seemed he had plenty of time for fun, plenty of time for seduction, and none at all for the letters, which remained untouched on the music rack.

After Wednesday, Zoe stopped asking Ethan if he'd read them. The other things she had found in the rolltop commanded her attention.

World of the Spirit, for instance.

The book that had set the public on its ear a hundred and forty years ago, the book she had expected to be the jewel of the Seymour Collection turned out to be a counterfeit. Its combination of inaccuracies, half truths and misconceptions was presented in a pedestrian writing style, and the text was less interesting than the notes some prior reader had penciled in the margins.

But if the first edition was a letdown, the letters stuck between its pages were not. Although they were written in German, so that Zoe couldn't read them, they were signed by Carl Jung.

Zoe found them Monday evening, and by Tuesday morning, the Jung correspondence was in the mail, on its way to Cosmo for translation.

The cloth-bound book was equally intriguing. It turned out to be Thomas Seymour's journal. The entries began in the grief-stricken days that followed Evangeline's death, and spanned the years 1908 to 1914.

In his first entry Thomas had written:

Vangie is gone, and with her my heart, my soul, my hope for happiness.

How can I go on without her?

Her father is devastated. *I* am devastated. He holds me responsible for my darling's death. He has agreed to my wishes for her final resting place. "As a reminder," he tells me, "of your guilt."

But reminders are unnecessary. My conscience cries out that I am to blame. I am at fault for what has happened, and in my heart of hearts I know that there can be no atonement.

In May 1908 Thomas had planted the lilacs. "I visit the knoll each morning, and again in the evening," he wrote. "It's the only place I find solace. I feel close to Evangeline there."

On the anniversary of her death, he elaborated on the sense he sometimes felt of her presence.

Evangeline lives on in my memory, in my heart. She lives on in her letters. They give me comfort. I read them often, and as I read, I can hear her voice, see her face, but tonight, for the first time since Evangeline gave me the music box, I found the strength to listen to the nocturne. For as long as the music lasted, I experienced a sense of peace, and then I remembered the promise she made. "Once I come home to you, dearest Thomas, I shall never leave you again."

Sometimes I feel her with me, reaching out to me, touching me, and I know, if only I had enough faith, if I were not hampered by finite concerns, Evangeline would always be with me.

In the weeks that followed this anniversary, Thomas's entries developed a different cast. He had come upon the copy of *World of the Spirit*, and after careful study he began acquiring other works, exploring the possibility of establishing contact with Evangeline.

He attended séances and met with mediums and spiritualists, but soon abandoned this avenue. "They are charlatans, one and all," he wrote, "skilled only at bilking the poor unfortunates who look to them for help."

Despite his disillusionment, Thomas persisted. More determined than ever, he concluded, "If I am ever to be reunited with Evangeline, I must find the way on my own."

His subsequent jottings tended to ramble as he tested theories, found them lacking, and made quantum leaps from one premise to the next. By the summer of 1909 he confessed that he had arrived at an impasse.

I am not giving up. I will never do that, but in the last few months I have begun to fear that I will not live long enough to discover the answers I seek, and so, after a great deal of thought, I have asked Ardith Mayo to become my wife. I have taken this step in the hope of fathering children who will carry on my pursuit, trusting that some day their efforts will lead to ultimate success.

Zoe read this passage to Ethan on Friday afternoon. He had just gotten home from the bank, and was trying to sweet-talk her into quitting work for the weekend.

For a half hour or more he followed her about the library, ambushing her at the bookshelves to steal a kiss, capturing her in a corner to hold her in his arms. He was at his most persuasive, and Zoe was not unmoved, but on this occasion she refused to let him distract her.

Thomas's journal, and that specific entry, provided a ready-made excuse.

Although Ethan listened impassively, he didn't interrupt, and when she had finished reading, he said, "Well, that explains how the library got its start."

"It explains much more than that," she replied. "It explains my visions, the way the nocturne affects me, the way I instinctively knew where to find Evangeline's grave. And it accounts for your interest in the occult."

"Are we back to that again?" Ethan groaned.

"Yes. Don't you see? Thomas was looking for a window to the afterlife so that he could communicate with Evangeline, and when he sensed that time was running out on him, he got married, hoping his offspring would inherit his psychic abilities—"

"Not very flattering to Great-grandma," Ethan cut in.

"Not flattering at all," said Zoe, "especially if she was the jealous type. And since Thomas was a casualty of World War I, that would explain the condition of the grave."

"Seems to me you're reading an awful lot into this. Great-grandma's gone from first runner-up on Hubby's hit parade to jealous *and* vindictive, and as for Great-grandpa, you've taken the things he wrote in his diary when he was out of his mind with grief, and from that you assume he never got over Evangeline's death. For all you know, he turned into a model husband. He could've been wild about Great-grandma—''

''He wasn't. Their suns were incompatible, and so were their moons.'' Ethan's pained expression told Zoe what he thought of this analysis, but she didn't give him the chance to reply that he considered astrology a shaky foundation on which to build an argument. Holding up Thomas's journal, she finished quietly, ''If you won't believe me, maybe you'll believe this.''

Before Ethan could say anything, she read him one of the later passages, an entry written a year after Hiram's birth, in which Thomas expressed concern over his wife's growing resentment of Evangeline.

I have been honest with Ardith from the start. When I proposed to her, I promised I would be faithful to her physically. I promised her my affection, but I made it clear that my love belongs to Vangie. I knew Ardith and I would never be lovers in the truest sense of the word, but I had hoped that our life together would be congenial. I thought Ardith understood my feelings and that we would always be friends, but now I realize my mistake.

I have given Ardith my name, my home, every material convenience she desires. I have given her the respect due the mother of my son, and a certain prominence in Long Island society. And she has repaid me with contempt for everything I hold dear.

Last night she informed me, if I do not give up my studies and curtail my visits to Evangeline's grave, she will leave me and take the baby with her. She says I have become a laughingstock, and if I challenge her, she is certain to win custody of our son.

Ardith is intolerant, but quite conventional. In the

years since our marriage, I have learned how desperately she craves acceptance. The good opinion of her
social set is essential to her, and she will go to any
lengths to preserve appearances. I do not know
whether she could ever bring herself to carry out her
threats, but for Hiram's sake I have decided to do
what I must to appease her, at least for the time being.

This is a painful choice, but it is the choice I am
compelled to make, and I am consoled by the knowledge that wherever she is, Evangeline understands
why I have made it.

Zoe closed the journal and shot an expectant look at
Ethan.

"You've made your point," he allowed. "Thomas was
a saint, and Great-grandma could've given villain lessons
to J. R. Ewing. But just because you're right about them,
that doesn't mean you're infallible."

"I never claimed I was."

"Maybe not, but at times you act as if what you know
about astrology gives you a monopoly on the facts. As it
happens, though, I've done a spot of investigating on my
own, and it turns out I was right about Evangeline not
drowning. According to her death certificate, she died of
pneumonia.

Zoe scarcely missed a beat. "It doesn't seem likely she'd
have gotten pneumonia if she hadn't gone through the ice,
so I don't see what difference the official cause of death
makes."

With that Zoe returned to the journal, and left to his
own devices, Ethan decided he sympathized with Ardith
Seymour.

He had checked out Evangeline's death certificate,
hoping the information it brought to light would discour-

age Zoe and maybe bring her down to earth. Instead, he was the one who was discouraged.

And annoyed.

He'd spent half the morning going through old records, and Zoe had shrugged off what he'd learned as if it didn't change anything. His great-grandfather's diary kept her so absorbed that the man who had brought her lunch and shared all five bedrooms at Gull Cottage with her and might want to share her life, didn't rate a second glance. She hadn't given him as much as a thank-you.

A few minutes later, when she read him another passage, Ethan responded coolly.

His great-grandmother couldn't have resented Evangeline any more than he resented Thomas at that moment.

As the youngest in his family, Ethan had had his fill of hand-me-downs: outgrown sweaters and coats, scuffed footballs and baseball mitts, scratched and dented furniture. When he was a kid, he hadn't minded. He'd realized that although his parents were comfortable, they were far from rich, and that raising three sons, keeping them in sneakers and peanut butter, providing music lessons and hockey camp, not to mention orthodonture and four years of college, was an expensive proposition.

But he wasn't a kid anymore and he had his pride. He wanted things to be the way they'd been last weekend.

He missed Zoe's smiles and her teasing, the way she'd listened to his anecdotes and even if he got a bit long-winded, never seemed to get bored.

He wanted to come first with her. Like any reasonably perceptive adult male, he recognized secondhand attention when he saw it—especially when he was the recipient. And like any reasonably good-looking man, he didn't relish being an also-ran. He didn't mind admitting that the experience rankled. He didn't like it and, he told himself, he didn't need it.

He refused to share Zoe with a ghost, and if that meant depriving himself of her company, her camaraderie, the intimacy they had enjoyed, then he'd damned well get along without her.

Chapter Thirteen

On Saturday Zoe brought up the idea of asking Cosmo to hypnotize her again.

Ethan was shocked. "Why would you want to put yourself through that? After what you went through the last time, I should think you'd have had enough."

"That's true, but still, there are a few mysteries I want to clear up."

Scowling, Ethan countered, "If reading that diary hasn't solved them, what makes you think hypnosis will do any good?"

"It might not accomplish anything," Zoe conceded, avoiding his gaze. "But as long as there's a possibility it'll answer my questions, I'd like to try it."

Answers were imperative, and the sooner she had them, the better, because her chief questions involved Ethan.

Why had he ignored her request that he go through Evangeline's letters? Why did he seem irritated by the excerpts she'd read him from Thomas's journal? Why had he turned down her invitation to have a late supper at Gull Cottage last night, and why was he keeping his distance today?

He hadn't kissed her since Thursday; hadn't even touched her. Was he tired of her? Had she done something to offend him?

Zoe could have asked him, of course. That would have been the simplest, most straightforward solution. It was also the approach she would have preferred—if only she'd thought he would give her a direct answer.

But since yesterday afternoon Ethan had been tense and moody, acting as if he were spoiling for a fight. She had been tempted to oblige him once or twice, when he'd snapped at her for no reason and impatience had nearly gotten the better of her. In the end though, it had seemed wiser to hold her temper.

She disliked feeling at odds with him, and the last thing she wanted was to add to the constraint.

THE MOMENT Zoe mentioned hypnosis, Ethan's vow to get along without her went out the window. The memory of her first experience with altered consciousness was indelibly etched on his mind.

He remembered her pallor, her wide, staring eyes, her tormented expression, and concern overshadowed resentment.

Whatever the consequences, Ethan knew that he could not let Cosmo put her under again. He resolved to do everything in his power to stop her, and since it seemed unlikely that Zoe would bow to his wishes, he resolved to take up the issue with Cosmo.

He phoned DiSantis that night and told him he had to see him. "If you're free tomorrow," he said, "I'll take the morning train into the city."

"If this is about the Jung correspondence, I've finished the translations," Cosmo replied. "I'll be out your way

Monday to deliver the letters to Zoe, so if you can wait till then, it'll save you the trip.''

"This can't wait," said Ethan. "It's a matter of some urgency."

"I see," Cosmo answered and then, recognizing the anxiety in the younger man's voice, "Can you give me a hint what this is about?"

"I'd rather not discuss it on the phone, but it has to do with Zoe."

"In that case, I'll come out to East Hampton first thing tomorrow."

"I'll meet you at the station," said Ethan.

By noon on Sunday, the two men were seated in the gazebo at the Seymour estate.

Ethan took a chair facing the driveway, keeping watch in case Zoe decided to stop by, and Cosmo slumped over the table opposite him, blue-jowled and haggard after an all but sleepless night, yawning over his sixth cup of coffee of the day.

When his cup was empty, DiSantis nudged the briefcase at his feet to one side with the toe of his shoe, stretched his legs under the table and fixed Ethan with a brooding glance.

Holding up a shaking hand, he declared, "Suspense does not agree with me, my boy. Neither does caffeine. I'd appreciate it if you'd put me out of my misery and tell me why you're worried about Zoe."

Ethan rearranged his chair an inch to the left to improve his view of the drive. Although there was no sign of Zoe, and he really wasn't expecting her to come to work today, he spoke in lowered tones.

"I don't know how much she told you about what happened the night you hypnotized her—''

"Nothing," said Cosmo. "She told me absolutely nothing."

Ethan looked at him, surprised. "You didn't ask her about it?"

"Of course I asked, but she put me off. She said she didn't feel ready to talk about it, so I didn't press her." Cosmo squinted at Ethan above the rims of his bifocals, then removed the glasses and polished the lenses with his napkin. "I gather she chose to confide in you."

"Yes," said Ethan. "Yes, she did, and I suppose the first order of business is to fill you in."

As briefly as possible, without digression, he repeated Zoe's account of her experience under hypnosis, and DiSantis remained inert and silent, glasses forgotten in one hand, napkin in the other, his face rapt yet oddly featureless without the dark-rimmed bifocals. But when Ethan described Evangeline and Thomas, certain details of the skating party seemed to galvanize Cosmo.

"Tell me," he said, "does the skating end with Evangeline going through the ice?"

"That's right," said Ethan. "How did you guess?"

"Let's just say I've had my suspicions." With brusque vigorous gestures, Cosmo fogged the lenses of his glasses with his breath and gave them one last swipe with the napkins. But through all this activity, his scrutiny never left Ethan. "I assume you don't follow *Passion's Children*."

"No, I'm not a fan, but Cora ran a few tapes of the show for me before she went back to New York."

Cosmo pursed his lips, considering this reply. "While you were watching the tapes, did you by any chance take Cora into your confidence?"

Ethan stared at DiSantis, perplexed. "Did Zoe tell you about that?"

"No," said Cosmo. "She didn't have to, and if you'd seen this week's episodes of *Passion's Children*, you'd know why."

"You mean Cora's written Evangeline and Thomas into the script?"

"The names have been changed to protect the innocent, but yes, I'm afraid she has."

Good Lord! thought Ethan. Zoe wasn't exaggerating about her aunt. And I was the know-it-all who didn't have enough sense to take her word for it. I accused her of imagining things—

No wonder she was upset!

Whether it was all the talking he'd done, or the realization that Zoe had had a perfect right to be furious with him, his mouth was suddenly dry.

After a pause for a swallow of coffee and a hurried scan of the driveway, he went on to describe Zoe's version of the skating accident, and in the telling, found himself recalling other things she had said.

It occurred to him that if Zoe had been honest about Cora, she might very well have told the truth about everything, and his doubts continued to evaporate as he discussed the importance Zoe ascribed to the nocturne, and mentioned that her discovery of the music box had seemed to lead her directly to Evangeline's grave.

"Where is this knoll?" Cosmo inquired.

Ethan pointed out the sloping green flank of hillside, and Cosmo rose and crossed from one side of the gazebo to the other, trying to see the crest of the hill.

"You can't really see the grave site from this side of the house," Ethan said, "but if you'd like to, we could take a walk up there later."

"I would like to see it, but Zoe's expecting me."

"Well, now that the brush has been cleared, the grave's easy enough to find. Feel free to check it out at your convenience."

"Thank you, my boy. I'll do that." Cosmo returned to his chair. "You did say that Zoe had never been up there before the night you found the music box?"

"To the best of my knowledge, that's the only time she's been there."

"That's extraordinary!" Cosmo murmured. "Utterly incredible!"

"That was my reaction too," Ethan admitted. "But if you think that's incredible, wait'll you hear the rest."

In hushed, solemn tones, he recounted the troubling developments of the past few days, building up to Zoe's notion about hypnosis. When he finished, Cosmo was sympathetic but unruffled.

"Listen, Ethan, I understand why you're concerned about Zoe's fascination with Evangeline and Thomas—"

"It's more like an obsession."

Cosmo slipped on his bifocals and chose not to quibble over semantics. "Whatever term you apply to Zoe's preoccupation, I'm more interested in your reaction."

"My reaction?"

"Exactly. Thomas Seymour was your ancestor, yet you've refused to read his journal. You seem determined to deny that he had a life, emotions, passions that he and Evangeline could have loved each other so desperately, a residue of their feeling for each other might survive, even today."

"I don't deny it. I just don't think it's relevant."

"Ahh," Cosmo sighed. "If you can't admit that the past can influence the present, perhaps it is you who should undergo hypnosis."

Ethan pushed to his feet so forcefully that his chair tipped over. He confronted DiSantis, posture rigid, every line of his body conveying outrage. "Not a chance, Di-Santis! Even if I believed in that kind of hocus-pocus—which I *don't*—I wouldn't be gullible enough to subject myself to it."

Cosmo registered the display of temper, but was not at all intimidated by it. With a benign smile, he remarked, "You're overreacting again."

Ethan's hands knotted into fists, then just as quickly relaxed. He subsided into his chair, thoroughly abashed. "I'm sorry," he muttered. "You probably won't believe this, but I don't usually fly off the handle like that. I don't know what came over me."

"Obviously your feelings are close to the surface."

"It's just— Everything seems to be happening at once! Half the time lately I don't know whether I'm coming or going."

"There's no shame in that. I've always seen confusion as a sign of an open mind."

Ethan shook his head. "I've always seen it as a sign of weakness."

"It isn't," said Cosmo. "Take my word for it. Even the fact you can admit that takes a good deal of strength."

"Maybe," said Ethan, "but that doesn't make it any easier to take."

Cosmo opened his briefcase and removed a sheaf of papers.

"What's all that?"

"The translations of the Jung letters." Cosmo looked up and caught Ethan's wary expression. He grinned as he extracted one of the pages and laid it on the table. "Don't worry. I'm not going to read all of these to you, but there is one note Jung wrote in his student days, after he'd happened upon a book pertaining to spiritualistic phenomena. It might help bring the issue of Thomas and Evangeline into perspective. I'd like you to apply your slightly muddled but admirably open mind to it and tell me if it clarifies your thinking.''

''Okay. I guess it's worth a try.''

Cosmo's glance sharpened at Ethan's halfhearted reply. ''Do you have reservations about Carl Jung's reputation?''

''To be honest, I don't know much about him, except that he was a contemporary of Freud's and he had something to do with psychiatry.''

''He was one of the founders of analytic psychology and a philosopher of the first rank. Now, knowing that, would you agree that he was a scholar of some renown?''

''Yes, certainly.''

''Then perhaps you'll also agree with his hypothesis that there's nothing earthshaking in the idea that there might be events that overstep the limited categories of time, space and causality.''

''What kind of events?''

''Well, for instance, animals have been known to sense impending storms and earthquakes. There have been documented cases of dreams that have foreseen the death of certain persons, clocks that have stopped at the moment of death, glasses that have shattered at the critical moment.'' Cosmo squared his bifocals on the bridge of his nose and bent over the paper. ''Jung writes that all of these things had been everyday occurrences in the world of his childhood. He'd always taken them for granted. But his friends refused to discuss them with him. They showed a curious resistance to the subject . . . even seemed to find it a cause of dread.''

Cosmo fell silent, and skimmed to the bottom of the page. "Jung goes on for a few more lines, but that's the gist of what I wanted to get across to you. So tell me, Ethan, what do you make of his quandary?"

Ethan shifted in his chair, more confused than before. "Frankly, I'm not sure what to make of it, but I can tell you this much. I don't think Jung's note establishes a case for spiritualism. The examples he cites could be explained scientifically, or they could be coincidence. Clocks stop every day. Glasses break. People dream. And if an infinitesimal percentage of dreams happens to forecast an actual event, it doesn't necessarily prove anything."

Cosmo tapped his forefinger against the paper. "For the moment, let's concentrate on what's happening with Zoe and take a closer look at an event that troubles you."

Ethan frowned. "There are several, but I guess the one that bothers me most is the way she found the grave."

"You can think of no scientific explanation for this?"

"No, I can't."

"Can you pass it off as coincidence?"

"No. But I can't just accept it, either. Even in the world of my childhood, I couldn't have taken something that strange for granted."

"So what you're saying is, instead of indentifying with Jung, you identify with his friends."

"That's right."

"And you found the incident with the grave so disturbing that you spent an entire day trying to prove Zoe was mistaken."

"Yes, I did."

"How did you feel while you were clearing the brush?"

"I wasn't happy, if that's what you mean. It was a backbreaking job and a scorching day, so physically I was uncomfortable."

"What was your state of mind?"

Ethan's mouth turned down at the corners. "That was uncomfortable, too. Mostly I wondered what I was doing there. I mean, talk about your no-win situations! If Zoe was wrong, that meant she was delusional. If she was right— Well, that possibility scared the hell out of me. Either way, I dreaded what I'd find."

"Naturally you did. The unknown is always frightening. We look around and things appear to be in balance. There's an orderliness to the universe. We can chart the stars and the planets. We can predict the phases of the moon. The sun rises in the morning and sets in the evening. Seasons come and go. We rely on the laws of nature, on time and space, cause and effect, and when we're confronted by an effect that has no apparent cause, one that's *un*predictable, that we *can't* explain, the world turns upside down."

Cosmo leaned back in his chair and steepled his fingers beneath his chin. "When an aberration like that happens, the immediate need is to scurry around, searching for an explanation that will set things right side up. And if we can't explain it, we tend to react to the imbalance in one of several ways. We can call it a miracle and chalk it up to divine intervention or the devil's handiwork."

"That's no good," said Ethan. "If we hadn't progressed beyond that, we'd still be living in caves and worshiping oak trees."

Cosmo nodded. "Then again, we can accept the event as coincidence, simply walk away and pray it doesn't happen again."

"Too passive."

"That's right, and if we're passive, we risk losing control of our environment, and the prospect of losing control can send us running scared in the opposite direction."

"Which is?"

"Denying anything out of the ordinary ever happened to begin with."

"I've tried that," said Ethan. "It's another blind alley."

"If you've discovered that, you may be ready to try a different route."

"I'm about at the end of my rope, DiSantis. I'll try anything as long as it's constructive."

"Then if I were you, I'd confront the unknown. I'd take a good hard look at whatever frightened me, and figure out why I dreaded it."

Ethan grinned ruefully. "Why do I get the feeling that's easier said than done?"

"You've got me there," said Cosmo. "It doesn't have to be difficult. I could show you a shortcut—"

Ethan held up a weary hand. "Don't bother saying it. I know what you're going to suggest."

"Very well, Ethan. Since you insist, I'll skip right to the bottom line. You claim you don't believe in hypnosis—"

"Dammit, DiSantis! Don't you ever give up?"

Cosmo favored Ethan with a sunny smile, and went on as if he had not been interrupted. "If you don't believe hypnosis is real, you have nothing to fear from it for yourself or for Zoe."

"And nothing to gain from it, either."

"On the contrary, you could make tremendous gains in terms of self-knowledge, self-discipline." Cosmo shrugged. "Who knows? If you're very lucky, you might break through those defenses you've erected and cultivate a nodding acquaintance with the truth."

Ethan had no clever comeback to this riposte. For long moments he stared at Cosmo, at his wit's end, and when he unscrambled his racing thoughts, the best he could manage was a grudging, ''Touché.''

While Cosmo downed the last of the coffee and stowed the Jung correspondence in the accordion file in his brief-case, preparing for the drive to Gull Cottage, Ethan's mind kept replaying his arguments, and the more he thought about them, the more rational they seemed.

The trouble, he decided as he walked Cosmo to the car, was that the older man had worn down his resistance.

They were creeping along with the bumper-to-bumper traffic on Main Street, headed toward Frigate Alley, and Ethan was thinking of all the comebacks he might have made, when a final question occurred to him.

''Is it possible,'' he inquired, ''that under hypnosis I might discover an explanation for what's been happening with Zoe?''

''I can't promise you that, but you may find that some things need no explanation.'' Cosmo inclined his head to-ward Ethan, fixing him with an owlish stare. ''Will you think about it?''

Ethan braked to avoid hitting a jaywalker. ''I suppose the least I can do is give it some thought.''

ETHAN HUNG BACK when they arrived at Gull Cottage. Uncertain of his reception, he loitered near the end of the walk while Cosmo rang the bell. Although the front door was ajar, there was no response.

Cosmo swung the door wider. ''Hello,'' he called. ''Anybody home?''

''Come on in,'' Zoe answered from the depths of the house.

Cosmo went inside, and Ethan trailed a dozen steps be-hind him, following the sound of Zoe's voice through the living room. When they reached the solarium, they found that she was on the phone.

When Cosmo walked into the room, she smiled, obviously delighted to see him.

"Long-distance," she mouthed, pointing to the receiver, and returned to her caller without spotting Ethan, who remained out of sight on the threshold, an unseen observer, admiring the fluid grace of her movements as she paced the length of the telephone cord between the fireplace and French doors.

"Really, Laurence, if he'd injured himself, you'd be the first to know.... I understand. Truly I do, but I assure you, Boris is fine."

Zoe stopped for a moment beside the hearth, coiling the cord around her fingers.

"No, he didn't see the vet.... Well, because I didn't think it was necessary. He only escaped for a couple of hours.... No. There's been no problem getting him to take his vitamins, and his appetite has been good.... You what...? He's right here with me, but you can't be serious.... Yes, of course. If you insist, I'll put him on."

She turned toward the cage, offering the receiver to the mynah, who was contemplating her every move.

"It's for you, Boris. Say hello to Laurence."

The mynah hopped toward the earpiece, drawn by the transatlantic baritone of his master's voice.

"Hello," Zoe prompted. "Say hello."

Boris ruffled his neck feathers and pecked at the receiver.

"How about some Shakespeare?" Zoe pleaded. "Double, double, toil and trouble—"

Boris cocked his head to one side, attentive to her coaching, and with an eloquent sigh, she held the receiver to her ear.

"He doesn't seem to be in the mood to talk.... Well, at these rates, I thought ... You called collect, Laurence.... Yes, I'm sure you will.... All right, but just a minute more."

Again she offered Boris the phone, and this time he responded.

"Ehh, what's up, Doc?"

Although Zoe jerked away the receiver before he could say anything else, her reflexes weren't fast enough to keep Laurence from hearing the Bugs Bunny impression, and from the width of the ocean away, via satellite and the electronic wizardry of AT&T, Ethan could hear Laurence McClellan's reaction.

"What a maroon!" Boris screeched. "What a nincompoop!"

Zoe shot a stern look at the mynah and a sterner look at Cosmo, who was holding his sides, quaking with suppressed laughter.

"Laurence?" she inquired brightly. "Did that convince you he's okay...? I read the instructions, but it wasn't me. I haven't watched TV since I got here.... I've been working long hours, so I've missed some of his lessons, but I made a tape of the soliloquy.... Yes, at least thirty minutes a day.... Well, as long as you called, there's a problem with the furniture—"

Zoe broke off in midsentence and held the receiver away from her ear. The dial tone was audible as she glanced at Cosmo and jiggled the disconnect button.

"We seem to have been cut off."

"I doubt it," said Cosmo. "If I know Laurence, your problem with the furniture was his cue to hang up."

"Told you so," said Boris.

Zoe made a droll face at the mynah, dropped the receiver onto its cradle, and turned away from the phone just as Ethan came into the room.

Her eyes lighted up when she saw him so that the clear blue depths were starred with an emotion richer than delight, stronger than mere fondness; an emotion so profound that he felt humbled by it.

"Ethan!" she cried. "I didn't see you there in the doorway."

But was it him she saw or a latter-day reflection of Thomas Seymour?

The question sprang into his mind, catching Ethan unaware, cooling his response to Zoe's greeting. And the coolness persisted. He could not shake it off. Even half an hour later, when the three of them were having lunch beside the pool, he was gripped by an icy reserve.

Nothing could dispel it. Not the warmth of the sun or Cosmo's cheery banter or the sweetness of Zoe's smile.

He contributed nothing to the conversation, and although Zoe and Cosmo must have noticed, neither of them commented on his silence. He began to wonder if he was destined to become a crusty curmudgeon like his Uncle Hiram, and when Zoe got up to serve the coffee, he jumped at the chance to leave the table.

"Let me take care of this," he said. "You and Cosmo must have a lot to talk about."

He took his time with the clearing up, and when he returned with the coffee tray, they were going over the Jung letters.

Zoe was enraptured. "These are fantastic!" she said to Cosmo. "They're even better than I hoped they'd be. You've done a wonderful job with them."

"They ought to be accurate," Cosmo replied. "I spent most of the week on the translations—I'm afraid to the detriment of the shop."

Zoe moved a stack of papers out of the way so that Ethan could set the tray on the table. "How are things at The Second Story?" she asked.

Cosmo stole a cookie off the tray. "I'm still searching for that illustrated edition of Chaucer."

Zoe wrinkled her nose at him. "Look in the *C*s, after the Caldwells and before Colette."

Cosmo chuckled. "Aside from the fact that I miss my smart-aleck assistant, I'd say everything at the store is fair to middling. It looks as if the retail business will survive till you get back."

"It won't be long now," Zoe replied. "I'll be finished with the library in a few days."

"That soon?" Ethan asked.

She nodded. She did not meet his gaze. "June's almost over," she murmured.

Until that moment, it hadn't dawned on Ethan how soon Zoe would be gone.

Of course, he'd known from the beginning that her stay in East Hampton was temporary, but after that first night at Gull Cottage, he'd begun to think of her as a permanent fixture in his life. And somehow or other, somewhere along the way, she had become essential to him; as important to his well-being as the air he breathed or the water he drank.

It seemed as if he had always known Zoe. In his complacency, he had assumed he always would. But now that a chance remark had punctured his complacency, he forced himself to envision a future without her.

When he got home that Sunday afternoon, he sat on the terrace wondering what life would be like when he reached out for her in the night and found that she was gone. What would it be like when he couldn't wake her with kisses in the morning and fall asleep with her in his arms?

And what would become of Zoe without him?

She was lovely and warm, intelligent, sweet, and totally desirable, so it wasn't likely that she would lack masculine attention. Not for long. Eventually another man would enter the picture. That much seemed certain.

For her sake, Ethan hoped she would find a man who would coax her away from her desk when she'd been working too hard. One who would remind her to eat and be kind to Merlin, and keep wolves like Haines Randolph away from her door.

And if this unknown man proved worthy of Zoe, he would also keep track of her shoes. He would be there whenever she needed him, holding her hand, ready to pick her up in case a wave at the beach knocked her down. He would provide an anchor to reality, and bring her safely back to earth when one of her far-out fantasies sent her soaring into the stratosphere.

And someday, if fortune smiled on him, this nameless, faceless rival might persuade Zoe to settle down. He might give her a home, roots, children—

But dammit, thought Ethan, *he won't love her the way I do!*

No other man could possibly love her as deeply, want her as passionately, need her as desperately as he.

What would he do without Zoe to tease him...challenge him...talk with him...laugh with him...love him?

He would still have his career, of course, and his family and friends. He would still have his music. And he would have memories. A wealth of memories.

Years from now, on rainy June evenings, when he was intoxicated by the fragrance of lilacs, he would go into the library and play the nocturne, and reflect on happier times—

My God! He was pathetic. He was as bad as Thomas Seymour. Only he had less justification. Thomas had plunged into mourning, but he had never abandoned hope, even though death had separated him from Evangeline.

Zoe, thank heaven, was very much alive. What's more, she was still in East Hampton. So why was he sitting with his chin on his chest, moping about her absence as if she'd already left? Instead of feeling sorry for himself, why didn't he take action? Why didn't he *do* something—anything short of a felony—to keep her from leaving?

Self-disgust brought Ethan to his feet, but it was a resurgence of optimism that kept him there far into the night.

He prowled from room to room till the small hours of the morning, plotting and scheming, trying to devise a foolproof way of inducing Zoe to stay.

He knew that she was committed to her work, but East Hampton was not the end of the earth. If she chose to open a bookstore here, he would offer financial backing. If she wanted to continue her studies with Cosmo, she could commute to the city two or three times a week. Or if she would rather keep her flat and her job at The Second Story, she could commute to East Hampton on weekends.

Although his own preference was that she make a lifetime commitment to him, marriage seemed an impossible dream. That led him to believe the wisest course would be to take what he could get. As long as Zoe was prepared to give him a few days a week, he would be willing to compromise.

He wasn't sure she would, however, and caution made him hesitate about setting his plan in motion. And he couldn't decide whether or not he ought to declare his feelings.

He wasn't too proud to go out on a limb, but once there, he was naturally reluctant to cut off the limb after himself.

At the bank the next morning he was not at his best; in fact, he was downright cranky. By noon his secretary was giving him a wide berth, and even then she walked on tiptoe.

The high point of his day came when he got back from lunch and discovered that someone had left a newspaper on his desk, folded open to the daily horoscopes.

He automatically glanced at the advice for his sun sign, and what he saw there made Madame Makarova's authentic Ukrainian borscht churn in his stomach like battery acid.

The column read, "Even Scorpios can't always win. The time has come to accept defeat, and bow out gracefully."

Accept defeat? Never! And he jolly well would not bow out, gracefully or otherwise. No syndicated soothsayer was going to tell Ethan Quinn how to run his life. *He* was the master of his fate.

He loved Zoe, dammit; loved her enough to fight for her. And if that meant he had to tilt at windmills, defy the stars or compete with ghosts, so be it. He would do whatever he had to do, and in the end, he'd win.

Ethan slapped down the newspaper and reached for the phone. He punched out Laurence McClellan's number with impatient jabs of a pencil. Cosmo answered on the third ring. Ethan heard Boris jabbering away in the background and didn't say hello, nor did he bother to identify himself.

Without preamble he declared, "You talked me into it, DiSantis. I've decided to try hypnosis."

Chapter Fourteen

"I ought to warn you, it may not be easy."

"What is this?" Ethan demanded. "Are you trying to talk me out of it?"

"Not at all," said Cosmo. "I'm glad to hear you've changed your mind, but I don't want to mislead you. There's more to hypnosis than you realize. It's taken you quite a few years to build up your defenses. They're not likely to go away overnight. We may not be successful on the first try."

"Whatever it takes, let's do it."

"All right, Ethan. As long as I have your full cooperation, when would you like to begin?"

"Today," he replied. "The sooner the better. There's no sense putting it off."

"I'm tied up this afternoon, doing some research for Zoe, but I could make it this evening. Shall we get together at your place, about seven?"

"Seven's fine, but I'd rather we met at Gull Cottage. Zoe will be working in the library, and I want to keep her out of this."

"If you have misgivings," said Cosmo, "if you're concerned about losing control, I'd like to reassure you. In the hypnotic state, your faculties won't be impaired. Part of you remains observant. You can't be made to do anything against your will."

"I understand, DiSantis, but just the same, I'd appreciate it if you'd keep this to yourself."

"Very well, Ethan. If that's the way you want it."

"It is."

"Then Zoe won't hear about it from me."

Or me, thought Ethan, as he hung up the phone. Not till he was certain he wouldn't do something embarrassing.

Despite Cosmo's assurances, the thought of going into a trance made him uncomfortable, and as the afternoon waned, he felt increasingly on edge. At five o'clock he left the bank, regretting his decision.

Hypnosis seemed an iffy proposition, and he wondered if he'd been too hasty. What if he never came out of it? Would he go through the rest of his life like some sort of zombie?

He might have reneged on his agreement, if it hadn't been for Zoe. Her bicycle was propped next to the front steps when he got home, and he went straight to the library, looking for her.

She wasn't there, but he found evidence that she couldn't have gone far. Her carryall was beside the steno desk. Stacks of books covered the desktop, and she'd left the electric typewriter on. There was even a half-finished index card rolled into the machine.

He crossed to the windows, thinking that she might be taking a coffee break outdoors, but the terrace was deserted, and so was the garden. He was about to turn away when he spotted two people at the top of the knoll.

The sun at their backs made it impossible to see the couple clearly, but he knew beyond a shadow of a doubt that one of them was Zoe. And the other must be DiSantis.

"Damn," Ethan muttered. Hadn't Cosmo heard a word he'd said about Zoe's obsession with Evangeline and Thomas? Didn't he realize the hazards he was exposing her to, permitting her to visit the grave?

Ethan swung away from the windows and hurried out the back door. Without stopping to close it, he strode across the terrace. He started up the hill, and when he was halfway to the top, Zoe spotted him and waved.

"Ethan," she called, running down the slope to meet him, "guess what I found."

Oh, God, what now? he wondered, lengthening his stride. Aloud he answered, "I can't imagine."

"Wait'll you see!"

Zoe waved again, and the sun glinted off the small, shiny object she held, but before he could detect any other details, she ran full tilt into his arms. Her lips collided softly with his chin, then skidded toward his mouth, but he scarcely had time to return her kiss before she moved away from him, fairly skipping with excitement.

"What do you think of this?" she said, dropping an ornately engraved locket on a delicate gold chain into his palm.

Uncertain what to think, Ethan glanced from the locket to Zoe, and then toward Cosmo, who was hastening to join them.

"Open it," Zoe prompted. "Take a look inside."

He ran his thumbnail along the seam in the casing, depressed the catch, and the halves of the locket sprang apart, revealing the intertwined initials *E.B.* on one side, and on the other the hand-tinted photographic miniature of a man.

Ethan stared at the picture, struck by the familiar cast of the man's features. If the hairline were different, if his own eyes had been blue, he might have been studying a picture of himself. This man's nose was like his, and the set of his jaw, the slant of his brows, the shape of his mouth.

"Where did you find this?" he demanded.

"In the rolltop desk. The locket must have been Evangeline's, so I assume that's a picture of Thomas."

"Zoe tells me he's the man she saw in her vision," said Cosmo. "Notice the resemblance?"

"How could I help noticing?" Ethan replied. "The similarity's uncanny."

"Do you honestly think so?" asked Zoe.

"Don't you?"

She framed Ethan's face between her palms and turned his head from left to right, making a feature by feature comparison of the face in the miniature with his own, and when she had finished, she stepped back and regarded him with serene, untroubled eyes.

"That morning I found you asleep on my sofa, there were a few minutes when I expected you to look like Thomas, but once you woke up, the impression didn't last. I suppose there's some similarity of bone structure, but aside from that, I don't see much resemblance at all."

"How can you miss it?" asked Cosmo. "A blind man could see they're as much alike as peas in a pod."

"I'm sorry I can't make it unanimous, but what I see are the differences." Zoe linked arms with Ethan. In a musing voice, as if she were thinking out loud, she added, "Maybe the way I see you is colored by your personality—and by the way I feel about you."

The discovery that Zoe was in no danger of confusing him with Thomas was a burden off Ethan's mind. And the compliment she had paid him made him feel taller, stronger, as if he could lick his weight in wildcats. With Zoe holding onto his arm, walking beside him, inquiring about his day at the bank, he practically swaggered down the hill.

But her compliment was a double-edged sword. It offered encouragement and let him know that his optimism was not unfounded, and it also left him with an obligation. He had to go through with the hypnosis.

Zoe had met him halfway—more than halfway, and in more ways than one.

First, she'd been so eager to show him the locket that she had run to him from the knoll and literally thrown herself into his arms.

And then she had admitted that she loved him. Perhaps not in so many words, but she had made it clear that her feelings for him were more than casual.

Knowing that, he couldn't back out of his arrangement with Cosmo. Not honorably. Not if he hoped to live with his conscience. And not if he ever hoped to live with Zoe.

LESS THAN TWO HOURS LATER, Ethan kept his appointment with Cosmo, who was not terribly pleased about being sworn to secrecy.

"I felt like a louse, sneaking out on Zoe," he grumbled as he let Ethan into Gull Cottage.

"So did I," said Ethan. Yet he had been too self-conscious to tell her the truth.

While Boris kibitzed from his cage, the two men dragged deck chairs into the solarium and sat near the French doors, eyeing each other as if they were adversaries.

"What excuse did you use for leaving?" asked Cosmo.

"I offered to feed Boris."

"Then you'd better see to him before you leave."

Ethan nodded. "How about you?"

"I told Zoe I had some reading to do at the public library."

"Did she buy it?"

"She seemed to, but I've no idea if the library stays open Monday nights. If it doesn't—if Zoe finds out I lied to her—I'm going to tell her the truth. I won't cover for you again."

"I wouldn't ask you to," said Ethan.

"I believe you," said Cosmo. "And now that we've got that straightened out, shall we get down to business?"

"Where do we begin?"

"You might try relaxing—unless you're comfortable sitting on the edge of your chair." Ethan sat back, and Cosmo smiled. "There's no reason to be uptight, you know. Until you trust me, there's no point in attempting to hypnotize you, so for tonight, all we're going to do is talk."

"What about?"

"Well, in case I haven't covered the most common misconceptions about hypnosis, let me reiterate that there's nothing to fear about entering a state of altered consciousness. You can't be forced to do anything that's not in accord with your value system, you can't be manipulated into revealing anything you don't want to reveal, and you will come out of your trance. Hypnosis is not permanent. The subject remains in control at all times."

"That's reassuring," said Ethan, but he did not look reassured.

"You're only half-convinced, but I consider that progress," said Cosmo.

For several seconds he fixed Ethan with a bright, inquisitive gaze, but as the seconds lengthened to a minute, and Ethan did not reply, Cosmo settled back in his chair and closed his eyes.

A conspicuous stillness settled over the solarium. Even Boris remained silent. Like Cosmo, the mynah appeared to be napping.

Ethan could hear his own heartbeat. He could feel beads of sweat popping out on his forehead. He gripped the arms of his deck chair, grappling with uneasiness. Part of him wanted to get up and walk away from Gull Cottage; another part wondered what might happen if he stayed.

After five minutes of silence he cleared his throat. The sound seemed unnaturally loud in the stillness.

"What happens next?" he inquired.

Cosmo opened his eyes. "I don't know about you, but I've always thought conversation required the active participation of at least two people. I say something, you say something in response, and so on and so forth."

"I've got to hand it to you, DiSantis. You have a polite way of telling me it's my turn to talk."

"I don't know how polite it is, but it's my way."

Ethan colored. "I don't mean to be difficult, but I'm not sure what's pertinent in a situation like this. Why don't you ask a few questions, and I'll try to answer them?"

"All right, Ethan, just to prime the conversational pump, why don't you tell me why you decided to do this?"

Ethan looked startled.

"If that question was too personal for you, I'd be happy to rephrase it."

"Yes," said Ethan. "Please do."

Cosmo shrugged. "When people undergo hypnosis, it's not uncommon for them to have some sort of goal. Some subjects use posthypnotic suggestion or self-hypnosis to cope with anxiety, others use the same mechanisms to reduce pain. Still others find that hypnotherapy enables them to overcome a phobia—"

"So your question is, what do I hope to achieve?"

"That's close enough," said Cosmo.

Ethan focused on the pattern in the carpet, then scuffed the design with the toe of his shoe. His expression was guarded. "I guess I look upon this as a learning experience."

"What is it you hope to learn about?"

He scuffed the pattern again; once, twice, three times. "Evangeline," he answered tersely. "And Thomas."

"If you want fo find out about them, why don't you refer to the things they've written?"

"The letters and the journal aren't enough. They can't tell me what I have to know."

"Aha! The light dawns." Cosmo removed his bifocals and rubbed the bridge of his nose. "Could it be that you're hoping to duplicate Zoe's experience under hypnosis? If so, I must inform you, that is not a realistic expectation."

"It isn't?"

"No, it isn't, but if there's something else you'd care to explore—"

Ethan gave Cosmo a hooded glance. "Zoe," he said. "I'd like to learn more about her."

"Read the instructions! Read the instructions!"

Both men laughed at the mynah's exhortation, and their amusement eased the tension between them.

Cosmo sent an appreciative grin toward the bird cage. "You know, Ethan, there's a kernel of truth in Boris's advice."

"How do you mean?"

"Just that Zoe comes as near to being an open book as anyone I've ever met. This may sound corny, but she cannot tell a lie. It's just not in her nature. That's one reason I hated fibbing to her tonight."

Ethan remembered an occasion when Zoe had succeeded in pulling the wool over DiSantis's eyes and his own, creating an illusion with nothing more than body language, and doing it flawlessly, with a facility that had duped three other witnesses. On at least one night, in this very room, she had fooled everyone but Boris.

And this was the woman Cosmo called an open book!

Ethan stared at the older man, trying to hide his skepticism. "Don't you think you're oversimplifying?"

"Not where Zoe's concerned. With her what you see is what you get. She may not always tell you what she's feeling. She may not want to divulge her thoughts, but she's painfully transparent. So if you want to learn more about her, all you have to do is take a look at her face. Whatever she's thinking, whatever she's feeling will be written there for all the world to read."

"Maybe for the rest of the world, but not for me," said Ethan. "To me, Zoe's an enigma. I'm never sure what she's thinking, what she's feeling, how she's going to react."

"Maybe that's because the two of you are so much alike."

"But we aren't alike. Not at all."

"Yes, you are," said Cosmo, "and I'll give you an example. You're in love with Zoe. She's in love with you. That much is obvious. But instead of seeing the obvious, each of you is the last one to recognize how the other feels. So you've set aside your personal distaste and agreed to undergo hypnosis, hoping to learn more about her, while she's been burning the midnight oil, reading Thomas's journal, seeking answers to her questions about you."

Ethan leaned forward, wanting to believe, not daring to believe. "What kind of questions?"

"Well, one of her concerns is that you don't respect her work."

"But I do respect it, too damned much. Sometimes I'm afraid for her."

Cosmo nodded. "Nature out of balance."

"That's it, DiSantis. That's it exactly." Ethan got to his feet, too keyed up to sit still. "If Zoe wanted to know more about me, why didn't she just ask?"

"Probably for the same reason you haven't approached her."

Ethan broke into a slaphappy grin.

"Ahh," said Cosmo. "I see that's convinced you."

"Not quite. If I may paraphrase a certain well-known astrologer, I'm only half-convinced, but I consider that progress."

"So do I, my boy. So do I. Which brings up another question. Can you tell me why you're here?"

"I wish I knew," said Ethan. "Maybe it's because I feel I have something to prove."

Cosmo nodded approvingly. "I appreciate your honesty, even if it doesn't establish a goal."

For the rest of that session Cosmo instructed Ethan in various techniques for relaxation, and as Ethan's trust became more complete, they took the first steps toward putting the techniques he was mastering into practice.

He achieved what Cosmo termed a hypnoidal state, but Ethan complained that he hadn't noticed much difference. "All I felt was drowsy."

"That's how you were supposed to feel," Cosmo explained. "It's true it was only a light trance, but it's the first stage of deep hypnosis."

By the end of the evening, they had reached an agreement that his goal in hypnosis would be self-knowledge, and although DiSantis was satisfied with their progress, Ethan was impatient.

Only three days were left in the month, and his sense that time was running out prompted him to declare that he was ready to go on to another level.

"Breathing exercises aren't my idea of a fun time," he said.

"Are you prepared to go deeper?"

"I think so. At least, I'd like to try."

"Then we'll plan on it for tomorrow."

Ethan frowned. "What's wrong with tonight?"

"I assumed you'd want to include Zoe. You did say she's the point of this exercise?"

"Yes, I did, but—"

"And you said you felt the need to prove something to her?"

"Yes, but—"

"How can you do that if she's not present?"

Ethan tugged at his necktie and acknowledged defeat. "I can't," he admitted.

"It's time to put your cards on the table," Cosmo said quietly. "I suppose you know she thinks you've been avoiding her."

Ethan did know. In the past several days, he'd seen Zoe only in passing, but even so, he had recognized the bewilderment in her eyes. It made him feel about two inches tall. The last thing he wanted was to hurt her.

"Will you invite her, or shall I?" asked Cosmo.

"I'd rather you'd speak to her. You'll explain it better." Ethan cleared his throat. "Tomorrow night, then?"

"Same time, same place." said Cosmo.

Ethan glanced around the empty solarium. "As long as Zoe's going to be in on it, we could meet at my house."

Cosmo shook his head. "We worked here tonight. You're accustomed to it. I think we'd be ill-advised if we made any unnecessary changes."

Ethan studied Boris, who was snoozing on his perch. "What if Zoe doesn't agree to come?"

"She will," said Cosmo. "I promise you, she will."

Chapter Fifteen

Persuading Zoe to sit in on the Tuesday session turned out to be relatively simple. When Cosmo confessed what he and Ethan had been up to, she was eager to attend. But once she was seated in Ethan's car for the trip to Gull Cottage, she chided both men for keeping her in the dark.

"You were so elusive last night, I've been beside myself with worry," she said. "Why didn't you tell me what was going on?"

Ethan tweaked the strand of red-gold hair that curled against her temple. "You didn't ask," he replied.

"Well, from now on, I will."

Ethan stroked her cheek with the backs of his fingers. "Word of honor?"

Zoe tilted her head to the side, inviting his caress. "Word of honor," she whispered.

Cosmo coughed to remind Zoe and Ethan that they had company. "Maybe I should give up astrology and hang out my shingle as a matchmaker."

Ethan flashed him a grin in the rearview mirror. "Maybe you should."

The fun and games ended when they reached their destination. Cosmo brought in another deck chair for Zoe and adjusted the blinds so that the light in the solarium was muted and restful, and Ethan moved Boris's cage into the living room and bribed the mynah with a handful of raisins to keep him quiet.

When he returned to the solarium, Cosmo motioned him to a chair. Ethan reached out to clasp Zoe's hand for a moment, then sat back, feet flat on the floor.

"Comfortable?" Cosmo inquired.

"Comfortable," he replied.

"Very good, then. I'd like you to start by taking a deep breath.... Hold it for a few seconds.... Now exhale slowly, letting your body sink into the chair.

"That's fine. Now another deep breath... Hold it.... Exhale slo-o-owly. Let out all the air and allow your body to sink deeper in the chair.

"Now I'd like you to close your eyes and imagine, if you will, that you're about to go snorkeling in a stream of pure, clear water. Take a deep breath... Hold it... And while you exhale, picture yourself stepping into the shallows at the edge of the stream. Feel how the sun has warmed the water. Feel how it relaxes your toes and feet as it laps about your ankles.

"Inhale as you take another step, walking into the stream. The water's up to your knees.... Exhale, and feel yourself sinking deeper, growing more relaxed.

"Now another step, slowly, effortlessly, moving with the current. Let it draw you deeper, farther from shore. The water's up to your waist now, and you can feel how buoyant it is. It supports the weight belt you're wearing, and everything inside the belt floats away.

"All your concerns... All your apprehensions... Let them go.... Concentrate on the warmth.... Let it wash over you.... Feel the buoyancy.... Let yourself drift with the current.

"Inhale.... Exhale....

"Every time you breathe out, you are more and more relaxed.

"Fine. That's fine.

"Feel the water flow past your body as you float farther from the shore.

"Breathe in.... And out....

"Let the water support you.... You feel weightless.

"In... Out...

"You're drifting deeper...deeper...deeper...."

HE SLID UNDER THE WATER and lay motionless on his back. His eyes were shut tight and his cheeks were puffed out. He was showing someone how long he could stay underwater without coming up for air.

Someone... Who?

Try to remember. Try to see.

He peeked through squinted eyelids. Soap burned his eyes and he screwed them shut again, but not before he caught a watery glimpse of his grandmother's face.

Grandma, lookit me swim! See how long I can hold my breath!

The shrillness of the little boy's voice reverberated off the tiles of the tub enclosure and echoed past his ears, even after he had pinched his nose and plunged beneath the water. Inside his head he was counting off seconds with more gusto than accuracy. Once he got past the teens, his concept of numbers was hazy.

He was smart as a whip. Everyone said he was. But he was only four years old—at least, he would be four on his next birthday, and that was just around the corner. In November. Whenever that was.

He let out an experimental puff of air and listened to the bubbles. Then he blew out a gusher of air, emptying his lungs, and shoved to the surface, giggling and blinking the water out of his eyes.

Lydia Quinn's face sprang into focus, flushed and still youthful despite her nimbus of snowy hair. Gramps called her an "eyeful." He said she was "the cat's meow," but to Ethan, she was simply Grandma.

"How long, Grandma? How long was I under?"

"About twenty seconds, love."

"How long's that? Longer 'n a minute, I bet."

"Not quite, but it's a new record for you." Smiling indulgently, his grandmother dried her hands on a bath towel and picked up her wristwatch. "Look here, sweetie." She pointed to numbers on the watch face. "The sweep hand went all the way from the six to the ten."

He nodded smugly, chest swelling with pride. "I betcha dumb old Jodie can't hold her breath that long."

"Ethan! I thought you liked Jodie."

He lifted one bony shoulder in a going-on-four-year-old imitation of his oldest brother's shrug, and his grandmother, wise woman that she was, did not pursue the subject.

Jodie was okay, he guessed. She had a neat tree house, and her mom made the best chocolate chip cookies in town. Maybe in the whole world.

But last week at Sunday school Jodie had kissed him.

Being kissed by a girl wasn't so bad. Not nearly as yucky as the guys said it was. In fact, he'd kinda liked it. But then Jodie had gone and tattled to the other kids—

"Come along, Ethan. Time to get out."

"Not yet, Grandma. *Please.*"

Without waiting for an answer, he launched his tugboat, pushing it around the edge of the tub, making chugging, tooting noises and creating a tidal wave of a wake behind the boat with his skidding, sliding body. When his grandmother knelt down, towel at the ready, he wriggled to the far side of the tub.

"Ethan Quinn, you little scamp. Stop that splashing and get over here."

"*Please,* Grandma, I hafta—"

Lydia put an end to his bargaining by pulling the stopper from the drain. "If you get out of the tub this instant, and put on your pajamas very quickly, we might have time for a story."

Although Ethan stalled for a few moments longer, pretending to think about the offer, both he and his grandmother knew there was no contest. He chose the story every night, and nine nights out of ten, the story he wanted to hear was not one from a picture book, but one that Lydia had made up. And that night was no exception.

He was out of the tub in a jiffy, and within a quarter of an hour he was in his pajamas, teeth brushed, recently combed hair already mussed, bouncing on his bed, waiting for his reward.

"I was quick," he boasted when his grandmother came into the room. "I was 'mazing."

"Yes, my little love, you were quick as a bunny."

Lydia folded back the covers and shooed him into bed, then sat beside him and tucked his spare pillow behind her back.

"Now then," she said, when he had curled up next to her, "which story would you like? *The Cat in the Hat*? *The Little Engine*—?"

"The princess."

"What, again?"

His grandmother invariably needed some coaxing, so he cuddled closer and patted her cheek. "Pretty please, with sugar on it."

"All right, snugglebug. The princess it shall be. But you'll have to help me. I'm not sure I remember how it begins."

Ethan realized Lydia was teasing, but neither of them laughed. Her reluctance and pleas for help were part of the ritual. They were part of his enchantment with the story, and he took his role as prompter seriously.

"Once upon a time, there was a bee-yoo-tiful princess—"

"Oh, yes, of course. Now I remember."

After a momentary pause to smooth down his cowlick, Lydia went on with the narrative of the story of the beautiful princess who had been imprisoned in her attic bedchamber by a wicked magician.

Deprived of the least comfort, cut off from the warmth of her parents and grandparents, her two older brothers and all her friends, the princess's only pleasure was listening to the troubadour who sang beneath her window each night.

"The troubadour's voice was so lovely, and his song was so poignant, without ever seeing him, the princess fell in love with him." Lydia hesitated, shaking her head. "Oh dear, oh dear. I forget what happened next."

"They 'loped," said Ethan. "One winter's night—"

"That's right. One winter's night, when the snowdrifts were as high as her windowsill, the troubador sang a new song to the princess. And how do you suppose it went?"

This time Ethan responded by snuggling closer to his grandmother, who sang out the answer in a husky contralto.

"Come to me, darling. Skate with me."

"And she did."

"That's right, my little love. That's exactly what the princess did. She climbed through the window into the troubadour's arms, and they ran away from the magician's house. They skated down the street away from the town. They skated and skated across the hill. And?''

At this point, Ethan usually recited the end of the story: "And if I'm not a'staken, they're skating still!''

Once he had done that, the bedtime ritual called for his grandmother to make sure he had his panda bear, tuck the covers under his chin, give him a hug, smooth down his cowlick one last time and whisper, "Sweet dreams, my little love.''

But on that night, when his grandmother came to the part where "They skated and skated across the hill,'' instead of responding on cue, Ethan announced, "The princess's name was Vangie.''

Lydia's harsh intake of breath seemed to consume all the air in his room. "Where did you hear that name? Who told it to you?''

"No one!'' he cried, alarmed by her intensity. "Honest, Grandma. I made it up.''

Lydia rose and left the bedroom without hugging him or wishing him sweet dreams. She didn't even stop to make sure he had his panda. And after that night, she never told him the story of the princess and the troubador again. No matter how much he coaxed and pestered, no matter how quickly he got into his pajamas or how many kisses he gave her, his grandmother remained adamant. But a few days later, while they were building a fort with Lincoln logs, she asked Ethan if he ever had any "strange'' dreams.

He stared at her, uncomprehending.

"Dreams that came true,'' she explained.

He added the pointy top pieces to his fort and began constructing the roof. "Once I dreamed dumb old Jodie fell off her trike. She cried and cried.''

"And?''

"And she did." He added a chimney to his fort, and sprawled in a belly flop on the floor to admire his handiwork. "'Member when Gramps lost his wallet? He looked for it all over the place."

"So did I," said Lydia. "We looked for it everywhere we could think of."

"And I found it, and Gramps was *so-o-o* relieved."

"Yes, he was."

Something in his grandmother's tone told him she wasn't smiling. Ethan glanced at her. She wasn't. He popped his thumb into his mouth.

"You never told me how you happened to look for the wallet under the car seat. I wonder, Ethan, did you dream it was there?"

"Uh-huh," he mumbled.

Lydia absentmindedly removed his thumb from his mouth and replaced it with a cookie. "What about Vangie? Have you ever dreamed of her?"

He picked several raisins out of his cookie and ate them, considering this. At last he admitted, "Sometimes I dream of the princess."

"And the troubadour?"

"Uh-uh, not him." He ate another raisin and rolled onto his back, studying a vase of red-bronze strawflowers on the end table. "Know what, Grandma? The princess has hair like that."

His grandmother stared at the flowers for the longest time, as if she were mesmerized by the color. And then she gave Ethan the last cookie on the plate and said, "This will be our secret, love. You must never, never tell anyone else about your dreams, and you must promise me you'll never tell a soul about Vangie."

"I won't, Grandma. Not ever."

More than twenty-five years later, under hypnosis, Ethan relived this moment, and he remembered his grandmother's horrified expression....

"THAT'S FINE, ETHAN. You've done very, very well. And now I'm going to count from one to five, and with each count you will become wider awake. At the count of five you will be fully alert, you will feel refreshed and rested.

"One.... Two.... Three.... You're still relaxed. You have a sense of well-being, but your eyes want to open. Four.... Almost awake now. Five.... Completely awake."

The count of five was Zoe's signal to rush to Ethan's side. She knelt in front of him, gripping his hand. "How are you feeling?"

"Hey, nothing to it. It was a snap." He attempted to illustrate this with a snap of his fingers, but couldn't produce any sound. His thumb and forefinger were not totally functional yet. He grinned, reassuring her. "That's what I get for trying to show off."

"Any aftereffects?" asked Cosmo.

"I feel kind of washed-out—"

"That will pass."

"And I've got a lot of questions." He looked from Zoe to Cosmo. "Were you able to follow much of what went on with me?"

"Enough," said Zoe. "You described most of it." She opened his fingers and laid her cheek against his palm. "You must have been an adorable little boy."

Ethan was moved by the comment, but with Cosmo sitting a few feet away, he couldn't do much about it. Besides, he had all those questions. And so he chose a response that made light of his emotions.

"Jodie always thought I was pretty cute."

"Whatever happened to her?"

"She grew up and married my brother."

Zoe smiled and brushed a lock of hair off his forehead. "Could I get you something to drink?"

"A cup of coffee would be great, and maybe a couple of aspirin."

"Do you have a headache?" asked Cosmo.

"Just a mild one."

"A nap might help."

"A few answers would help more."

Zoe squeezed Ethan's hand and got to her feet. "I'll have your coffee in a minute. Will your questions keep till I get back?"

"All but one. I went into this looking for explanations, and I found some. But why is it they lead to more questions?"

She laughed. "That ought to keep Cosmo busy for at least half an hour."

"Don't worry," said Cosmo. "We won't talk about anything interesting while you're gone. Matter of fact, I think I'll tag along with you. I'm sure Ethan could use a few minutes rest."

Ethan could and did. He slept for forty-five minutes, and when he woke, his headache was gone, but his questions still remained.

He was also starving, but Zoe had anticipated this. He followed a mouth-watering mixture of aromas to the kitchen, where she and Cosmo were putting the finishing touches on a late supper.

"None of us had dinner," she said, "and I remember how hungry I was after my experience with hypnosis."

The three of them sat at the game table in the family room and ate spaghetti marinara with mussels and garlic bread and tossed salad, and they drank most of a bottle of

Chianti, and after the meal, feeling mellow, Ethan finally got some answers to his questions.

The dreams he had as a child—still had—the "strange" dreams that came true, dreams he tried to forget, that he told no one about— "Is it possible that my grandmother had them, too?" he inquired.

"Absolutely," Cosmo replied. "Psychic abilities tend to run in families, and your grandmother was Thomas Seymour's daughter. I imagine she meant well, but she didn't do you any favors, forcing you to keep your dreams to yourself."

"The gift of clairvoyance can be frightening enough to an adult," said Zoe, "and you were just a little boy."

"But the promise you made your grandmother certainly explains why you've refused to read Thomas's journal," said Cosmo.

Ethan glanced at Zoe. Their gazes caught and held. "It also explains why I've overreacted to your interest in the journal."

"That's quite an insight, but I got the distinct impression that you objected to more than the journal."

"You're right," he admitted quietly. "Your interest in Evangeline was disturbing, but I actually resented Thomas."

"Why, Ethan? Why did you resent him?"

"Because I wanted your attention. Because I was afraid of losing you. Because I was jealous. Because—" Ethan drew in a ragged breath. "Because I love you, Zoe."

"Oh, Ethan, I love you, too."

The look that passed between them was filled with reverence and yearning. They were too absorbed in each other to notice that Cosmo had left the table. He went upstairs without bothering to say good-night, and within moments of his departure, Zoe was in Ethan's arms.

"Am I imagining things," he wondered, "or did you just say—"

"I love you," she repeated.

"But what about Thomas and Evangeline?"

"What about them?"

"Well, do you think we're—"

Zoe silenced him with a kiss. "It's you I love, Ethan Quinn. I've been searching for you all my life."

Ethan caressed her cheek and touched her hair, marveling at the ruddy-bronze curls. The color reminded him of strawflowers, of the princess he'd seen in his dreams—the princess whose name was Vangie.

Zoe had helped him regain so many memories; memories of Vangie and of his grandmother. He was overcome by gratitude and by a love too deep to define. Nevertheless, he had to try.

He buried his face against Zoe's vivid curls, exulting in her nearness. His voice was gravelly with emotion as he declared, "I love you, Zoe Piper. In a way, I think I've always loved you. I know I always will."

"Then that's all that really matters."

Zoe's answer was slurred by the brush of Ethan's lips, her murmur absorbed by his kiss. And in the magic of her response, he recognized the truth in Cosmo's prediction.

Some things, he discovered, needed no explanation.

Epilogue

Neptune was transiting Capricorn. Venus was sextile Mars. The sun was in the heavens, and all was right with the world.

Cosmo had gone back to the city, Boris to the solarium, and although the entire Seymour Collection was cataloged, Zoe had chosen to stay with Ethan. Since Tuesday evening, they hadn't been separated for more than a few minutes.

Zoe couldn't think of anyone else she'd want to spend that much unbroken time with, but Ethan was the exception that proved the rule.

She loved every minute she spent with him. Especially the nights. But she loved the mornings, too. And the afternoons. And the evenings.

She loved Ethan. Whatever the time of day, she loved being with him. And she'd missed him today, while she was out buying her trousseau.

He'd offered to come with her, but she had vetoed that plan. "It's bad luck for the groom to see the bride's dress before the wedding," she'd told him.

Ethan hadn't argued, partly because he felt ill at ease hanging out in the lingerie department, but mostly because he loved her, superstitions and all.

He had kissed her soundly, and said, "Hurry back, sweetheart." Then he'd gone off to supervise the crew of workmen he'd hired to restore Evangeline's monument, while she went off on her shopping trip.

She didn't really need much—just a nightgown or two and the wedding outfit. And since there wasn't a whole lot in East Hampton she could afford, she made quick work of her purchases. But even so, it was almost one before she got home.

By then the workmen were on their lunch break, but Ethan was still on the knoll. As soon as she'd put her things away, she ran up the hill to see him.

Ethan spotted her before she left the garden and walked down the slope to meet her. "Hi, sweetheart," he called, opening his arms to her. "Wait'll you see what you've accomplished."

When she reached him, he swept her off her feet and swung her around and around. By the time he put her down, she felt slightly giddy.

"Is it finished?" she asked, clinging to him for support.

"Come see for yourself."

Before she could get her breath, he caught hold of her hand, and sprinted toward the knoll, towing her after him.

Her first glimpse of the restoration was colored by laughter, although she tried very hard to control it. But Ethan was grinning, his eyes were shining with devilry, and she was young and blissfully in love with him, and he was in love with her.

Even when they were standing beside the marker, she could not contain her joy, and when she saw how meticulously the pieces of the monument had been fitted together, how carefully the seams had been concealed, she felt even more elated.

"It's beautiful," she said, and a ripple of laughter slipped out.

And chuckling, Ethan replied, "Yes, the workmen did an incredible job."

She pressed her lips together, holding back another burst of laughter. "Correct me if I'm wrong—"

"With pleasure."

The wink Ethan gave her was almost her undoing. A smile quivered on her lips and her voice was uneven as she asked, "Shouldn't this be a solemn occasion?"

"Why solemn?"

She tipped her head toward the marker. "Isn't it obvious?"

"Not to me, but I'll show you what is." With his hands on her shoulders, Ethan turned her full circle on the hilltop. "Look around, Zoe. What do you see? Green grass, blue sky, not a cloud on the horizon. The day couldn't be more perfect if we'd had it made to order. But the best part is, next spring, when the lilacs are in bloom, you'll be here to share them with me."

"Then you don't think it's wrong that we should be so happy here?"

He wrapped his arms around her, and pressed his cheek close to hers. "I think this is why Uncle Hiram left me the library. I think Evangeline and Thomas are delighted for us. I think they want us to be happy, and I can't imagine a more appropriate memorial to them."

Ethan had spoken of Thomas and Evangeline in the present tense, and that, too, seemed appropriate. Zoe sighed with contentment and relaxed against his chest. "This *is* a lovely spot."

"Mmm-hmm." He nuzzled the side of her neck. "And if that's not enough for you, think about this. As of tomorrow we get Merlin back from Cora, and you don't have to bird-sit Boris anymore.''

"As of tomorrow I'll be a married lady."

"Married, yes, but I hope not too much the lady."

She rubbed her cheek against his shoulder. "Does that mean you won't mind if I go barefoot sometimes?"

"I'll insist you go barefoot, except at formal dinners. Think of the money we'll save on shoes."

"Tomorrow," she murmured.

"I'm sorry, sweetheart, but I'm afraid you'll have to wear shoes to the wedding. At least during the actual ceremony."

"Of course, Ethan. Otherwise our marriage might not be legal. But there's something else about tomorrow—"

"The sun'll come up," he suggested.

"Besides that."

"It's the first day of July."

"That's it!" She pulled away from him and started down the hill.

"What's it? Where are you going?"

"Gull Cottage. The new tenant's moving in tomorrow, and I'm supposed to meet the rental agent there at two."

He glanced at his watch. "I'd better drive you. You're going to be late, as it is."

The rental agent was waiting at the cottage when they arrived. So was the contractor, who was painting the ceilings in the bedrooms where the roof leaked.

Ethan dealt with the painters while Zoe went over the inventory with the agent. His task was easy. The missing furniture made Zoe's job complicated. Just consoling the realtor might take the rest of the afternoon.

Ethan spent the time tending to Boris's needs, teaching the mynah a few choice phrases, swapping insults with him, and listening to his complaints. Today Boris was harping about crow's-feet. Tomorrow it would be food additives or nuclear waste.

By five o'clock the inventory was finished. Zoe handed over the keys, making her the official ex-tenant of Gull Cottage.

The painters were still hiding the evidence of the damage done by the rain, and the rental agent was in the kitchen, having a nip of the cooking sherry, when Zoe and Ethan sneaked out through the French doors, and when they arrived at the car, Ethan was startled to see that Zoe looked as if she might weep.

"Don't tell me you're feeling sentimental about this place!"

"I am, a little." She looked at the house, blinking back tears. "The last month hasn't exactly been a picnic, what with Boris and the leaky roof and the phantom furniture mover paying us calls, but I got to know you here, Ethan. I fell in love with you here. And you fell in love with me. How can we leave without doing something to commemorate all of that?"

He opened the glove box and handed her a Kleenex. "For old times' sake, would you care to take one more trip down the Nile in Cleo's barge?"

A tear rolled down her cheek. "N-no, thank you. That might disturb the painters."

"Well then, we could go back inside, and I could carry you out over the threshold."

She blew her nose. Another tear spilled over.

"You could carry me."

This provoked a sob.

He leaned across the stick shift, bringing his face close to hers. "I can understand the sentiment, but why the tears? Do you have serious regrets about leaving?"

She shook her head. "I'm not crying for myself. It's j-just that I feel so sorry for the new tenant."

"Cheer up, sweetheart. You just got through reminding me that we fell in love there. Who's to say the same thing won't happen next time around?"

A smile shone through the tears. "You're right, Ethan. It just might happen."

He drew her close, dissolving into tender laughter. "If you say so, love, it probably will."

HARLEQUIN
American Romance®

COMING NEXT MONTH

#305 MOTHER KNOWS BEST by Barbara Bretton

Author of the "Mother Knows Best" helpful-hints column, Diana had a master plan: finish her book, lose ten pounds and on Labor Day, begin the Great Husband Hunt. But then a month at seaside Gull Cottage fell in her lap, and two months early, at exactly the wrong time, Diana met Mr. Right. Don't miss the second book in the GULL COTTAGE series.

#306 FRIENDS by Stella Cameron

As children, Tom, Shelly and Ben had been inseparable. Then they became adults and their friendship faced a challenge. Ben was destined for fame, while Tom and Shelly were destined for love. But would their love break the bonds of an unbreakable friendship?

#307 ONE MAN'S FOLLY by Cathy Gillen Thacker

Diana Tomlinson was justice of the peace in Libertyville, Texas, but her life was far from peaceful. Newcomer Mike Harrigan was insistent about his foster ranch—even though the town was up in arms, all hell had broken loose and there had been a rash of burglaries. Diana knew that where there was a will there was a way—but as she got to know Mike and his trio of boys she found her will rapidly fading....

#308 WHITE MOON by Vella Munn

Lynn Walker was a championship barrel rider without a horse—her dream was just out of reach. Then Bryan Stone found her a mare to match her spirit and her strength: proof that he believed in her and her dream. There are many ways to say "I love you," and White Moon was Bryan's.

Harlequin American Romance.

Gull Cottage

SPEND THE SUMMER
AT GULL COTTAGE . . .

Now that you have learned the secrets of Gull Cottage, met its resident mynah bird, who warned Zoe Piper against summer romances, and traveled into the past with Zoe and Ethan Quinn, come back again to the luxurious East Hampton mansion and meet its next summer renter, Diana Travis.

It starts off as a month to finish her household-hints book and "practice" motherhood on her twin toddler nieces, but then Diana meets Gregory Stewart—and July becomes a month she'll never forget. Don't miss #305 *Mother Knows Best* by Barbara Bretton, coming next month from American Romance.

For the best in summertime reading, catch all the books in American Romance's GULL COTTAGE trilogy: #301 *Charmed Circle* by Robin Francis (July 1989), #305 *Mother Knows Best* by Barbara Bretton (August 1989), and #309 *Saving Grace* by Anne McAllister (September 1989).

GULL COTTAGE—because a month can be the start of forever . . .

Have You Ever Wondered If You Could Write A Harlequin Novel?

Here's great news—Harlequin is offering a series of cassette tapes to help you do just that. Written by Harlequin editors, these tapes give practical advice on how to make your characters—and your story—come alive. There's a tape for each contemporary romance series Harlequin publishes.

Mail order only

All sales final
